SPRING SHADOW

SPRING
SHADOW

SUSAN C.
MULLER

Books By
SUSAN C. MULLER

The Secrets on Forest Bend
The Witch on Twisted Oak
Voodoo on Bayou Lafonte
Circle of Redemption
Redeeming Santa
Winter Song
Spring Shadow
Summer Storm
Autumn Secrets

*This book is dedicated to all the heroes and heroines
who gave their lives in service to others,
and whose names are inscribed on the
Houston Police Officers Memorial.
May you rest in peace.*

PROLOGUE

T HE PEEPHOLE ON the hotel room door offered a fish-eye view of the hallway.

His eyes burned and his back ached, but he didn't move, refusing to lower his vigilance. Sweat coated his hands under the latex gloves. The air conditioner finally kicked on and filled the room with its cold, metallic smell. His shoulders flexed instinctively, allowing a breeze to flow down the back of his neck.

With the ding of the elevator, his body snapped to attention. Was this it? The brass ring surrounding the glass viewer had warmed from his body heat and he pressed his eye tight against it as he waited.

There she was. He took a deep breath, willing his heart into a steady rhythm. After all his planning, preparation, he couldn't afford to screw this up now. She passed in front of him on the way to her own room, close enough to smell her perfume.

She was alone and not staggering as if she'd been overindulging like the last time he'd seen her. But she looked tired. She needed to learn. This reckless behavior had to stop.

Wasting her gift with late night partying was unacceptable, and slipping out a back door to avoid him couldn't be tolerated.

All this would soon change. He would be her teacher. But first, she needed to learn. Here in Houston or home in Nashville, his word was law.

A muffled *click* reached him as her door closed.

The only illumination inside the room came from the thin line of light that seeped under the door and the glowing red numerals on a bedside clock as he groped his way to the end table and added the time to his note.

CHAPTER ONE

THE ELEVATOR DOORS closed with a soft *swish,* allowing Noah Daugherty to meet his partner's eyes in its reflective surface.

"And you don't know why the Chief wants to see us." Any demand to report to the top floor should be met with trepidation. He didn't like it in grade school when he was called to the principal's office and he didn't like it now.

Conner Crawford stared straight ahead, but brushed imaginary lint from his lapel. "No more idea than the first two times you asked me, unless you've been up to something you failed to mention."

"Huh, I thought maybe you'd stepped in some kind of shit and chose not to tell me about it." That wasn't true. If one of them was in trouble, it was much more likely to be him. Still, while he wouldn't say he hadn't done *anything,* he hadn't done anything lately, or that the Chief was apt to know about.

Noah cut his eyes to the side. At a hair under six feet,

Conner was a good two inches shorter than him and at least twenty pounds lighter, yet could hold his own in any situation. Noah never worried about his back with Conner around.

Not even the type of situation that might be waiting for them in the Chief's office.

The trip from Homicide on the sixth floor to the Chief's office on sixteen took long enough for a knot to form in Noah's gut. He had just reached for the worry stone in his pocket, but found only crumbled doggie treats, when the doors opened.

Now what? His fingers were coated with a smelly brown dust and he had nowhere to wipe them. He patted Conner on the back. "Don't worry, partner. I'm sure it's nothing."

The hum of a busy office swept over him after the cocooned silence of the elevator. Phones rang and printers beeped while uniformed officers, sergeants, and civilian clerical staff stopped to gawk at the two doomed men. Rumors traveled fast on the upper floors.

Noah paused at the life-sized statue of a patrolman holding the hand of a young boy and touched one finger to its cool bronze surface for luck, then made a beeline for the Chief's office.

Inside the floor-to-ceiling glass doors, a city councilman cooled his heels in a straight-backed chair. Noah glared at the civilian receptionist until she dropped her Sudoku puzzle. "Detectives Daugherty and Crawford. We had a message the Chief wanted to see us."

The desk-jockey eyed him without a smile. "Go right in. They're all waiting for you."

Oh, shit. That didn't sound good.

He tugged open the heavy oak door and waited for Conner,

but his partner waved him ahead. *Bastard.*

Across a room the size of a basketball court, the Chief pinned him with a stare worthy of an Academy Award. Next to the Chief's desk stood his lieutenant, Nate Jansen. Noah's feet sank into the thick-pile carpet and walking across it felt like trudging to his doom.

As he got closer, the man sitting in front of the Chief's desk twisted toward him and the glare from the wrap-around windows bounced off his bald head.

The Chief of Detectives. Could this day get any worse?

"Come in, come in. We've been waiting for you." The Chief's voice boomed across the room and the corners of his mouth curved up in a fake smile. "Good to see you again, Noah." He held out his hand. "And you too, Conner." He gave a perfunctory nod.

Noah? Conner? Were they—what did his nieces say— BFF's now? He'd never actually met the guy one-on-one before. Three chiefs had come and gone since he joined the force twelve years ago. This one had only been in Houston six months.

"Nice to see you, too, sir." Two could play that game. He nodded to the other men. "Lieutenant, Chief." At least he'd *met* the Chief of Ds, although he had only come on board with the big boss a few months ago.

"It's a pleasure, sirs." How did Conner manage that? He actually sounded like he meant it.

The Chief nodded toward Jansen. "The lieutenant tells me you're quite musical."

So that's what this was about. Noah bit back a sigh of relief. It wouldn't pay to let the Chief know how nervous he'd been. He waited, expecting a request for his band of Homicide musicians to play at some birthday party or fundraiser.

For anyone else, the answer would be, "No." They only played for sick kids at the hospital. But this was the Chief. His boss's boss's boss.

The Chief arranged his face in a more serious expression. It was like watching him sort through a box of masks and pick the most appropriate one. "We have a situation here that needs to be handled delicately, and Nate thinks you're just the man for it."

Noah couldn't do much about the two big-wigs, but he planned to give his Lieu the business when they got back down to six. And he'd give his eyeteeth to be able to see the expression on Conner's face about now.

"If we're not careful, this could give the city of Houston a black eye."

Now he was responsible for the entire city?

Jansen and the Chief of Ds nodded like bobble-headed dolls.

"There's a free city outdoor concert planned for this Saturday night at Eleanor Tinsley Park. I'm not sure what they're calling it, The Shadow of Spring, or some such foolishness. The first day of spring was the end of March, six weeks ago. Anyway, three bands will be playing and the lead singer of one of them, Paige Reimer. . ." He glanced at Noah. "You've heard of her, haven't you?"

Noah joined the bobble-heads and nodded, although he'd only heard of her for the first time on the drive in to work.

"She's had some trouble lately. Seems she has a stalker. The asshole got up close and personal last night. Slipped a threatening note under her door. She got scared and called the concert promoter who called the mayor and threatened to pull all of his performers if we couldn't guarantee their safety. Then the mayor called me with a tirade that lasted fifteen minutes."

The Chief glared at Noah as if the problem had been his fault. "You understand—I don't like it when the mayor calls me and throws his weight around?"

The leather swivel chair groaned as the Chief sank back and folded his arms across his substantial belly. "Damn fool women. If they wore more clothes they wouldn't have such nonsense. Anyway, we've got to keep her safe while she's here, and I thought you could blend in, join her band and keep an eye on her while your partner looks for the son-of-a-bitch. Just be sure you keep this quiet. We don't want the media to get wind of this. They'd be all over it and that'd be a black eye for the city."

The skin on Noah's face felt tight, flushed. His fingers curled into fists and he shoved them deep into his pockets before the Chief noticed. "I'm a homicide detective, sir. Not a rent-a-cop bodyguard." He waited for backup from Conner, but the silence from his partner was deafening.

The expression on the Chief's face wasn't encouraging, either.

"Would you rather wait and investigate my death?" The voice behind him was soft, but full of power.

Noah spun around in time to see a vision walk through the door. She was tall, probably five nine, and her blond hair flowed in waves past her shoulders. But it was her eyes that held him. They were the most startling shade of blue he'd ever seen. For a moment, he would have sworn someone hit him in the gut with a two-by-four.

Her long legs ate up the distance between them. The guitar case hanging over one shoulder thumped against her side with each step. Skin tight jeans, cowboy boots and a frilly blouse that appeared sexy yet didn't actually reveal anything completed her outfit. A beautiful package around an angry expression.

"No, not at all." Noah swallowed a fist-sized lump and let his eyes beg Conner for help.

"What my partner means is we're trained to investigate. That's a different skill set from protection. You'd be safest with someone experienced in that field."

About time Conner made himself useful.

Up close, her eyes were an even deeper blue, but anger had turned them to ice. "Your boss seems to think you can keep me safe *and* look for the son-of-a-bitch who's trying to terrorize me."

There went any hope she hadn't heard the Chief. On the other hand, maybe he wasn't the only one she was fuming about.

"Although I don't know about letting you play in my band. Standing on a stage in front of thousands, even faking it, is a lot different than playing kiddy songs for a captive audience."

Noah didn't answer, but held out his hand for the guitar case on her shoulder. She stared at him and let him wait with his hand out for several seconds before handing it over. He set the case on the Chief's desk and opened it.

No way was this her performance instrument. One strum told him it was a piece-of-crap out-of-tune throw down designed to make him look bad. He strummed again and adjusted the tuning pegs. Two more tries and he had it the way he wanted.

Now what was her signature song? He'd heard it on the radio twice that morning, probably because she was due in town. At the time, the lyrics had grabbed him. He took a deep breath and sang.

"When the wind reaches out to grab my hand,
And the stars light the way to Heaven,
I'll think of you lost in that distant land,
I'll dream of you searching for me."

When he finished the song, Conner was the only one in the room without a shocked expression. It hadn't been note perfect, but close enough for a spur of the moment gig.

Paige's mouth hung open as he handed the guitar back. He winked at her. "Not exactly what I sang at Carnegie Hall, but you get the idea."

"Spit it out. I know you're angry." Conner might *look* cool and calm as they made their way back to the elevator, but Noah wasn't fooled.

"We were out, free, but you let your pride drag us back in. You couldn't stand to be told you weren't good enough for something. Anything."

Was it pride? Or was it the desire, just once more, to do what he had spent so many years training for before life interfered and he took a different path? On the other hand, it might have been those blue eyes, calling to him. If that was true, he was a fool and deserved Conner's condemnation.

He'd learned the hard way—a woman who looked that

good shouldn't be trusted. Now wasn't the time to forget. "We weren't out. The decision was made before we got on the elevator. No matter how persuasive your argument."

"Probably, but now we'll never know. Do you realize how hard it is to protect someone who's a public figure? She's going to be up on that stage where anyone could get to her if they aren't worried about consequences. We need to find this guy *before* she makes an easy target of herself. It's already Monday afternoon. That only gives us a little more than four days."

"This perp is some coward who slips notes under doors in the dead of night, not a criminal genius."

"He may be a coward, but leaving a message while she's sleeping is already a step up from anonymous phone calls or emails. Plus, he knows what hotel she's in and her room number. Information they don't hand out with the concert tickets."

"Everyone who's working with her on this concert could discover that much. Give me a day to get close to her and the band and I'll spot who likes to sneak around in the dark."

"Be careful. We've seen it too many times. These creeper types have a way of escalating overnight into something dangerous. Especially when you appear out of nowhere, sticking close to her."

"Don't worry. I'll blend in like I've always been there. I can out-country Willie himself if I need to."

"You don't even *like* country music."

"You don't know what I like. I enjoy all kinds of music." At one time he was a classical music snob, but he couldn't listen to it since Betsy died. Only now, after almost eight months, could he bear to hear it again.

"Well, then, *I* don't like country music."

"Get off your high horse. She sings ballads, almost lyrical, with only a touch of Country." The tune was haunting, and her voice like a crystal bell, but it was the words that drew him in. He'd love to find out who wrote that song.

They both clammed up when the elevator deposited them back in their squad room. The noise level dropped as every detective strained to hear what the Chief wanted with them.

Let them wait.

Noah stomped to his desk to collect his weapon and clip a radio to his belt. Conner could deal with the office rumor mill. He was headed home to feed his dog, change into jeans, and pick up his guitar.

Apparently he'd just become a country/western singer.

His father would roll over in his grave.

CHAPTER TWO

NOAH SLIPPED HIS key in the lock and was immediately blasted with a barrage of barking. A five pound Yorkie paced on her zebra-print bed and eyed him suspiciously.

He fumbled in his pocket for the remains of a liver treat. "I know, I know. I'm not supposed to be home this early."

Any change in routine upset Sweet Pea. She and Noah had reached a truce of sorts over the last two months, but the least deviation from the norm seemed to remind her that Betsy had rushed out one morning, late for work, and never came back, and Noah had turned into an angry, grouchy man.

Things were better now, but Noah had no doubt he was still on doggie probation.

"Let me change my clothes and I'll take you for a quick walk, then I've got to go back to work. No telling when I'll be home. You know those musician types. Probably sleep all day and party all night."

When had he started carrying on conversations with the dog? Probably when he'd discovered he sometimes went all day, especially on weekends, without talking to anyone but the TV. Sweet Pea at least let him know by her expression what she thought about him, and that was more response than he got from the sportscasters and talking heads he yelled at.

Forty-five minutes later, he had changed, walked the Yorkie around the block and sat on the floor for a game of tug-o-war with Mr. Squeaky Man. "I'm going to put out your supper, but if you eat it all now you'll be hungry before I get home, so here's a little of the dry stuff to tide you over. Don't give me that look. You used to like it."

Sweet Pea's whimper stabbed at his heart as he grabbed his guitar. She'd been left alone all day and now he was heading out again with no idea how long before he'd be home.

Rush hour traffic was well under way, but Noah was headed the opposite direction. He sailed down I-45 until he reached downtown gridlock and came to a screeching halt.

The wait gave him time to stress over the case. There were too many ways to get tripped up working undercover and no backup around when it happened.

But there it was, and he was stuck with it.

Didn't matter if he liked the job or hated it, believed Paige or doubted every word out of her mouth. He'd been given a case, and he'd work it to the ground just like he always did. He'd never given a case half measure before and he didn't plan to start now.

That didn't mean he couldn't resent the whole situation.

Now all he had to do was figure out how he would handle his cover story.

No one in the band would know he was a cop or even that Paige had a stalker problem. He was just a local, hired to fill in for a band member who'd broken his leg.

Odd man out. Sort of like entering a small school in the middle of the year. He wasn't there to make friends, but he needed to find out as much as possible about everyone around Paige. And he needed to keep his facts straight while doing it.

He'd stay as close to the truth as possible, just move the timeline around. His mother was an opera singer, his father a concert violinist, he'd studied at Julliard, but what had he been doing these last years? He'd been playing in New York? No, too likely one of the band members had worked there. California was just as bad. New Orleans. That should work.

Then he'd come home to help with his dying mother. Since she passed, he'd been playing pick-up gigs. He could pull that off if no one questioned him closely.

Damn. He should have done a Google map search of New Orleans. How long since he'd been there? Five years? Six?

There were so many little clubs on back streets, he'd be okay.

It would be nice if he could trust the band members and roadies to help him—the more eyes on Paige the better—but too many stalkers were someone close who managed to go unnoticed.

Paige and her band were rehearsing in an old building that had once housed a failed nightclub. The faded brick dinosaur was located in the buffer zone between the thriving downtown area and wood-framed houses with peeling paint and yards full of cars parked on hard packed dirt.

He slipped in the side door in time to hear her voice echo through the cavernous space.

"I heard him myself, not like the last yahoo I had to take on someone else's say-so. This one's got the skills and enough talent to pick up what he needs to follow along."

"If he's so good, why's he available at the last minute?" The voice had a deep, accented drawl.

Okay, job number one: find out who yahoo was and get Conner to check him out. Get him to look into the guy with the broken leg while he was at it. Yahoo number two might think he didn't need replacing.

Hell, Lyle Lovett played and sang sitting in a chair after a bull stomped on his leg.

Conner could check out Paige while he was at it. It might not be fair, but being a cop made you skeptical of everyone.

Noah's footsteps rang out on the wooden floor and Paige stopped talking. All eyes turned his direction.

Yep, just like being the new kid in school.

"Evening, guys, Paige. I'm...Noah...Daniels." Damn, first sentence out of his mouth and he'd almost screwed the pooch by saying Detective and giving his real name. "I understand you're short one guitar player."

"Hi, Noah. I was just telling the guys how lucky we were to find you, last minute like this. I'll let everybody introduce themselves. There'll be a test later." She winked.

A cymbal crashed and he jerked his eyes up and back to the drummer's platform. A tubby man with a Beatles bowl-cut grinned at him. "Jeff Cooper, from Denver."

One by one, they introduced themselves.

The last was the lead guitarist; a tall skinny guy with a frown that would curdle milk. "Kevin O'Malley, New Orleans."

Well, fuck. Now what?

Disappointment surged through Paige like a physical presence. After years of trying to outrun her past, every decision she'd made the last few days had been wrong. Starting with coming to Houston early so she could visit her mother.

What made her think that was a good idea? Just when they'd taken the first tentative steps toward reconciliation, some giant hand had scooped up a pink gum eraser and rubbed out large chunks of her mother's memory. Now they were back to the days of accusations and recriminations, suspicion and distrust, a confusing mash-up of love and hate.

So what had she done? Compounded the error by letting performance anxiety cause her to demand protection after a threatening letter was slipped under her hotel room door.

She'd tried to correct her mistake by going to the police chief's office and calming the situation, only to let the fool's insult get under her skin. As if what she or any other woman wore gave some pervert the right to harass her.

Add to that, a cop with a voice that flowed over her like satin sheets on a hot night, and she'd been too dumbfounded to put her foot down. Instead of convincing the Chief that the best way to insure her safety was to get the public to help watch for her stalker, she'd acquired a babysitter.

Now she'd stepped into a pile of shit clear up to her kneecap. Her only hope was to keep him focused on the singing and protection part of his assignment.

Paige watched Noah win the guys over, one at a time. Well, all but Kevin who looked like he'd been sucking on a pickle. Nothing unusual there. Kevin didn't like anybody, especially anyone who might make the band look bad, and, by reflection, her.

Noah shouldn't fall into that category. He definitely had the chops to play. Now it seemed he had the skill to blend in with an already close knit group.

What did it mean that he could lie so easily, pretend to be something he wasn't?

Was any of his story true? The dying mother, the murdered father? She'd have to be careful what she said around him.

He wasn't to be trusted.

Noah took his guitar from the case and she nodded to herself. She'd horded a little nugget of worry his instrument wouldn't be performance quality. So many amateurs didn't know the difference, and as a cop, he likely didn't have a lot of cash to spare. But he'd just pulled out a Taylor, series 300 if she wasn't mistaken, acoustic. Sweet choice. At first glance it looked like spruce, but no, something else. Hawaiian Koa?

She wasn't any expert on wood, but she'd swear she'd checked out one like it when searching for a back-up instrument for herself. Maybe she'd misjudged his financial status.

He didn't seem to be married. His partner wore a ring, but he didn't. Not on his left hand, anyway. Not that a ring was any guarantee.

Forget the ring and the guitar, what about a gun? Did he

carry one and if he did, where did he hide it? Not in those jeans.

She had to keep him busy, and that required focusing on more than playing in the band. He was supposed to be her protection also, yet he was sitting, one hip parked on a table, laughing, not even looking her direction.

Everything about him was different from the up-tight, suit-wearing detective she'd met a few hours ago. He strolled in easy, like he'd been on stages all his life. His hair looked like he'd raked his fingers through it so that it fell, sort of casual looking, and he sported an earring in one ear.

Nope, not the same man at all.

He'd look fine standing up on that stage, though. Tall, buff, good looking. Not in a movie star kind of way. More like the guy you wanted to meet, but were a little afraid of. The type it was best to avoid.

An asset to the band, too. A better voice than poor Harvey. She hadn't realized how weak Harvey was until she heard Noah. His voice was strong, solo-worthy. But did he know how to control it? She couldn't risk him overpowering her on stage.

Saturday night was a big break for her career. She'd worked too many years and given up too much to risk letting a mistake blow this chance.

They'd get along fine as long as he remembered why he was there.

She ran her fingers over the smooth wood of her own guitar, a move that always soothed her.

This was her show after all. She was the star and anybody who worked for her better not forget it.

As long as he remembered that, they'd get along just fine.

Noah cradled the phone against his shoulder as he swung his bare feet up on his desk and leaned back in the Henry Miller chair Betsy had bought him for a housewarming gift. Sweet Pea shot him a dirty look and adjusted her position on his lap.

"Four fucking hours to rehearse four songs. That's all the time they've allotted us for the concert, four songs worth."

"Us?" Conner didn't even try to disguise the chuckle in his voice.

"Her. The band. You know what I mean. If she'd pick the four songs and stick with them it would be one thing, but she keeps trying different ones. Says she needs to figure out how my voice will fit in. I tell you, I trained two years under Antonio Baldaci. Antonio fucking Baldaci, and he didn't hold a candle to her in the perfectionist department."

"So how do you think it's going?" Conner sounded tired. What did he have to be tired about? He spent the afternoon sitting at a computer, not standing on a stage playing catch-up and tap-dancing around questions.

Noah crossed one ankle over the other. Sweet Pea opened her eyes but didn't move. "Okay, I think. If this assignment had come down the pike two months ago, I'd have been in trouble. But I've been playing enough lately to build up some callouses. My hands and fingers are sore, but I'll be ready to go again by morning. If she would just pick one fucking song and stick with it."

"The assignment, nitwit, the assignment. Are you so worried you won't be the best at something you've forgotten the reason you're there?"

"That's what I'm getting at, numb-nuts. I have to be able to play the part, don't I?" Was that it? Or had Conner hit on some deeply buried character flaw he didn't want to examine too closely? "Those guys are good, and if I can't win their confidence I'll never learn any of their secrets. Which brings us back to the reason for my call. What have *you* learned?"

"First, Paige is clean as a new morning. No wants. No warrants. Not even a parking ticket."

"Good to know. And the rest of them?"

"Harvey Simmons, the guy with the broken leg, seems to be resting comfortably in Nashville."

"What do you mean, seems to be?" Noah reached into his bag of Cheetos, bit one in half, and gave Sweet Pea the nub.

"He answered his phone when I called and pretended to be an insurance salesman. He's happy with his coverage, by the way. They were really nice to him in the hospital and he walked out, or maybe limped, without having to pay a dime. Wait till he gets his first bill. Then we'll see how satisfied he is."

"He might have been home this afternoon but what about last night? It can't be more than a three hour flight from Houston to Nashville. And what if that was a cell phone or he had call forwarding? He could be here in Houston and we'd never know."

"Thus the 'seems to be,' part. The Nashville police are going to find a reason to ring his doorbell, but that will have to wait for morning. Which, by the way, is only a few hours away."

Noah glanced at the time displayed on the lower corner of his computer. Not even eleven. The news had only been over for twenty minutes. Conner was turning into an old lady. Wait until that baby came. He better learn to operate on little sleep. And his five a.m. jog might be with a baby stroller.

Sweet Pea whined and Noah gave her another Cheeto nub. That made four; her limit unless he was willing to risk waking up to a stinky, orange mess of diarrhea. "You had half a day, you have to have learned more than Harvey likes his insurance company. What happened to him, anyway, how'd he break his leg?"

"Hit and run. He'd walked Paige back to her apartment after a gig and a car sideswiped him as he stepped off the curb. They never did find the guy who did it, but the car was a dark colored Ford Taurus, probably 1995 or thereabouts."

"You think it could tie in with our case?"

"It happened after midnight on a dark street and Harvey had been drinking. Nashville police didn't seem too sympathetic. Acted like Harvey was an idiot who brought it on himself by not paying attention. Gave him a ticket for public drunkenness. Still, you know how I feel about coincidences."

Yeah, me too. "Could he hold a grudge against Paige for the accident?" That would be a stretch.

"She wasn't the one who hit him, and she drove him to the hospital."

So, probably not Harvey, but he'd love to know who drove that car. "What about the rest of the guys in the band, anything suspicious about them?"

"They're musicians, I found a lot of stuff: DUI, smoking weed, skipping out on a hotel bill. The only one with any violence was that O'Malley guy and it wasn't much. He came off the stage after a drunk threw a beer bottle and hit him in the head. In the end, he didn't do anything but shove the guy out the door."

"In other words, I have to watch out for all of them." Fuck, why couldn't one of them have a record for domestic abuse or stalking? Nothing was ever easy. None of the band members had stood out as creepy during rehearsal, but Paige was always nearby and any pervert worth chasing would have been on his best behavior.

While Noah had good instincts and could usually recognize a scumbag whether hiding behind a business suit, clerical collar, or guitar, true creeps knew how to keep the freaky side of their personality well camouflaged. With several people to keep an eye on, he could use some help from Connor in narrowing down the field.

"I should know more tomorrow. Speaking of keeping an eye out, how's our girl? Is she tucked in safe and sound?"

Our girl? Conner was riding a desk, he was the one on the front line. "She's tucked in, but I don't know how safe. You're the one who arranged her lodging."

"I did everything I could. She's in a new hotel. Her room was reserved in Lieutenant Jenson's name and is on the seventeenth floor. No chance of a window break-in and no connecting door. I checked it myself. I even left her one of those alarmed door stops. The thing goes off if someone tries to push the door in. A retired cop is working security and for twenty bucks he agreed to keep an eye on her room. She refused to have an officer bunk in with her so that's the best we can do."

"You're shittin' me. An ex-cop hit you up for twenty bucks? He'd know it came out of your own pocket." Noah had slipped many an informant his hard-earned money, but one of their own? He crushed the empty Cheetos bag against the side of his chair, spreading a cloud of orange dust over his pants. Sweet Pea jumped at the noise and almost fell off his lap.

He sighed and ran a hand over the Yorkie's head until she settled down. No point getting angry, but he'd remember if the guy ever came to him for help. For now, he had to concentrate on this case. "I had her call me after she was safe inside. She promised she'd engaged the dead-bolt and pulled a chair in front of the door, but I agree, that's all we can do. I don't understand why they come to us for help, then ignore our advice."

"She should be fine for tonight. You coming in tomorrow?"

"I'll stop by around nine if you give me your word you won't rag me about how I look."

Silence floated down the phone line, then Conner started chuckling. "You're not wearing that stupid earring, are you?"

"Hey, I'm undercover. I haven't worn it since that drug buy over a year ago. It took me fifteen minutes to get it in and now my ear's so sore I can't touch it. But these boots were even worse. I stuck my little Smith and Wesson inside one boot and my badge inside the other. By the time I took the boots off, they'd dug an inch into my skin."

"I still think you should have taken my Walthrup pp. It's lighter."

"And I still think you're full of shit. Either way, I'm better off with what I'm used to."

Not that it mattered. He'd never had to use it before and he certainly didn't plan to use it now. Not on some sneak and peek pervert.

Although the last one he met almost finished him off.

CHAPTER
THREE

LIGHT FROM THE neon sign seeped through the blackout curtains and formed an odd pattern on the ceiling. Paige tried to force it into some type of recognizable picture, but failed. Not a dog or a horse. A face?

Only if it were painted by Salvador Dali.

The bed was comfortable, but the pillow was all wrong. She punched it several times in an effort to tame it, then pulled a second pillow on top of the first only to yank it off and toss it to the side two minutes later.

Maybe the room was too hot. No, the AC was set at sixty-nine. Any colder and she'd wake up freezing. If sleep came at all.

Was that a noise in the hallway? If so, it wasn't repeated. She sighed and threw back the covers. What was this, the third or the fourth time she'd checked the door? A thin stream of light showed at the bottom, but no note had been pushed through the opening.

Why hadn't she listened to reason and let a policewoman stay in the room with her? Having one cop watch her every move was bad enough. Two was out of the question.

If it were only her, she'd consider heading home with her tail between her legs. But it wasn't only her. She owed it to the guys not to let her mistakes ruin this opportunity. They were on the cusp of an actual career. What happened next could make them or break them.

She'd seen too many one-hit-wonders not to know they had to strike while they had their fifteen minutes. *Dreaming of You* wasn't even a true hit. More like a semi-hit. Popular in the South and West, but still unknown in large parts of the country. She had to do everything she could to get her name out there.

So far she was in the hole. She'd spent more money promoting than she'd made. Money she didn't have. After selling her mother's house, car, TV, pots and pans, and any knickknack worth more than a dollar twenty-five, she had enough to keep her mom in comfort for only another two years. And the doc said she could live ten more, slipping farther away with each passing day.

The thought of warehousing her mom in the type of place covered by social security alone made her sick. But that's the only choice she had. She was dead broke.

Hell, the guys had paid for their own tickets and hotel rooms. She sure couldn't afford to front them the money. It would take every penny the city was paying to reimburse them. None of it was going into her pocket.

If they left now, it wasn't only money they'd be out. Their reputation would be in the tank.

She punched the pillow again and flipped it over, looking for the cool side.

Worrying wasn't doing her any good. Time for drastic measures. A bottle of sleeping pills waited in her make-up bag. Taking one meant being groggy in the morning, but after so little sleep two nights in a row, tomorrow would be hell without it.

Fifteen minutes later she teetered on the verge of sleep when the hotel-room door rattled against its frame. Lifting her head caused the room to spin and her eyelids seemed to weigh ten pounds each. Her head dropped back on the pillow with a *thud.*

She didn't move again until almost nine a.m.

Sitting up was tough, but standing was agony. Each move caused the room to swirl around her. With one hand on the wall for balance, she shuffled to the desk. Thank God she'd filled the coffee maker last night. She forced her trembling finger to punch the red button, then flopped back in the chair to stare, hypnotized, as the black liquid trickled into the pot and the aroma drifted through the fog of her brain.

Taking the damn pill had been a mistake. She detested not being in control, even if the feeling would pass after a cup of coffee and a shower.

Two more minutes, one more, and the Heavenly brew would work its magic.

The first cup was half empty yet her hands still cradled the container as if drawing strength from contact with its cardboard surface, when a knock sounded at the door.

"Room Service," the male voice called out.

"What?' Her voice cracked and she tried again. "Who is

it?"

"You left an order for breakfast to be served at nine o'clock. Low fat strawberry yogurt, a fruit cup, and one slice of whole wheat toast, plain."

That's true, she had. "Can you leave it outside the door?"

"Yes, ma'am. If that's what you want." His voice sounded sullen. Probably worried he wouldn't get any extra tip added on the seventeen percent the hotel already charged.

Dishes clattered as he set the tray on the floor, but if he walked away, the carpet muffled the sound. She neared the door, her eyes on the tiny peephole.

She felt rather than heard the crinkle as her bare foot stepped on the folded paper just inside her room.

A scream caught in her throat but died away before the sound escaped.

Noah knew it was coming, still, he wasn't prepared.

He wasn't sure where the first catcall came from, but the wolf-whistle originated behind him. He refused to turn around and search for the person who gave it, but Lefty Bob's desk was in that vicinity.

Conner glanced up from a stack of papers, closed his eyes, and dropped his head into his hand. "Shorts? I thought you were playing in a band, not running track."

"I'm supposed to meet Paige outside the hotel work-out room at eleven. It's got to look like we're heading in at the same time. She says she has to get out of her room and get some exercise or she'll go mad and this is the only way I can keep an eye on her."

"Well, sit down so I don't have to look at your hairy legs and I'll go over what we've learned so far."

There wasn't anything wrong with his legs, was there? Betsy always claimed he had great legs. But she might have been a little biased.

"Okay, hit me with it. Let's start with the note. What'd you learn?"

Conner shuffled through the papers in front of him and pulled one out. "It's written on a plain piece of computer paper, probably thousands like it, but the same brand the hotel uses. Forensics believes the note was written first and the time added later."

"So where was he watching from?"

"People were coming and going in the lobby until around ten o'clock but she got in after midnight and no one on duty noticed anyone hanging about. There were still people in the bar, but that's on the top floor so they wouldn't know when she came in."

Noah drummed his fingers on Conner's desk. He wasn't asking where the guy *didn't* watch from.

"The door to a room across the hall and two down from her opened at 10:37 and again at 12:24. Nine minutes after she came in. Enough time for her to go to the bathroom, brush her teeth, whatever, and crawl into bed. She didn't see the note until the next morning."

Now they were getting somewhere. "Who rented that room?"

Conner smiled and Noah could feel his partner's excitement at the first break in the case. If they could solve it before the weekend, he wouldn't have to stand up on a stage and pretend to be somebody he wasn't. Was that relief he felt, or disappointment?

"No one. The room was empty."

"So some Joe Blow just walked up and picked the lock?" How did that help wrap this up?

"It's not that easy. The lock can be opened, but not by just anybody. You or I couldn't do it. The lock mechanism has a battery. It is possible to build a contraption that sends an electronic charge that fools the lock and opens the door. However, even that only works a fraction of the time, and you have to be damn good to build one that works at all."

Screw Conner. He might have to come across the desk and shake the information out of him. "Then how the hell did the creep get in and, for that matter, how did he know that room was empty?"

"Now you're asking the right questions."

Why did he have to ask questions at all? Couldn't Conner just give him the fucking information?

"Our guy hacked the hotel computer, found Paige's room number, and the nearest empty room. Then he printed a master key that opens all rooms."

"How about he stole a key from housekeeping or security or something?"

"All those type of keys have a code number. This one didn't. He. Made. It. Even harder than the electronic device. And hotels are extremely careful about putting up firewalls to keep hackers out of their system."

"So, he's a smart creep. Not the first time we've dealt with that."

"And bold. He waltzed in and out of that hotel like he

owned it."

Great, a double threat. "What about prints, was he smart about that, too?"

"Prints, pubic hair, bodily fluids all over the room. It would make you sick. I may never take Jeannie to a hotel again. But no prints on the door, table, or pen. Oh, yeah, he used the pen in the room to insert the time into the note later. He left a flattened area in the carpet in front of the door where he stood, but no useable footprints."

"I need to get moving if I'm going to meet Paige at the hotel in time. Is there any *good* news you can tell me?"

"Just a question to ponder."

Again with the questions. "What?"

"If he had a key that opened any door, why did he slip a note in but not go inside?"

Noah speed-walked from the parking garage through the spacious foyer of the conference area. Men in khakis with golf shirts wandered from one exhibit booth to the next while men wearing ties that matched or contrasted with dress shirts of royal blue, lavender, mint green, or any shade except white, stood on the other side of the booths and explained the newest in oilfield safety equipment. Mannequins wearing hard hats, orange vests, goggles, and hand-held radio equipment or fire extinguishers stood poised, ready to jump into the next disaster.

The oil patch was apparently still an old boys club.

Noah slowed as his phone chimed, indicating a text. He melted into the doorway of an empty meeting room to check it.

On my way

"Here for the conference?"

He jerked his eyes up from the screen. A man in his mid-thirties wearing a Cheshire-cat grin approached him with his hand out. The guy wore a shirt whose color ranged somewhere between pink and purple. The color probably had a name. Betsy would have known it. He didn't.

The guy's name tag read, *Hello, I'm Evan. How can I help you?*

By getting out of the way, Evan. That's how

Evan dropped his hand when Noah didn't offer to shake it. "I can make you the best price on fire-retardant foam of anybody in the industry. And it's a top-of-the-line product."

Noah glanced down at his gym shorts, running shoes, and sports bag. Did he fucking look like a conference attendee?

"Right now, I'm headed for the Health Club. I need to work off some of last night's over indulgence."

"You must be staying here if you're using the Health Club. Maybe I'll see you tonight after dinner. The bar on twenty-five serves a killer pear martini."

Noah glanced back at the hard-hat wearing mannequins. Evan better learn to drink beer or bourbon if he planned to make it in this industry. "You never know, fella. It could happen."

He side-stepped the guy and doubled his pace. It wouldn't do to have Paige get there before him.

When she rounded the corner, her eyes flitted to him and back to the Fitness Center door. She slowed her steps and fumbled in her pocket for the key card, dropping it on the navy and cream patterned carpet.

Noah reached down and scooped it up, the plastic cool in his hand. "Let me get that for you." He slid it in the slender opening and the door clicked open.

Inside, the receptionist sported a skin-tight tank and leggings of the same royal blue as the carpet. The hotel logo was embroidered in cream across her generous left breast along with her name, *Kitty*. How much sexier Paige looked in simple yoga shorts and a matching athletic-gray T-shirt.

Kitty flashed him a smile full of over-white teeth against artificially tan skin while ignoring Paige. "Good morning. May I help you?"

Noah stepped slightly in front of Paige, blocking her from the receptionist's view. "Mr. and Mrs. Nate Jenson, room 1712."

Paige gurgled a strange noise, then remained silent.

"So, that would be Nate and. . .?" Kitty held a blue pen with a flower on the end poised over a ledger.

He dragged a name from the recesses of his memory before Paige could speak. "Kathy."

"Go right on in. You have the place to yourself for the moment. No one else is working out. Do you need me to show you how to operate the machines?"

"I think we can manage. We'll call you if we have any trouble." He took Paige's hand and led her through the frosted doors into the gym area.

"Nice legs," she muttered as he stowed his bag near the elliptical machine.

What the hell was it with his legs today?

They started on matching treadmills, but Paige set her speed to an easy jog with a definite incline while he kept to a brisk walk with no elevation.

"Don't strain yourself," she commented.

This was going to be a long day if she kept up with this attitude. "I'm not here for the exercise. I'm here to protect you, and I'd just as soon not be out of breath if trouble pokes its head around the door. Beside, this is one of the few times we can be alone together and I'd like to ask you some questions."

"You're right. I had a bad night and I'm being a jerk."

An alarm bell sounded in his head. "What do you mean, bad night? Did something happen?"

"I heard noises in the hall half the night and when I got up, a note had been slipped under my door. No, not from my friendly stalker. It was the hotel bill." She gave a weak laugh, but it was unconvincing. "I didn't know that at first and it scared the tar out of me."

"The night security guard is an ex-cop, and he's keeping an eye on your room. He promised to patrol your hall at least once an hour. You probably heard him."

"It would have been nice if you'd told me earlier. I might have slept better."

What could he say? She was right.

"So you think I'm safe?" Those blue eyes begged for an affirmative answer and he'd give anything to be able to offer her one. But life didn't come with guarantees.

"I'd rather you would agree to have an officer in the room with you, but as safe as possible otherwise. Can we talk about who might be doing this?"

She lifted her chin and spoke through clenched teeth. "If I knew that, I'd have told you."

He couldn't do anything right today. "Do you have a bad feeling about anybody? Is there anyone you deal with, even a clerk at your favorite store, who gives you the creeps? Someone you try to avoid?"

"Sometimes fans get a little over zealous, but I'm new enough at this to still be thrilled they want to see me." She slowed her treadmill to a walk, but kept the incline. A slight sheen of sweat coated her forehead and her T-shirt seemed to cling a little tighter. "And any clerk I deal with would be home in Nashville."

"What about your band members, have you fired anyone lately?"

"When I was first starting, we had a lot of changes, but I'd say it was mutual. Different approaches, you know, or they got a better offer. I'm pretty much set with the bunch I have now. They're along for the ride and they like where I'm taking them. I make sure to give them plenty of recognition every chance I get, so I don't see any reason they'd resent me." Her voice was ragged. Either this small amount of exercise was hard on her or she was more worried about this stalker than she admitted.

He'd have Conner work on those early band members. Maybe they weren't too happy she was moving up the charts without them.

"Let's talk about the note you got the other day. '*Time for you to learn your lesson, Bitch.*' Then it listed the exact time you came in. Sticking it under your door is pretty strong for a first contact. Are you sure you haven't heard from this guy before?"

"He didn't sign his name, did he? So, how would I know?"

Why couldn't she just cooperate? Why did he have to work so hard to keep her safe? "Have you gotten any fan letters that called you Bitch, or use that style of block printing?"

The speed-controls on her treadmill suddenly took all her

attention and she was able to avoid his eyes.

Every damn time. "What do you know that you're not telling me?"

"I've gotten a couple. I don't think the first called me bitch, but they both used block printing. I threw them in the trash."

Shit. The guy might not have been as careful on the first ones. They could have scored a fingerprint or something. "Can you remember what they said?"

"I'm not sure. Maybe something about being disappointed in me?"

That felt like someone who had known her a while, not just a random fan.

"What about phone calls? Anything suspicious?"

Her eyes widened and she stumbled before righting herself. "I've had a rash of calls that show *Private Caller* or *Unavailable.* I don't answer and they stopped about two weeks ago."

She slowed the machine to a brisk walk. "Now it's my turn to a question. Who do you think is behind this? What type of person?"

If only he had more to go on. "So far, it looks like some type of Einstein with a set of brass balls the size of truck tires. Know anybody who fits that description?"

A small smile might have crinkled the corners of her mouth. "No. I absolutely don't."

A swish sounded behind them and Noah glanced in the mirror. The frosted glass door swung open and a pot-bellied heart-attack-waiting-to-happen nodded to them before jumping on a nearby elliptical machine.

Paige opened her mouth to say something, but Noah

shook his head. Within two minutes the guy had sweat pouring down his neck and dripping off his nose. Another two minutes and he left to go sit in the sauna.

"This isn't going to work. If I have any other questions, we can talk over the phone." Phone interviews were never as successful. He couldn't see the person's face to judge for lies. In fact, this whole set-up was a cluster fuck.

How could he investigate, protect her, and stay undercover at the same time?

Paige fumed as the doors slid closed behind her. Noah had insisted she take the glass elevator so he could keep an eye on her, something not easily accomplished with a bank of five elevators, yet he sat with his back facing her direction and fiddled with his cell phone. Probably playing Angry Birds.

When her car reached the second floor, she saw her reflection in the gift shop window and realized he'd been watching her the whole time.

Irritation flooded over her and she turned her back, refusing to look at him.

Every time she thought she had him pegged as an incompetent loser, he did something to indicate he knew exactly what he was doing.

That should have been a relief, considering he was her protection, but somehow it was more of a worry. She'd overreacted to a stupid note. Even if it was some troll who saw her come in and thought it would be funny to scare her, so what? She wasn't frightened.

She could handle herself. She had before and would again.

But no, she'd called the concert organizer in a moment of panic and he called the chief of police.

Now it was too late and she was stuck with a nosey shadow who couldn't be brushed off.

Just when things were getting interesting.

She lived by only one hard and fast rule: never shit where you eat. Band members were totally off limits. But he wasn't technically a band member, was he? A few more days and she could leave this town with all its creeps and perverts behind.

How long had it been since she'd let her hair down; had a little fun? All she did these days was work, work, work. He might have been a nice distraction. A way to take her mind off her stalker and the pressure of a possibly career-making performance.

Until he started talking about checking into her past, and that couldn't be allowed.

Check into her past

Noah hit send and regretted it immediately. Conner wouldn't appreciate long distance instructions.

In less than a minute he had his confirmation.

What the f do U think I've been doing for the last 3 hrs?

Yep, he'd stepped on a nerve with that one.

Learn anything?

That U R a prick

He could keep this up, but it wouldn't do any good. Conner would tell him when he had something.

For now, Paige was as safe as he could make her. He'd watched her as far as her floor and the hotel security guard had taken over from there.

He walked Sweet Pea, fed her and put down fresh papers, then changed into jeans. He'd proven he could look western by wearing cowboy boots yesterday. Today he'd switch to low-cut rough-out boots. His back-up piece and badge would still be hidden, but more comfortable.

One last check of his email showed Conner had sent him a list of names for Paige to look over. He printed it out, folded the paper into a small square, and stuffed it into his pocket. He'd slip it to her sometime tonight.

The back door was open and he had one foot on the step when a silver Kia careened into his driveway. Long legs unfolded from the driver's side door, followed by a brown ponytail and a purse the size of Rhode Island.

Two young girls, one blond and one brunette, hopped out of the back seat.

"Hi, Uncle Noah," two little voices squealed.

"Hi Punkin', Princess. How was school today?" A slow smile spread across his face, the warmth traveling down to fill his chest and drown any remaining resentment about his new assignment.

"Kimmy threw up on Trevor and Miss Howard got it on her new shoes when she tried hold the trash can." Emma gave a gap-toothed grin.

"I went to the nurse and got a Band-Aid." Iris held up an arm with a pink Snoopy Band-Aid.

"I'd call that a good day for both of you."

Rachelle stood on tiptoe and kissed him on the cheek. "Hey, big brother. I didn't expect to find you home this early."

Then why was she here?

"I have half a left-over tofu casserole I was planning to have for supper tonight, but Frank said to swing by and stick it in your fridge and we'd go out. He had his mouth set on some fried catfish."

Thanks, Frank. You don't want it so you palm it off on me.

"Where's he taking you?"

"Probably to Mel's. That's his favorite. If you're off work, why don't you join us?"

If he accepted, could he send the casserole back to their house where it belonged? There was a good reason half of it was uneaten.

He tried to avoid taking the dish, but when it became obvious she wanted to come inside and put it up herself, he lifted the bowl, still cold from her refrigerator, and stuck it in his own nearly empty fridge. If she opened the freezer and saw the last one she'd sent him, covered with ice crystals, it would hurt her feelings. He'd eat the damn thing before he let that happen.

Those vile things were nearly impossible to get rid of. They stunk up the house if he dropped them in the trash, gummed up the disposal if he tried to run them through, and would undoubtedly make Sweet Pea sick if he was stupid enough to feed them to her. He'd give one to Conner if Jeannie wasn't pregnant, but he couldn't risk what that glop might do to an unborn child.

He swung back toward her before she made it inside the kitchen door. "Thanks for the invite. I'd love to, but I'm headed to work."

"In jeans and a T-shirt, carrying your guitar? That must be an interesting assignment."

The girls had squeezed past him and were on the floor, playing with Sweet Pea. When was the last time he'd mopped? If Rachelle guessed how dirty his floor was she'd have a fit.

Since their mother's death from cancer, she'd decided keeping her kids away from red meat and dirt was the way to assure them a long life. He couldn't blame her. With all the things they'd both lost in life, if avoiding beef and germs helped her get though the day, he understood.

But backing off on the accelerator might be a more effective way to keep them safe.

"I'm doing a favor for the new police chief." That much was true. He tried not to worry her, but he didn't like to lie to her, either. Sometimes what he said, or didn't say, was a balancing act.

"Cool. You're stepping up in the world. Is it some kind of a big party or what?"

The late afternoon sun gave the sky a rosy glow. He took a deep breath of clean, spring air, stalling while he figured out what to say. "Pretty big, I guess. I don't know for sure yet. I'll tell you about it later, when I know more."

"Just so long as you don't forget you're babysitting Saturday night."

His jaw dropped, but he was powerless to control it.

"Ah, Noah. You didn't forget, did you? We never go anyplace, and it's our anniversary."

"No, no, I didn't forget." He just didn't remember it was *this* weekend. "I'm looking forward to it."

That gave him three days to solve this case

CHAPTER FOUR

NOAH CIRCLED THE parking area twice. Near as he could tell, no strangers hid in cars or lurked behind support columns, but shadows were long and the light in the garage dim. He kept his window down, but the only sound was his own tires. While the whole area smelled stale, no tell-tale exhaust fumes warned of an idling engine.

He parked and strolled past Paige's rental car. With a casual flick of his wrist, he dropped his keys near the passenger side door and stooped to retrieve them. No one crouched in the backseat, no suspicious wires hung underneath, and no black box stared back at him with a red, blinking light.

He'd been watching too much television.

A chirp caught him off guard and he grabbed for the phone in his pocket.

Leaving now

Noah rushed back to his truck, replying *ok* to Paige.

A moment of embarrassment washed over him as he

texted *now* to Garcia. He should have asked who the ex-cop security guard was before mentally chastising Conner for giving him money.

He'd seen Garcia around plenty when he first made detective. A nice guy, always ready to help a newbie without making him feel like a complete incompetent.

Then the guy's wife got Lou Gehrig's disease and he took early retirement to help take care of her. That had to have been, what, five years ago? Now the wife was little more than a shell and his pension didn't cover all her expenses so he worked at the hotel while an assortment of his kids, in-laws, outlaws, neighbors, and church members took care of her overnight.

Come daylight, he rushed home to take over. When he slept was anybody's guess, but it wasn't while on duty. He'd earned the twenty bucks Conner slipped him plus the forty he'd given the guy himself by checking on Paige several times during the night and watching when she entered or left her room.

But there were still plenty of hours a day when he wasn't on duty.

All of this was a joke. If she was honestly in danger, she needed to scrap this silly concert and go home. No amount of people could protect her from a determined assailant. Reagan and John Lennon had learned that.

One guy, working undercover, didn't have a chance.

Noah had to admit; he approved of Paige's driving. He'd followed plenty of people over the years and most of them drove like fools. Betsy was an exception. She was a good driver, unless he had to follow her for some reason. Then she drove like she was trying to lose a tail.

But most people drove either too fast for road conditions, or too slow. They sped around other cars on slick streets, then cut back in front of them with only inches to spare, or drifted into an oncoming lane while studying passing shop windows.

Paige kept her rental at a steady three miles over the limit, passing slower motorists only when necessary and giving him plenty of time to make the same move before cutting back into her lane. Her head bobbed in time to whatever music she had playing, but she didn't talk on the phone or constantly fuss with the radio or air conditioning knobs.

He realized he was desperate to find some fault with her when disappointment flooded him after she executed a perfect left turn across heavy traffic outside the rehearsal hall.

Why did he care? Did he resent this assignment that much?

Resent it or not, he'd agreed to it. Now he needed to keep his head in the game.

He waited in the car as she entered the building, following her only with his eyes. Five minutes later he joined the group on stage.

All the admiration he'd built for her as a strong, decisive woman fled when she pulled out two new songs she thought might fit better with his voice and skill level.

The next four hours passed about as they had last night. He was more confident his playing was up to par, but Jeff, the drummer, and Kevin, the lead guitarist, tried harder to start up conversations. He could handle Jeff, but if Kevin asked too many questions about New Orleans, he was in trouble.

After an hour, Paige finally gave them a fifteen minute break. Kevin and Jeff made a break for the bathroom like their socks were on fire. Although he'd been in enough bands to know what was likely going on, Noah strolled after them, just to make sure.

A sweet, spicy smell greeted him as he pushed through the men's room door. Jeff already had a joint lit while Kevin tugged at the collar of his shirt and fumbled with a doobie the size of his thumb.

"Hey, man. Want a hit?" Jeff extended his joint Noah's direction.

"Better not. Smoke does a number on my voice."

Kevin narrowed his eyes. Suspicion clouded his face. "Paige doesn't give a shit."

Noah forced a wheeze into his voice. "She will when I cough up a loogie on stage."

Damn, he hated this undercover shit.

By nine o'clock, Paige had finally settled on four songs and they played them all through once more before she called it a night. Noah reached for his guitar case when Kevin threw out the first notes of *The House of the Rising Sun*.

Which would be worse, ignoring him and looking like a prick, or joining him and encouraging camaraderie? When Craig, the keyboardist, and Paige joined in, he had no choice. The jam session was in full swing.

From there, Kevin went straight into *When the Saints Go Marching In*. Noah followed up with his own personal favorite, *Jambalaya*. In his opinion, Hank Williams, Sr.'s best work. The others must have agreed because a chorus of hoots and *all right's* followed him.

There must not have been any songs about Denver, because Jeff called out, *"Rocky Mountain High,"* and the band joined him.

Craig suggested, *All my Exes Live in Texas,* and that brought a good laugh and pointed looks at the keyboardist. There were plenty of songs about Dallas and Houston, but none any of them considered righteous. *Galveston* was too lame to even mention.

Another half hour passed and they were all best buddies, like it or not.

By the time they had finished playing every song written about any city one of them had ever been to, Noah's stomach was grumbling. When Craig suggested a nearby Mexican restaurant, he made only a token objection.

He was about to take his first mouthful when the door opened and three women pushed inside. The other guys, even Kevin, perked up immediately. Maybe being married didn't mean as much to some people as it had to him.

"I call the blonde on the left," Craig said.

"Fuck. Then I call the smoking hot brunette in blue." Jeff motioned with his chin.

Noah glanced over to see who they were talking about. The women were all dressed in casual, but attractive outfits, but none looked the least bit provocative. And not one glanced their direction.

Betsy had said several times it just wasn't fun to go out with her girlfriends anymore. Was this type of behavior the reason?

He was still studying the trio when Craig's choice looked up and met his eyes. Recognition hit him with a punch in the gut.

Laurel Bledsoe. What the hell was she doing here? Last time he saw her, she was just getting her feet back under her after her jerk of a husband deserted her. Would ignoring her undermine her new self-confidence? And which would be worse, hurting her feelings or having her come over to say *Hi* and blowing the whole assignment?

He gave an infinitesimal shake of his head and held his breath for a minute, then another. He was safe. She wasn't going to acknowledge him. Why did that disappoint him so much?

Noah lowered his head and kept his attention on his *fajitas,* willing his eyes not to turn her direction.

Fifteen minutes later, Craig pushed his chair back. "My lady has about finished her drink. I think I'll mosey over there and offer to buy her another."

"She married," Noah said.

"How do you know?"

"She's wearing a ring." Was she? He should have checked. How long did it take to get a divorce in Texas, anyway? Especially if your douche-bag husband kept throwing up obstacles.

"Eat up, boys," Paige said. "I hear there's a happening bar on the top floor of my hotel."

Fuck no. He needed to get Paige inside where no one would recognize her.

He kept his cap pulled low on his forehead as he pushed

through the brightly painted doors. The restaurant wasn't much more than a hole-in-the-wall. The food smelled delicious, but that didn't make up for the dingy surroundings. Really, an embarrassment. Once he was in charge, and he would be soon, make no doubt about it, he'd see to it Paige frequented only the best places.

She didn't seem to understand that in this business, perception was everything. Act like a star and people believed you were a star. He had his work cut out for him, but the faster she learned, the easier he would be on her.

The collar of his shirt choked him but he didn't dare loosen it or the spider-web tattoo would show. He'd considered having it removed, but kept it as a constant reminder of the damage a youthful mistake could cause.

That's all this was; a youthful mistake on Paige's part. She hadn't realized how much she owed him. How much she needed him. But she would…soon.

He struggled to remain calm on the outside as Paige threw her head back and laughed, a rich, throaty sound that should have warmed him. Anger bubbled up from some distant core of his being and threatened to burst forth. He inhaled a deep breath and steadied his heart rate.

This wasn't the time or the place.

Just stay cool for a while longer and he'd know how far she'd fallen and how much rehabilitation she needed. After that…

He chugged half his glass of tea, letting the icy liquid cool the steam building in his head. The menu was sticky under his fingers. What did that say about the hygiene practiced in this dive?

Still, he had to order something or he'd stand out.

"*Carne Asada*," he mumbled when the waiter came around. If the incompetent fool tried one more time to push a margarita on him, he'd never see any tip at all. As it was, the guy was down to ten percent.

The food was about what he'd expected from a place like this—fat, grease, and spices. He shoved it around on his plate, eating little. The waiter kept his glass of tea filled and he twisted it, using the condensation to make concentric circles on the plastic table cloth. He smiled at the sight of the interlocking rings. If the design had been a Rorschach test, his answer would have been, "A pair of handcuffs."

He split as soon as possible and waited in a darkened corner of the lot. When Paige left the restaurant and started her car he was ready, motor on but lights off.

What he hadn't expected was to see the new guy follow her out of the lot and to her hotel. Especially after spending most of the evening sneaking glances at the blond bimbo at the next table. That might be a fatal mistake for somebody.

He'd taken care of bad influences before, he could do it again.

CHAPTER
FIVE

OAH LIFTED HIS glass of Dr. Pepper and gazed around the
hotel bar. Flashing neon lights, loud music, and half
the oil well safety convention trying to pretend they
were still young and hip.

What the fuck was wrong with Paige? She wanted his
protection, but refused to follow his instructions, insisting
they stop here for a nightcap. How was he supposed to keep an
eye on her in a place like this?

His claim to be a recovering alcoholic served two purposes.
He didn't have to pretend to keep up with the others while
secretly pacing his drinks in order to keep a clear head, and it
explained his flimsy résumé for the last few years. Maybe that
would help keep Kevin off his back.

The deception accomplished something else, also.
Something he'd discovered by accident. Most people accepted
his story and left him alone with his soda. Occasionally,
someone encouraged him to drink. Even tried to trick him

into indulging. That almost always turned out to be a person he needed to watch closely.

Kevin, on the other hand, didn't give any excuse. He just stuck to iced tea.

The music changed to something with a slow but driving tempo and Paige placed her hand over his. She nodded toward the miniscule square of wood that served as a dance floor. "Let's go," she said. Her expression booked no room for argument.

The other guys had all danced with her at least once. He could hardly refuse.

The movements felt stiff, awkward at first. How long had it been since he'd danced? More than a year for sure. After a few false starts, the beat of the music traveled up through the soles of his feet and the moves became smooth, natural.

He moved Paige around the floor, using the opportunity to scope out other areas of the club. While the bar and dance floor were brightly lit, almost garish, the far corners remained in shadow. If anyone lurked there, watching, he couldn't tell.

The song ended and he escorted Paige back to the table before heading for the bar. A waitress wearing black jeans and a vest with no shirt had been keeping the table well stocked, but he had other ideas.

A wall-sized mirror mounted behind the bar not only showcased an assortment of high-end liquors, it reflected a far corner of the room where he thought he'd spied a familiar face.

Before the bartender returned with his drink, a mint-green shirt appeared at his elbow.

"You've got the moves, all right, but you didn't seem too happy with your partner."

"Well, she's my boss, so I didn't have much choice."

"Evan, from yesterday morning," the guy in the colorful shirt said.

Noah glanced at his own T-shirt and jeans, then at Evan's dress shirt with the contrasting white collar and cuffs buttoned up tight. Didn't the guy know how to cut loose?

"I remember. I'm Noah. Guess I brushed you off earlier, but when the boss calls…"

"Hey, tell me about it. We all have a boss, some better than others." Evan leaned across the marble counter and flagged the bartender. "Another pear martini, please." He glanced at Noah's drink. "What have you got there? You really should try one of these martinis. It's their specialty."

"I better stick with my Dr. Pepper. Can't afford to put a foot wrong in front of the head honcho, you know."

"Then wait half an hour and cut out. Some of us know a bar in Montrose where no one cares who you dance with or what you drink."

Noah took a long swallow of his soda. A gay bar in Montrose wasn't exactly his idea of fun, but no point burning bridges. This guy had turned up twice now, once too often to ignore. "Sounds tempting, but I'll have to pass this time. We're playing at the Shadow of Spring Festival on Saturday. It's a pretty big gig for me. I wouldn't want to mess it up."

Evan leaned his back against the bar, cutting his eyes from Noah to Paige's table and back. "I thought you musician types were more open minded than most."

"Some are, some aren't. Just like the rest of the world."

"That's Paige Reimer, isn't it? What's she like to work for? I heard she was a real bitch."

All of Noah's senses snapped to attention. "I haven't seen

that side of her, but then I've only worked with her for a couple of days. The other guys have been with her for years. You'd do better to ask one of them."

Noah watched in the mirror as Evan studied one band member after the other. "Nah, I'm planning to go to that Spring Festival thing this weekend and I wanted to figure out which band to watch. There's too many playing to see them all, and I like to support musicians that I could admire as a person."

"Isn't the conference over by then? Won't you be ready to get back home?"

"It's just a four hour drive back to Dallas. Even if I stay for the concert, I'll be home by midnight."

Fuck. Dallas was Paige's hometown. The place where she'd played in school talent shows and garage bands. Sung the National Anthem at ball games. Gotten her first break. She'd only been in Nashville a few years.

"All I know to tell you is that she's a workaholic, a perfectionist." He'd heard of people supporting bands for all kinds of reasons, even their stand on social issues, but this felt like more than a coincidence.

Evan watched Paige as she tried unsuccessfully to flag down the waitress. Noah didn't have to be a lip reader to spot the curse word as she gave up and dropped her arm.

The dim lighting and the smoky tint to the mirror made it difficult to be sure, but Noah thought he saw Evan roll his eyes before picking up his glass and returning to his dark corner.

Paige let her head fall back so the last few drops of ice cold amaretto margarita could slide down her throat. She slammed the empty glass on the table. Where was that waitress? At this rate she'd never drink enough to manage a full night's sleep.

Coming to Houston early so she could visit her mother had been a mistake. Seeing her the way she was now brought back all the old memories. The fears, the insecurities, the night terrors. It was as if they both had regressed ten years. Her legs trembled as much as they had when she was seventeen, alone and in trouble, only to have her mother verbally attack her and belittle her just as she'd done all those years ago.

Instead of centering her mother in *today* as she'd hoped, her visits seemed to draw her deeper into the past. Each day she went to the nursing home, and each day the woman she'd loved despite her flaws slipped farther away. Would her mother be better off if she stopped visiting entirely? Could she live with herself if she never saw her again?

Noah kept frowning at her and glancing at his watch. Fuck him. He probably fell asleep as soon as his head hit the pillow. Only those who spent hours staring at the ceiling had any idea how long a night could be. If overindulging in an adult beverage gave her a solid four or five hours with no nightmares, whose business was it but hers anyway?

As long as she didn't let the hangover interfere with the next day's rehearsal.

She licked her finger and slid it around the rim of her glass, picking up the last few grains of margarita-flavored sugar. One drink at the restaurant, but that was an hour ago. Two here, but interspersed by a dance with each band member. Noah was the best dancer once he loosened up and let the music take over. But it took him half a song to give in and go with the flow.

She should be glad he never completely forgot why he was

here. So why did she try so hard to make him? He was her protection, not a challenge to overcome.

The music started again and she felt the rhythm of the drums course over her. She closed her eyes and swayed in time to the beat. When she opened them again Kevin was watching her and smiling. He raised an eyebrow and nodded toward the miniscule dance floor.

No, she didn't need to dance. She needed another drink.

One more and she had a fair chance of decent night's rest with no demons waiting their turn. She stuck her finger in her mouth and let the sweet-tangy-gritty goodness melt on her tongue. Where was that waitress?

Jeff and Kevin left before the waitress took her order. Craig was too much of a gentleman to desert her. Noah stayed because it was his job. She might as well be alone…again. Still, it gave her time to enjoy one last drink. And put off facing an empty room and another round of dreams worthy of Stephen King.

A piercing screech sent a bolt of pain through her head and she massaged her temples.

Maybe she didn't need another margarita after all. Her lips were numb already, her usual benchmark. Four might be overdoing it. Especially with the amaretto added. All this noise was too much for her. She couldn't concentrate.

Noah grabbed her arm and tried to pull her to her feet. No way. She wasn't getting up. Her head was pounding. If only that sound would stop. The red pulsing light didn't help any, either.

What the fuck was going on? The bar band wasn't good, but it wasn't that bad.

"We have to go." The fact that Noah was shouting registered in the back of her mind, but with so much noise in the room, his words were muffled. She lifted her head and saw Craig jump up, his chair toppling behind him. The crash of the chair hitting the floor melded with that of other chairs scraping back or falling over and people rushing past, their voices urgent and frightened.

Noah tugged on her arm again. "Now! Grab your purse and let's head out through the kitchen stairs. This is getting too dangerous. We've got twenty-one flights to go down and more people will be pushing into the stairwell on every floor."

She couldn't think with that blasted alarm pounding in her ears. Alarm? She shook her head and all the commotion made sense. "Is it a fire?"

"It's a fire alarm. Whether there's a fire or not, I don't know. But we have to act as if there is."

Climb down twenty-one flights of stairs? She was having trouble navigating her way across the room. Drinking as a nighttime sedative wasn't working. She had to find a better way.

Noah steered her through throngs of people, holding her up with one hand and using his shoulder to clear a path.

The stench of burnt grease assaulted her as they pushed through the swinging door to the kitchen. Was this where the fire started? Maybe they should go a different direction.

She twisted her head toward where Craig had been standing a moment ago, but the keyboardist wasn't anywhere to be seen. "Let's go back," she begged Noah.

His only response was to speed up, dragging her behind him.

"You there, stop," he called to the back of a white chef's coat disappearing through the exit door. Noah reached out with his free hand and grabbed a handful of the starched fabric. "Get back in there and turn off all the appliances before you set a real fire."

The young sous chef eyed Noah and the exit door, but didn't move. Paige's heart pounded as she tried to catch her breath, but the grease smoke made her cough.

Noah reached over and ripped the man's name tag off his coat. "If you don't and a real fire starts, I'll personally hand your name to the fire marshal. The only danger here is from your incompetence. Now do your job!"

All the color drained from the young man's face, but he pivoted and ran back toward the kitchen, brushing Paige roughly with his shoulder.

Before she had time to react, Noah was pulling her through the exit and down the stairs. Inside the stairwell the air was damp and stuffy, but without the acrid stench of grease smoke. The constant ringing of the fire alarm and the din of people fleeing was muffled, also.

She hated to admit that Noah had been right, but the service stairwell had been a good idea. They had gone down three flights before they saw another person.

When they reached the seventeenth floor, she tugged on his hand. "I need to stop by my room and get my guitar."

The jerk didn't even answer her, just yanked her past the exit and kept rushing down the stairs.

By number twelve, people poured in from each floor. The noise level rose to an overwhelming din, echoing back and forth so it seemed to be coming from every direction at once.

Couple that with the increasing stench as more bodies pressed into the confined space, and Paige had to swallow down a bubble of panic threatening to escape and erupt into a scream.

At floor ten, the mass of humanity forced them to slow to a steady trot. Good thing. She couldn't have kept up the punishing pace a minute longer. By seven, her calves were screaming in pain.

Somewhere between floors four and five, the horde of people came to a complete stop, then inched down, one step at a time. She leaned against Noah, gasping. "I can't keep going. I have to rest."

"Look behind us. If you quit now, you'll be trampled. Pretend this is that elliptical machine you liked so well."

Asshole. If she got out of this hell-hole alive, she was going to fire him.

Noah gulped in the cool night air. The pounding of a hundred sets of feet tromping down an enclosed cement stairwell still reverberated in his ears. But even outside, there was no relief from the shrieking alarm as more police cars and fire engines sped up to the hotel.

Flashing lights colored Paige's face a sickly shade as she sagged against him but they couldn't stop now. "Just a little farther. I'm parked around the corner."

"Can't we sit here?" She swept her arm toward groups of people sprawled on the grass.

"Not yet. We have to keep moving while we have the chance." It wasn't her fault. She didn't understand. But he didn't have time to explain now.

He slipped his arm around her waist and half dragged, half carried her to his truck. Once inside, he peeled away, weaving through unfamiliar streets. Neither spoke for several minutes. He kept his eye on the rear-view mirror. If anyone followed, he couldn't tell. The fire had turned already heavy traffic insane. Cars cut across lanes and took illegal turns. In the dark, any bozo could tail him with lights off and he wouldn't know.

By the time they reached the freeway, Paige's breath had evened out. "Where are we going?" she asked.

That was the sixty-four dollar question, wasn't it? So far, he'd just been driving, but at some point he had to pick a destination. Police headquarters wasn't an option. Even if they weren't being followed, news of her heading inside there would leak out and the Chief had insisted he keep this mess quiet.

Conner's house was closest, but that was out of the question with Jeannie due in what, two, three months? The last big case they'd been on had put her in danger and Conner had to whisk her out of her teaching job and into a hotel for several days. A move he was still paying for.

There were a few convoluted short-cuts he knew about to his house that would make a tail obvious. Plus, Sweet Pea would serve as a back-up alarm that couldn't be silenced.

"Somewhere safe," was his only answer. He couldn't afford to say more. If he told her what he had in mind, she might get the wrong idea. Plus, if he spotted anything suspicious, a last second change in plans could send her over the edge.

He watched her from the corner of his eye, but she didn't speak again for the next twenty minutes while he ran yellow lights, backtracked, and made sharp turns out of the center lane.

"You're either the worst driver in the city of Houston—and that's saying a lot—or you don't believe that fire alarm was the real thing." She didn't turn her head or move anything except her lips.

"Did you smell any smoke?"

"All I smelled was a hundred pair of sweaty armpits and a like number of stinky shoes, all of which got riper with each flight of stairs."

"Exactly."

"Still, that doesn't mean the alarm had anything to do with me."

"Do you really want to take a chance? Pulling a fire alarm is serious business. Think how easy it would have been for someone to get hurt during that evacuation." Noah executed a three point turn and backed into the narrow driveway.

Paige jerked her head toward the gray frame house. "Where are we?"

"My house."

CHAPTER
SIX

H ACKLES ROSE ON the back of Paige's neck. Did he really think she would spend the night at his house? If he did *anything* improper, she wouldn't just fire him as a bodyguard, she'd see he lost his badge.

The night fell silent as Noah switched off the ignition. The high seat of the truck offered an excellent view down the driveway and surrounding neighborhood. Nothing moved. Suburbia was deep in dreamland. Only an occasional porch light indicated this wasn't a ghost town.

She reached for the handle, but Noah placed a hand on her arm. "Wait."

He didn't move or take his eyes off the street for three minutes by the dashboard clock. Just when she thought she might jump out of her skin if she had to sit still and silent for one more second, he nodded and released her.

"Go! Head straight to the back door. I'll be right behind you." He slid out with the grace of an athlete. She threw open the door, but was yanked to a stop by the seat belt she'd forgotten to unfasten. He rounded the truck and grabbed her hand. "Now," he growled.

She fumbled blindly for the release button. The latch sprang loose and the belt snapped back. He pulled her across the driveway at a dead run and she stumbled behind him, legs as uncooperative as a newborn colt. He paused in the shadow of a tree, then darted up the steps. By the time he unlocked the back door and turned off the alarm, she'd regained her balance.

Her heel and little toe were on fire. After traipsing around with Noah, both were sporting blisters that stung like a mother. As soon as she got a chance to sit down, she was taking off these espadrilles and throwing them away. Even if she had to go barefoot the rest of her life.

She wasn't sure what she expected when she stepped inside, but a miniature Yorkie, polka-dotted hair bow and all, wasn't it. The dog lifted her head from a zebra-print bed, as surprised to see her as she was to see it, then burst into an ear-splitting round of barking. A sound that couldn't possibly have come from a body so small.

"Shhh. Quiet Sweet Pea. It's okay. She's with me."

Sweet Pea? This man who looked as if he could bench press a Harley, yet sang like Pavarotti, had a dog named Sweet Pea? What else was he hiding?

Staying here could be fun after all. No telling what other secrets she might uncover.

A sliver of ice lodged in her chest. As long as he didn't discover more about her than she did about him.

Noah scooped up the five-pound terror and cleaned several soiled papers from around the floor, murmuring softly to her all the while. Sweet Pea quieted, but continued to shoot Paige disapproving looks.

He must not bring much company home if that little shit-factory treats everyone this way.

She studied the dog suspiciously. "Does she do any tricks?" Love me, love my dog? He was trying. She could, too.

"Only one. She'll drop like a used dishrag and play dead for a liver treat." Noah sat Sweet Pea on the floor, formed a pistol with his fingers, and said, "Bang."

The dog's legs went limp and she instantly fell to the ground, even if it was only a matter of a few inches. Five seconds passed before she gazed up at Noah with enormous chocolate eyes.

"Good girl." He crooned and held out a treat.

"Will she do it for me?"

"If she thinks she'll get another treat."

Paige pointed at the dog and said, "Pow."

Sweet Pea didn't budge.

"You have to make you finger into a gun and say *Bang*. It's got to be both. One or the other won't do it."

She tried again and Sweet Pea flopped onto the floor. A childish laugh bubbled up as she watched the dog stand on her hind legs to grab the treat Noah held out. The little thing was kind of cute, especially with those pleading eyes. On the other hand, she was awfully tired and exhaustion left her with a big, gooey soft spot.

Paige sank into the nearest chair and eased off one shoe, examining a blister on her heel. "That's it, Mr. Madden, we're officially quits."

Noah twisted toward her, a puzzled look on his face. "You

play video football?"

"Football? What are you talking about?" He wasn't making any sense. Maybe he was as tired as she was.

"Why are you so angry at Madden?"

"He made these stupid shoes. Sure, he probably didn't envision using them to run down twenty flights of stairs, jog around the block, and jump out of a pick-up, but he should have designed them for that possibility." She toed off her other shoe and tossed it in the direction of the trash can Noah had just used. It hit the side of the metal can with a *ping* and thumped to the floor.

"He might have been too busy with all his sports casting and video game duties to think about a fire alarm in a hotel. Maybe, just maybe, he could have some ideas on athletic shoes, but I can't imagine him having any input on something like that." Noah nodded toward the exaggerated wedge she waved in one hand, then reached across her to pick up a video game with a picture of a football player on the front.

Paige kneaded her arch as a cramp hit. "I believe there's some possibility we're not talking about the same person."

Noah had the nerve to chuckle. "I hope not, because you'd have lost a fortune if you bet on his picks last year. Although he had a couple of long shots nobody else saw coming."

He carried the dog to the back door and set her outside. "Guest bedroom and bath are down the hall. Sheets are clean and so are the towels. Give me a minute to make sure Sweet Pea is finished with her business and I'll find you something to sleep in. It's late and I think we've had enough excitement for one night."

Plenty of excitement. That was the problem. How was she

supposed to fall asleep now? A strange house, a strange bed, a strange man with an even stranger dog down the hall, and the effects of three Margaritas long gone.

Noah brought her a gown—pretty, soft, but not what she was used to—and she thanked him before closing the door to her room. Now what? If she turned the lock he would hear. Would that be rude or practical?

She'd just stretch out on the bed for a few minutes. Once the house settled down and they both had time to fall asleep, she would slip into the kitchen and search out the bottle of scotch or bourbon he was bound to have stashed somewhere.

For the first time in her life, she hoped a man snored. For now, the bed welcomed her and exhaustion wrapped around her like a warm blanket.

This house was a home, comfortable and inviting. The tension she carried in her neck and shoulders melted away, like butter on a hot sidewalk.

She was safe here.

The sound of running water filtered through Noah's sleep-fogged brain. Was Betsy taking a shower; getting ready for work? He opened one eye to see Sweet Pea staring back at him. And the far side of the bed undisturbed.

Fuck. How many times did he have to go through this? Every time was a punch in the gut. Would he ever get used to it?

At least it didn't happen often anymore. About time, after all these months.

He groaned and sat up, feet hanging off his side of the bed.

"Come on, Pea. Our house guest is gonna need coffee after all she drank last night."

He pulled on yesterday's jeans and padded into the kitchen. Once Pea had made her rounds of the back yard, he put the coffee on to brew.

The aroma of French Roast filled the kitchen. Noah topped off his favorite mug and inhaled deeply. Maybe this day wouldn't be as bad as he thought.

Paige slipped almost silently into the room. Her hair fell in damp ringlets against her shoulders. A pink nightgown was draped over one arm.

"Thanks for the loan," she said. "Hope this isn't going to get you in any trouble."

"Not much chance of that. Not anymore." He had lent it to her, so why was the thought of her wearing it so unnerving?

He took the gown from her, folding it carefully, and laid it on the seat of a kitchen chair. "Coffee?" he asked.

"I don't suppose there's any chance you have some Earl Grey Morning Blend?"

Noah grunted, sat his mug on the counter, and rummaged in a top cabinet. "I'm not making any guarantees on how fresh this stuff is."

He felt her eyes on his back as he prepared a cup and set it in the microwave. Betsy had always used a tea kettle, but that was one of the only things he'd thrown away. The sight of it, accusing him every morning, had been more than he could stand.

"How long has she been dead? Less than a year, I'm guessing."

Every muscle in Noah's body froze. "August twenty-eighth."

"Some kind of accident?"

What was this lady, Sherlock Holmes in drag? "Long haul truck driver, dozed off at the wheel. How'd you know?" If she'd been snooping through Betsy's things while he was asleep, it wouldn't matter how much danger she was in. She was on her own.

She nodded toward his right hand. "You still wear your ring, even if it's not on the left hand. And you treat her things like they were made of glass. You wouldn't if you divorced. There's no sign of sickness in this house. It's like she walked out the door and never came back."

Yep, that's exactly what happened. But no matter how intuitive Paige Reimer was, she didn't know the full story. Or why the whole fucking thing was his fault.

Something he'd have to live with the rest of his life. However short he might decide that would be.

Conner punched Noah's number on speed dial, then leaned back and propped his feet on his open bottom drawer. The squad room was semi-quiet. Most of the detectives were out working their cases. That meant their lieutenant would be free to pester him all day about their lack of progress.

Where the hell was his partner and why didn't he answer his damn phone? He'd worked every bit as late as Noah and yet he was here at his desk, toiling away.

"What?" Noah panted on the fifth ring.

"I might ask the same thing. Where are you and where's Nightingale?" Stupid codename. Like anybody couldn't figure out who he was talking about.

"Home, with me. We just got in from taking Sweet Pea for her morning walk."

He dropped his feet to the floor and hunched over the phone, almost whispering. "You took her out walking where any fool could see her?" *Naw.* He must have misunderstood. Even Noah wasn't that stupid.

"Well, I couldn't leave her here by herself, could I?"

"She shouldn't be there at all. She should be somewhere safe. Under protection." Conner almost choked on the words.

"She *is* under protection. Mine. And Sweet Pea's."

Wonderful. Protected by an idiot and a five pound ball of fur with only half her teeth. That should do the trick. Conner took a deep breath. No point screaming over what was already done. "The fire in the hotel was definitely a false alarm so it should be safe for her to go back to her room. The Fire Marshall is blaming it on those oilfield equipment rowdies. Most of them were drunk enough to blow the numbers off a Breathalyzer." The faster Noah got her back to the hotel, the better he'd feel about this whole situation.

"The drunk ones were up on twenty-one, in the bar. Where was the alarm pulled?"

"Seventeen, but there were drunks everywhere in the hotel." He should know. He spent half the night questioning them.

"Paige's room is on seventeen. And I know how you feel about coincidences."

"There were plenty of conventioneers on that floor, and she's Nightingale." he muttered automatically. Couldn't Noah at least pretend to cooperate?

Besides, what made Noah think Nightingale was safe at his house? A teenage-pervert-hit-man from their last big case had managed to slip into Noah's home several times with no problem. Sweet Pea wasn't much help then.

The Chief would eat them both for lunch if he discovered Noah had taken the woman he was assigned to protect to his own home overnight. It wouldn't matter that Noah hadn't glanced at another woman since Betsy died. That was still improper. Well, Noah might have *noticed* Laurel Bledsoe, the neighbor from their hit man case, but he was still too crabby for anything more to have happened.

Maybe he was wrong. Noah *had* seemed somewhat more alive since that brief encounter, whatever it amounted too, with Laurel.

This was a circle fuck. Nightingale had the mayor's ear. And the mayor controlled the Chief who controlled the Chief of D's who controlled their lieutenant. Who had the power to squelch his leave request for when Jeannie had the baby.

· *Awh, shit.* If anything had happened with Nightingale, they were both screwed, one way or the other.

Noah valet-parked his truck. A huge waste of money he was never likely to get back no matter how many expense account forms he filled out. But he didn't want Paige walking through the garage where anyone could see her, and he wasn't about to drop her off and tell her to wait for him.

He kept his left hand on the small of her back as they strolled through the lobby. His right hand remained loose, in easy reach of his weapon. A low hum of disgruntled voices drew his eyes to the reception desk and a young woman decked out in a suit with the hotel's logo on one shoulder.

Deep, plush carpet, heavy drapes, and overstuffed chairs, all designed to muffle noise, failed miserably as a line of angry customers waited as the clerk tried to explain that while she was sorry for the inconvenience, no one got their money back because of a fire alarm in the middle of the night.

Noah tried to steer Paige toward the elevators before anyone noticed her but she refused to be hurried.

"Quit shoving me. If you knew how bad my feet hurt, you'd offer to carry me."

If only he could. But that would attract more attention than waiting while she strolled like a pregnant snail across the wide expanse of restaurants and shops. Her feet hadn't hurt that bad when they walked Sweet Pea an hour ago. She just wanted someone to notice her and ask for an autograph. Not if he could help it.

He kept up the pressure on her back until they were hidden by the bank of elevators. Now, if they could manage to get on one before she was recognized.

The doors opened to a car full of conventioneers and Noah stepped in front of Paige, blocking her from view as the oil field rowdies got off.

"Well, that was rude." She tossed her hair back as they entered the empty car.

"It's not my job to be polite, just to keep you safe." Protection was hard enough when the person understood and cooperated. Paige had asked for help, but now acted like this was all an imposition.

"And I've got a career to think about, and employees to pay.

I can't afford a bad reputation as a stuck-up, crass celebrity."

The car stopped twice on the way to seventeen. Each time they faced a wall of disgruntled guests pulling rolling suitcases and carrying duffel bags or hanging clothes, waiting for the down elevator.

Each time he blocked her from view. And each time a low, growling sound came from behind him.

When the doors slid apart on seventeen, he tried to clear out a path, but tripped on a suitcase someone had carelessly dropped directly in front of the opening. Didn't these people have any manners?

And how many changes of clothes did they need, anyway? They had packed more than he had in his closet. He'd never get her out of here.

Paige pushed past him as he struggled to regain his footing. At least one of the waiting crowd recognized her, grabbed a cell phone, and snapped a picture.

"Why, thank, you, honey." Paige beamed at the lady. "Would you like a selfie?"

Before the love-fest was over, Paige had posed with everyone there.

Why couldn't she have at least worn the golf cap he offered her?

But, nooo. That might muss up her hair. And she'd just washed it. What a cluster. How could he protect someone so clueless?

As they marched down the hallway, he weighed his choices. Which was more important, getting her inside before someone noticed her room number, or checking out the room before she entered?

He'd just slipped the key in the lock when she shoved past him and into the room.

"Sorry, Darlin'. Gotta pee. That last cup of tea went right through me."

Looked like the choice had been made for him.

He was still checking the hall when a scream split the air and his blood turned to ice. He pulled his Glock from its holster, dropped the safety, and racked it in one swift move.

"Paige!"

CHAPTER SEVEN

Paige's knees buckled and she grabbed the wall as Noah rushed past. A tiny portion of her brain registered that he clutched a gun the size of her favorite Kate Spade bag, waving it from one side of the room to the other.

And all she'd been worried about was hiding the box of tampons she'd left sitting on her pillow.

Instead, displayed prominently on the ivory comforter of the enormous, multi-pillowed bed, was a single rose. Not even a red rose. A black one. With the stem broken near the top so the blossom hung to one side like a broken neck.

Bile threatened to pour out of her and she stumbled toward the bathroom before she collapsed completely.

"Wait." Noah's voice sounded behind her, a distant echo from the bottom of a deep well. "I need to check for intruders before you go in there."

But she couldn't stop. Besides, it wasn't necessary. She could feel the stillness in the air. No one else was in the room.

Whoever had been here was long gone.

She stretched one leg behind her and kicked the door shut. This was humiliating enough without him watching her hug the commode like a Saturday night drunk.

When nothing was left of any meal in recent memory, she lay back on the cool tile, trying to douse the heat that spread over her entire body. How long could she stay here? Would he leave if she just didn't come out?

A hesitant tap sounded on the closed door. "Paige, are you alright?"

Guess not.

"Five minutes. Just give me five minutes, okay?"

The carpet was too thick to hear footsteps, yet she felt him move away.

She counted to sixty slowly, then again, and one more time, before pushing herself off the floor. Two minutes left to make herself presentable. She brushed her teeth and splashed cold water on her face, then brushed her teeth again, but the foul taste remained.

Her hands shook and her knees were as week as if she'd run a 10K. Uphill. In July.

Every emotion in the dictionary swirled around her and she couldn't pick just one to settle on. Fear. Anger. Humiliation. Denial. Each seemed the most dominate until the next took over. But exhaustion trumped them all.

One swipe of powder and a dash of lipstick. That was the most she could manage.

Hand on the door knob, she took a deep breath. Time to face Noah, with his endless questioning and probing. And what good did it do? There wasn't anything she could tell him.

Noah sat at the desk, intent on his phone. Playing Candy Crush? No, she had to quit underestimating him. He was most likely texting his partner or someone.

He glanced up. "Feeling better?"

Real concern coated his voice. She tried to answer, but only managed to nod.

"Try this, I made you a cup of tea." He held out a paper cup of steaming liquid.

She clutched the cardboard as if it were a life preserver. Maybe it was.

"I need you to look around. Is anything different than you left it? Is anything missing?"

Well, there wasn't a dead rose on her bed when she left, did that qualify as different?

She'd left the bed in a wadded mess of pillows and blankets, with jeans and blouses strewn everywhere. Smoothing out the comforter and arranging the pillows she could understand—it made a better showcase for the rose—but what had the weirdo done with her clothes?

A quick check showed her clothes hung neatly in the closet and her bras and panties folded in the dresser. The idea of him touching her things creeped her out, big time. She'd be damned if she'd tell Noah about this. Some things were too personal to share. Designed strictly to embarrass her with no real information to further the investigation. "No, everything looks about the same."

Only one thing sent slivers of ice deep into her soul; the realization that the pervert had taken the box of tampons with him.

Damn that woman. Noah clenched the fist he'd shoved into his pocket. If it wasn't for the look of terror on Paige's face when she spotted the rose, he'd throw this job right back in the Chief's lap. No matter the consequences.

First she wouldn't wear even the slight disguise he'd ask her to put on. Then she insisted, against his instructions, on speaking and even posing for photos with every Tom, Dick, and Mary they passed.

Now she was lying to him.

Something in the room was changed or missing. And the thought terrified her. So why wouldn't she tell him?

This was all about to fall under the category of *not my problem*. As soon as the Chief learned about this latest break-in, Paige would have round-the-clock protection whether she wanted it or not. All they had to do was keep her safe until she went home to Nashville on Sunday.

Then he could get back to his real job. No more playing country/western singer. No more band practices. And, best of all, no more trying to keep up with a string of lies.

He picked up the phone he'd dropped on the desk when Paige finally came out of the bathroom. None of this was going to happen until he notified Conner, and so far his good-for-nothing partner had ignored three texts, one marked *Urgent* and another marked *911.*

Time to go over Conner's head and straight to their lieutenant. Just as he began to scroll down his Contacts list, his phone vibrated and strains of Beethoven's 5th broke the silence.

About damn time.

"Where have you been? Don't you know what 911 means?" He really shouldn't yell at Conner. Especially in front of Paige. The woman was already traumatized. Although putting a little fear of God into her could only help when he had to break the news that she was about to have twenty-four hour surveillance.

"I've been talking to Nightingale's old boyfriend, another name I can cross off my list. He's got a part in a play on Broadway so he has a hundred or more alibi witnesses every night. And, yes, I double checked with his director. Lover-boy had some interesting things to say about our sweetheart. None of them flattering. Although he did hint, rather broadly, that she was a good lay. Such a gentleman,"

When did any ex have something nice to say about a former lover? God, was he going to have to get back into that life again? He'd rather die alone. If only he didn't have to worry about Sweet Pea he'd be ready now. But the time was fast approaching when he'd have to make that decision and he'd never reach his street-cleaning quota before that self-imposed date if he remained on guard duty.

He really should dig up a Bible and see if his distant Sunday School memories about forgiving not seven times but seven times seven were correct. He had a lot to make up for if he was going to be allowed to join Betsy and removing forty-nine miscreants—not jaywalkers or pickpockets but true degenerates—from the streets of Houston was little enough to expect of himself whether he chose to take that final step or not.

Paige watched him from the other side of the room. Could she hear what Conner was saying? He needed to change the subject before Conner blurted out something else indelicate.

"You can bring me up-to-date later. Now we have a bigger problem. Our stalker broke into Paige's room last night and left her a calling card—a dead rose."

"Nightingale. Did the creep leave a note?"

"Not this time. Just a black rose with the stem broken."

"Wait a minute. Wait a minute." Conner's voice perked up with enthusiasm. "Was the rose dead or black?"

"Isn't that the same thing?" Noah crossed to the bed and eyed the flower, a menacing scar on a pristine surface.

"No, you can buy black roses."

Who in the world would send someone a black rose? He took the pen from his pocket and lifted one petal. The onyx segment moved easily and his pen slid over a velvet surface. He leaned forward, careful not to touch anything, and sniffed the blossom. Not much of a scent, but some.

Definitely not dead. Now what? Leave it to Conner to know some obscure fact. "You're right. This flower is alive. Can you trace it?"

"Maybe. I'll get right on that as soon as I tell the boss about Nightingale's visitor. Guess there's no doubt now about the fire alarm."

"Right, our stalker obviously knows where she is. I don't think you need to bother with code names anymore."

Conner leaned against the entrance to Jansen's office, waiting for his lieutenant to get off the phone. Jansen wasn't bad, as bosses go. He could usually be depended on to cover the back of anyone on his squad, as long as it didn't put himself crosswise with the big brass.

And Conner's news was likely to do exactly that.

Jansen took his feet off his desk, hung up the phone, and swiveled his chair toward him. "Don't hover there like the messenger of doom. Come in and give me whatever bad news is written all over your face."

The wood of the door frame bit into Conner's shoulder as he pushed off and forced his feet over the worn carpet to the lone visitor's chair. "There's a problem with Nightingale."

Jansen's bushy brows knitted like two fuzzy caterpillars crawling across his face. "What?"

"Paige Reimer."

"Why didn't you just say so?"

The stupid code name wasn't *his* idea. The Chief thought of it. Aw hell, what difference did it make now? "The false alarm in Paige's hotel wasn't an accident. Someone broke into her room last night and left a black rose on her bed."

"Was she in the room?" The twin caterpillars eased back to their original position.

"No, thank goodness. Noah had whisked her off at the first sign of trouble." *Please, for the love of all that's holy, don't let him ask where Noah took her.*

"Well, as long as she's safe." Jansen swiveled his chair back toward his desk, as if finished with the conversation.

That's it? That's all he had to say after some pervert set off a fire alarm in a crowded hotel, endangering hundreds people and using the distraction to break into the room of the one person the chief ordered them to protect?

Okay, the man had other things on his mind. For weeks an orchestrated gang had been backing a pickup into jewelry stores and cleaning out high-end merchandise then disappearing before patrol units could get there. Last night the scum-bags had made the jump from robbery to homicide when a store owner tried to chase them down.

The media was screaming for blood. Lefty Bob and Earl Sparks were on the case, but Jansen was the one on the hot seat. Still, the man didn't get to be lieutenant unless he could grasp more than one case at a time without crib notes.

Ancient plastic squeaked as Conner leaned forward in his chair to get Jansen's attention. "She's not safe, Sir. The stalker found her in one day. Then he escalated by actually going into her room. Whether she likes it or not, she needs round-the-clock protection in the room with her."

Jansen massaged his forehead, making the caterpillars dance. "Then do it. Keep her safe until the damn concert, then escort her to the county line when it's over. Meanwhile, you can pretend to investigate. Go look for a place to buy dead roses."

"Can you talk?"

Noah stepped into the hall and waited for the door to click behind him. "Yes, she's packing. She's not happy about the full-time bodyguard, but she understands. Her protests only rated a three on the Richter scale. What'd you learn?"

"I have good news, bad news, and no news."

That was progress, at least. So far there'd only been no news and bad news. He could use some good news, if he had any hope of avoiding playing Saturday night. "Shoot."

'I've only had time to do a cursory search of the Internet, but it looks like our stalker had no need to buy the black rose from a store. They're dyed that color. I'll keep looking, but if he's smart enough to make a key-card, he can probably manage to dye a rose black."

Of course the creep would have dyed it himself. Anything else would have been too easy. They'd never trace the purchase of a single rose.

The door across the hall opened and a middle-aged man wearing a hotel bathrobe that gapped open farther than Noah cared to see gave him the stink-eye while placing a room-service tray on the floor. The tray contained remnants of a romantic dinner complete with a bud vase and one red rose. Hell, their asshole didn't even have to leave the hotel to find a rose. He could have walked down the hall and picked one up.

"So what's the good news?" They could sure use some about now.

"Everything's all set with the new hotel. They're giving her a penthouse suite. There'll be plenty of room for her to have some privacy while still allowing someone to stay in the place with her. The room will be listed under my name and should be ready when you get there. They're expecting you. Just stop at the desk and grab the key, no need to register."

All this was great, and Conner must have worked his butt off to get it set up so fast, but what good did it do, really? They'd tried the cloak-and-dagger stuff already, and the creep had laughed at them. "Will an officer meet us at the hotel?"

"No, you'll have to stay with her a while. Every spare unit is out looking for our smash-and-grab murderers."

A couple of hours bodyguard duty was fine with Noah. That would leave him time to stop by his desk to write some kind of bullshit report and still get home early to feed Sweet

Pea and give her some much needed attention. Best of all, he'd be free to babysit the girls while Rachelle and Fred went out for their anniversary Saturday night.

"Are you ready for the bad news?"

Shit. That damn Conner. Noah paused while a businessman steered his rolling briefcase toward the elevator. As long as he could hear that squeaky wheel, the guy could hear him. Plus, the hall now smelled like last night's shrimp, caviar, and illicit sex. Although that last was probably his imagination.

With all that had happened, the stalker could be anybody and he wasn't taking any chances on being overheard. He didn't speak until the elevator dinged. "What is it?"

"Did you know the mayor's mother used to be a friend of Paige's mother when they both lived in Dallas?"

What the hell did that have to do with anything? "So?"

"Paige's mom is now in that exclusive Alzheimer's place in The Woodlands. That's why Paige came to Houston a few days early for the concert."

Probably the same place Betsy's mom stayed. Not that it mattered where she lived anymore. She didn't remember him at all and thought Betsy was away at band camp. For a while he'd taken photos and tried to jog her memory, but really, why bother? Sometimes not remembering was a blessing.

Conner's voice jerked him back to the present. "You there, partner?"

"Just waiting to hear something pertinent to this case." Noah leaned one hip against the wall. He'd learned the hard way Conner couldn't be rushed. He'd tell the story as he saw fit.

"While the Big Kahuna, the Chief of D's, and our Lieu all concur our only responsibility now is to keep Paige safe until she leaves for home, the mayor doesn't agree. It seems his mother is insisting we find the son-of-a-bitch who's stalking her childhood friend's daughter. Those were her words, by the way, not mine."

Fuck. There went Saturday night.

The stairwell door creaked shut, cutting off the meager supply of fresh air the quarter inch opening provided. The mid-day heat emphasized the lingering stench of last night's panicked exodus—fear, sweat, stinky feet, and old-fashioned body odor.

One little pull of the wrist and two thousand people had danced to his tune. Now, that was power. He got a hard-on just thinking about it.

Paige thought singing to a few hundred amounted to something significant. She was wasting her talent for pennies because she wasn't willing to go for the gold ring with one bold move. And she was too stupid and too disloyal to let someone who knew better take over.

Her talent lay in singing, not planning.

First he had to break her down. Then he could build her up according to his blueprint.

He'd waited in the stairwell for hours, but he'd learned plenty. The new guitar player wasn't just a replacement. Not with a weapon that size on his hip. His long-tailed shirt and blue jean jacket hid it pretty well, but the way he rested his hand on the slight bulge gave him away.

Hired help or cop, either way the guy was a bodyguard. And she'd spent the night with him. Something he couldn't allow.

He cracked the door open again to see if the guitar player was still in the hall. For this to work, *he* was the only one she could look to for help—or anything else.

She'd never learn her lesson with the bodyguard around. Which meant his next job was to isolate her. If he could do that without taking down the big guy, all the better. If not, he was prepared to do whatever was necessary.

The elevator dinged and a uniformed porter pushing a baggage trolley hurried past his hiding place. He was out of sight before the bellman noticed him, but it had been close. They'd be leaving any minute now. He ought to be able to get to his car in time to watch them pull away. Once he followed them to the new hotel, he could start work. Finding her room number and tracing bodyguard's license plate would be a snap.

All he had to do then was wait. Wait until the bodyguard looked away. Wait until she was alone. Wait for opportunity to smile on him.

Noah sank into the overstuffed chair. He'd kept surveillance from worse places. The noise and fumes of downtown Houston were a distant memory from this high up, replaced by the aroma of fresh fruit from a bowl on the table in the corner, and the gentle hum of the air conditioner.

Tinted windows blocked the glare of the sun, but gave the sky a somber look that fit Noah's mood.

This hotel's signature color was deep maroon—too close to dried blood for Noah's taste—but thankfully used only as accent pieces. His chair, the sofa, and the cushions on the desk chair were cream with maroon piping—was that what Betsy had called it when they recovered the ottoman?—at the seams. From his vantage point, Noah could see Paige bustling around in the bedroom.

She'd brought more suitcases than a traveling salesman. He hadn't liked the idea of a bellman helping them with the luggage, but he couldn't manage it all and keep a hand free to protect her, so they'd followed in formation behind the overflowing cart, attracting more attention with every step.

Once in the room, everything she'd just packed, she had to unpack.

He'd always left his clothes in the suitcase when staying in a hotel, but she hung up every garment. And now she was ironing. Blue jeans. Who ironed blue jeans?

Time to get down to business. "Do you think you could leave that for later and come in here with me?"

She stood in the doorway, jeans in one hand. "I can't just sit around. I'll go crazy. Every time I stop, I see that rose. Shouldn't you be out looking for the sicko that did this instead of doing nothing?"

A slow burn crept up the back of Noah's neck, but he tamped it down. She was only lashing out. She had no idea what he did or didn't do. "I am doing something. I'm protecting you. And I could do it better if you'd come over here and sit down so I could talk to you."

She wadded the jeans she'd just ironed and threw them at him. "I'm not in the mood to visit."

This time he couldn't keep the anger out of his voice. "I'm not interested in visiting. Do you think this is a game? You'll never be completely safe until we figure out who's doing this.

Conner's back at the station running down every lead we have, but they're few and far between. I need to do a serious, in-depth interview with you to see if there's someone in your past, someone you may not have thought about, who might wish you harm."

The color drained from her face in an instant. He might as well have slapped her. When would he learn to temper his words? He dealt with drug dealers, cheats, and murderers every day and kept his cool.

Why did he let this woman get under his skin?

CHAPTER
EIGHT

P AIGE HAD GUARDED secrets all her life. Starting as a child she knew instinctively not to tell the neighbors when her dad was passed out, not napping. Or when her mom was too beat-up to go to work.

It meant no friends over. Actually, no friends at all because they asked questions.

The one time she did tell was a disaster. Her mom caught her crying in the bathroom and wouldn't leave until she told what her father had done to her.

Her mom grew a pair and kicked him out, but then started drinking and so in a way she lost both parents.

Noah was an expert at asking questions. Keeping things from him might be difficult. But she had to try. Her carefully constructed life would fall apart like pulling a pick-up stick from the bottom of the stack if she let her guard down for even one minute.

Things had been going so well. With each passing year her

secrets were easier to keep. She almost forgot them herself. Only at night did they come back to haunt her. Now, for the first time, she was faced with an immovable object, sitting across from her, waiting for an answer. Not talking, not even blinking. Just waiting.

If she told part, could she hold back the rest? She took a long drink from the glass of ice water she gripped like a security blanket. The cold liquid eased the tightness in her throat. She could do this. She was as adapt at keeping secrets as he was at rooting them out.

She leaned back in her chair, keeping her arms close to her side but clutching the glass in front of her with both hands.

"You know the story, everybody does. I dropped out of high school in Dallas half-way through my senior year. I heard about some guys with a garage band who were looking for a singer. I worked days flipping burgers and nights singing for birthday parties or frat parties or pool parties. After a couple of years, I moved on to a better band. I still worked days, but sometimes we actually got paid for playing gigs and the bass player didn't have to hock his guitar to pay his rent."

"And the guys in the first band didn't resent you moving on?"

"Are you kidding me? They left me, not the other way around. They were tired of scrimping. They wanted real jobs and to have Friday night off to spent with their girlfriends. The band dissolved around me. I didn't leave it. I spent months looking for another band."

Months in which her mother rode her constantly to find a man to support her. Settle down. Have kids. Yeah, right. Like that had worked out so well for her.

"What about the second band?" Had he actually shifted slightly in his chair or was that her imagination?

"You don't understand. It was never a set band. Everything was fluid. Guys came and went. They found better gigs or they quit the business. Sometimes they just stopped showing up. I couldn't begin to tell you the names of everyone who passed through."

A drop of condensation rolled down her glass and plopped onto her linen trousers. She kept her eyes on the spreading wet spot to avoid looking at Noah. It didn't keep him from asking more questions.

"Why did you stay?"

Images of late nights, loud drunks, getting stiffed on fees, hitting the bartender up for a plate of fries because she couldn't afford to buy a meal flooded her mind. "What, and quit show business?"

He didn't crack a smile. Maybe he hadn't heard the old joke. Maybe he didn't get it. Maybe he understood it too well. He'd studied at Julliard, hadn't he? If he wasn't lying about that along with so much else.

"So how'd you get to Nashville?"

"I got paid twenty-five bucks to sing the National Anthem at a minor league ball game. The video hit YouTube and I was the darling of the Internet. I couldn't wait to turn in my waitress uniform and head for bigger things. Only in Nashville, they didn't care how much people in Dallas loved me. I was a nobody. I had to start from scratch. Five years later, here I am. An overnight success."

She'd done it. She'd gone through the whole story and didn't let anything important slip.

Noah pushed out of the chair, stretching to his full height, and ambled into the kitchen. He stood at the Keurig and made himself a cup of coffee before returning to the living area. "Let's start over. This time why don't you tell me all the things you left out?"

Noah kept his eyes riveted on Paige. If he made her squirm, so much the better. Some nugget of information was hidden in all the crap she'd just given him. There'd be another nugget the next time she told the story. And the time after.

All he had to do was ferret them out and string them together and he'd learn what she was trying so hard to hide. But her stubbornness was dragging this out too long.

His desire to be finished with this job before the weekend had seemed ample time to catch a low class deviant. Yet here it was, Wednesday afternoon, and he was no nearer closing this case that when the Chief handed it to him on Monday. Meanwhile, the pervert had escalated from slipping notes under doors to breaking and entering.

What did he have planned for tomorrow, or the concert on Saturday afternoon?

No matter what Paige thought, she was an amateur at this game. He hadn't started yesterday. "What did the guys in the second band say when you ditched them for Nashville?"

"They each chipped in $20 for gas and wished me luck. I even slept on one guy's sofa a couple of times when I came back to check on my mother."

Now they were getting somewhere. "Who was that?"

"His name is Hank, and don't even go there. His wife was

the drummer."

Don't go there my ass. He's the first one I'm checking.

"So you showed up in Nashville. Then what?"

"I went back to my old standby. You know: *Do you want fries with that?*"

Like pulling teeth. She wasn't going to give him one iota of information he didn't specifically ask for. He had all night. He could outlast her. "And a world famous talent scout waltzed in and asked you to fill in for the ailing star of the *Grand Ole Opry?*"

She lifted her glass and swirled the melting ice cubes, creating a slushy sound, like walking on wet snow. "Sometimes I worked nights and auditioned days. Other times I worked days and sang for pennies in dark, dirty dives where you wouldn't want to touch the seats for fear of catching something." She slammed her drink on the glass end-table so hard Noah expected to see it crack.

Paige didn't even glance down. "And *any* spare minute, day or night, I practiced or wrote songs until one day a guitar player I had worked with called and asked me to take over for their singer. No, she wasn't a star, just a third rate nobody with a drug problem. But I was a fourth rate nobody so it was a step up. That guitarist was Kevin and we sweated blood to make the band into what it is today. Two years later I went to a record producer and begged on my hands and knees for him to listen to *I'll dream of You*. That was a year ago and I haven't looked back."

Noah sat bolt upright, almost spilling his coffee. "You wrote that?"

The glacial ice that had covered her eyes the first time they met returned.

He'd made plenty of mistakes dealing with her, but this was the biggest. He'd insulted her. Getting back in her good graces wasn't going to be easy.

His phone rang before he had a chance to try. Conner always did have the worst timing.

"What ya got, partner? Please tell me it's something good." Noah carried his phone onto the small balcony, leaving the comfort of the suite and emerging onto a hot, windy, cement rectangle the size of his desk top.

No point letting Paige hear the conversation. She was either in on this mess and knew exactly what was going on—in which case she didn't need to find out how little they knew—or she was as in the dark as they were and would only become more upset.

"I've got the exact time our stalker friend entered Nightingale…ah hell, Paige's room. With any luck, maybe, just maybe, we can eliminate a few suspects."

"Spill it. What time?" Noah plugged one ear with his finger and dipped his head to shelter the phone from the wind and the grit it stirred up.

"Door opened at 11:31, then again at 11:38. The guy spent seven minutes in her room. Seven minutes. He wasn't worried about her finding him there. Can you account for anyone during that time?"

"Not sure. What time did the alarm go off?"

"Alarm was pulled on the seventeenth floor, but the far end of the hallway—a one minute walk from her room—at 11:29"

Conner might get on his nerves sometimes with his fussy

ways, but he was always thorough. He could look at a problem and know what facts were important.

"Most of the band left about five minutes before that. Only the keyboardist was with us when the alarm went off, and I lost him during the rush down all those stairs." Why the hell hadn't he let Paige stop on seventeen to grab her guitar? They might have caught the guy in the act.

Or Paige might have gotten hurt and his primary job was to keep her safe.

A perfect example of *damned if you do and damned if you don't*. Whatever he'd done, it would have been wrong. The Lieu was going to eat his lunch for this one.

"Keep digging and let me know when you find something. Meanwhile, I'll keep my eyes open on this end." He slid the balcony door shut behind him and found a different Paige Reimer waiting for him.

"You're no closer to finding him than the day I walked into the Chief's office, are you?"

Now what, a lie or the truth? "We're checking on a few things, but no. We don't have any solid leads at this time."

The glacial ice began to melt from her eyes and trickle down her face. "And you were right when you said I'd never be safe until he's caught. He followed me from the first hotel to the second. What's to stop him from following me here? Or back to Nashville?"

She was a desirable woman. Even with red eyes and tears ruining her make-up. But he'd dealt with desirable women before and not been distracted, even if she was harder to ignore than most. It was the hurt in those eyes and the fear in her voice that cut straight through him.

He stepped closer and, against his better judgment, patted her on the back.

"I can't promise you we'll catch the guy. Conner will be working behind the scenes. You couldn't ask for a better detective. He's like a kid with a new toy. He won't let go. And I'll still be working undercover in the band. We'll do our best to catch him, but until that time, you should be safe. You'll have a uniformed officer with you at all times, and creeps like that aren't likely to stray far from their home base."

Her shoulders stiffened and she pulled away from him. She thrust her hand into her pocket, yanking out a slip of paper. "Here's Hanks's name and number. He can give you the most complete list of bandmates from Dallas. Kevin is the one to talk to about Nashville. If you have any other questions, ask. I'll do my best to answer."

Now she decided to be cooperative? After he'd wasted days dragging information from her in bits and pieces? The woman's flip-flopping was driving him crazy. He hoped it wasn't too late.

Sweet Pea gave Noah her best, "Why are you late? Where's my dinner?" glare, but by the time they started on their evening walk she seemed to have forgiven him. Still, there wasn't any doubt he was on probation, so he didn't try to hurry her as she sniffed her way around the neighborhood.

Why rush her anyway? This was the most pleasant evening in months. The moon had turned the sidewalk into a ribbon of silver and the Henley's night-blooming jasmine filled the air with perfume. Harley Robson was changing the oil in his clunker of a car and had the radio tuned to a ball game. The announcer's familiar voice was better than Xanax.

The light bulb had finally been replaced in the nearest streetlamp, and his yard looked welcoming in its soft yellow glow.

Everything was under control. Paige had an armed guard so she was safe for now. With the names she'd given him, Conner had a place to start investigating.

He should be able to sleep well tonight.

Sweet Pea whined and he let her lead him down an extra block. Before they rounded the next corner he saw Ryan Howell's house, boarded up and decaying. Well, what did he expect? The home of a serial killer/hit man who left bullet holes in the walls when he shot his own parents before nearly killing a police officer wouldn't attract many buyers.

That's what happened when you thought you had all the bases covered and let your guard down. Even for one minute. Someone broke into your home and tried to kill you and your dog while you were sleeping.

Fuck. Just what he was doing now.

He scooped Sweet Pea into his arms and trotted home.

Conner would be pissed by the late phone call, but it wasn't the things Paige told him that pricked at his mind. It was the things she'd glossed over.

CHAPTER NINE

ONNER HAD SILENCED his phone, but not turned it off and it now sat on the coffee table beside him. He'd spent the last two nights on the computer or on the phone, tracking down Paige Reimer's past.

This night was for Jeannie. He'd promised her. She only had two more weeks of teaching second graders and every day seemed to be harder. Each evening her feet and ankles looked more swollen and the dark circles under her eyes grew more pronounced.

He'd gotten spoiled. She had sailed through the first two trimesters with few complaints. He should have known it couldn't last. That cute little baby bump had turned into a basketball. She wasn't due until the end of July. Was it possible to get any bigger and not explode?

After he whipped up his specialty—a one-pan ground meat and rice concoction he called Shipwreck Supper—and served her on a TV tray, he stuck the plates in the dishwasher and joined her on the sofa to watch her favorite program. Over the last couple of years he'd actually come to enjoy the show and could discuss with her which couple were the best dancers and if they had chosen the right music.

He didn't tell her what he honestly thought of the costumes.

A swell in the music covered the slight buzzing when his phone rang. Jeannie didn't seem to notice it, but he did and there was no mistaking the glow he caught from the corner of his eye when the screen lit up.

One quick scoop of his hand and the phone was out of sight as he pushed off the cool leather. "I'm going to get a little ice cream. How about you? Can I interest you in some Black Cherry Sorbet?"

"Yumm, that sounds great. Two scoops, please." She didn't take her eyes off the TV. "And, Honey, tell Noah *Hi* and that he missed a good dinner."

Conner answered the phone on the way to the kitchen. No point hiding it now. "This better be good. I promised Jeannie my undivided attention for this one evening."

"Why would you do a fool thing like that? Don't you know any better than to make promises when we're on a case?" Noah sounded out of breath. Walking Sweet Pea would never have winded him, and jogging was out of the question with his knee still healing. Was he only now heading home?

For one second Conner felt guilty, but it passed. He'd worked at home every night this week. "We're always on a case."

"Maybe, but most of our victims are already dead, so there's no hurry. Add that this one is a friend of the Mayor and the case becomes a little more urgent."

"Spit it out, partner. Tell me what you need so I can get back to the foxtrot."

Silence greeted him on the other end while Noah chewed on that piece of information, but Conner let him wonder. No reason to explain. Noah was the one who interrupted *him*.

"Uhh." A question mark hung in Noah's voice. "I'm texting you two names. One you already know. But they have the names of all the band members Paige has worked with in the past. Somebody might be a tad disgruntled she made it and they didn't."

For this Noah had called him at nine o'clock? It could have waited until morning. Had his partner completely forgotten what it was like to have somebody you cared about waiting for you in the other room?

Noah wasn't the same ball of barely contained anger and frustration he'd been for so long after Betsy died, but cliché as it might seem, the man needed to get a life.

Who was he kidding? He wouldn't take it half as well if some sleep deprived driver snatched Jeannie from him. If his religion didn't prohibit it, he might even consider the same action that until recently Noah had seemed to be contemplating.

"I'll get right on that first thing in the morning. Is Paige tucked in tight with round-the-clock protection?"

Between the hum of the dishwasher and dance music from the TV, Noah's chuckle was barely audible. "You remember a five foot nothing patrol officer named Tracy Barrows?"

"Is she the one they call The Wolverine because she looks like a miniature poodle but could tear a sumo wrestler apart with her bare hands?" Applause drifted in from the other room.

"Oh yeah, that's the one. I pity the fool who tries to break into that room."

"I guess we can relax and just concentrate on our jobs now that we know she's safe." *That was a hint you idiot, in case you missed it.*

He waited, but no reply came from the other end. Noah was definitely still there. He could hear him breathing.

Conner tucked the phone against his shoulder as he opened the freezer. A blast of icy air filled his nostrils, blocking out the scent of ground meat and garlic bread, but still no sound from Noah.

He'd rather have a beer than ice cream. But if Jeannie couldn't, neither could he. He'd already pulled down two bowls when he gave in. "Spit it out. What has your gut in a knot?"

"There's something in Paige's past she's not telling me, and I can't figure out what. She told me about the band members so I don't think that's it."

"What else is there besides the band? Something farther back? High school? That doesn't seem likely."

"She hasn't talked much about her mother. I think I'll pay a visit to the lady. I know she's suffering from Alzheimer's, and might not remember last week, but ten years ago could seem like yesterday to her. No telling what might slip out."

Conner shouldered the freezer closed. "You check the old lady. I'll work on the band. Between us, maybe we can find something because right now we've got bupkis"

"Mrs. Reimer is in the same nursing facility as Betsy's mom. Guess I could pay a visit to my mother-in-law at the same time. Won't that be a fun start to my day?"

Sundowners Syndrome, the phenomena of worsening conditions for those with dementia as the sun goes down, left Betsy's mother with severe mood swings and agitation, making Noah's usual evening visits a mistake for both of them.

He downed a cup of coffee and skipped breakfast. After a quick walk with Sweet Pea and a game of toss-the-toy, he headed for The Woodlands.

The worst of the morning rush hour was over, school kids were at their desks, and no eighteen-wheeler had overturned. He flew down I-45 at a record pace.

Where was a traffic jam when you wanted one?

As he jogged up the steps of the nondescript tan brick building, he realized the last time he'd been here he'd still been using a cane. Had it really been that long? Much as he hated coming here, he owed it to Betsy to do a better job of checking on her mother. She'd have been disappointed in him and that was worse than facing a belligerent old woman who didn't remember him.

The place was spotlessly clean and brightened by cheery yellow paint, colorful artwork, and vases of fake flowers, yet it still managed to smell of sickness and desperation. Locked doors and a sign-in system to rival Ft. Knox didn't lighten the mood any.

Noah swung left down a familiar hallway and came to a stop in front of room 127 just as an aid stepped out. "Detective Droughty, how nice to see you again." Her salt and pepper hair sported a lavender clip, holding it back from her face.

"Nice to see you again, too, Nancy." He always trusted the

older ones more. They seemed willing to take the necessary time while the young ones constantly acted like they were in a rush.

"How's Francine doing today? I thought I'd come earlier in the day and maybe catch her in a better mood."

"Oh, she's past all that now. Day, night, it doesn't affect her anymore."

She must have seen the look of horror on his face because she put her hand on his arm. "Sometimes getting a little worse can be a blessing. She's happier now."

He stepped into the room and saw his mother-in-law, the woman who'd thrown a fit at the idea of her talented daughter wasting herself on a cop, sitting in a wheelchair, staring at nothing. The same woman who'd sworn men were no damn good. They'd leave you every time.

Had the insidious disease been working on her even then? Was it hereditary? Would Betsy have gotten it in time? He couldn't have lived with that: watching her waste away. Losing her all at once was better.

No it wasn't. At least then he'd have had a lifetime of memories to call on instead of only three years' worth.

"Hi, Francine." He spoke softly, hoping not to startle her.

"Who are you?" Venom dripped from each word.

The first time she hadn't recognized him had been a kick in the gut. One more link to Betsy lost forever. Now he was used to it. "I'm Noah. Betsy's piano teacher." It was a lie he'd worked up as an excuse for his monthly visits.

"Oh." She softened a minute amount. "She's not here. She's at band camp. She's been gone a long time. I think she'll be home soon."

"I know. I promised her I'd look in on you while she was away. See how you were doing. Do you have everything you need? Can I get anything for you?"

"No. You better go. It doesn't look good for me to be here alone with you." She averted her face and returned to staring at the wall.

Noah waited in the doorway for a few seconds but she continued to ignore him so he backed away.

If Paige's mother wasn't more alert, he could kiss that line of investigation goodbye.

CHAPTER
TEN

NOAH STOOD IN the hall and peered into Estelle Reimer's room. The small space contained heavy, oversized furniture. The four-poster bed was covered with a busy, flowered spread that matched the drapes. Every flat surface had knickknacks and doilies, but not one family photo that he could see. The scent of perfume, strong enough to overpower the hospital odor, wafted through the door.

The effect of so much clutter made Noah claustrophobic. He fought the urge to turn and run.

From what the nurses told him about Estelle Reimer, Paige and Betsy had a lot in common.

Mrs. Reimer was what Noah's father would have called a handsome woman. From the records he'd checked, Paige must have been a late-in-life baby, putting her mother in her mid-sixties and in the early stages of the disease. She didn't yet have the slack jaw, vacant eyes, and stooped posture of Betsy's mother. But that didn't make her any more likeable.

He'd heard many times—before you marry a woman, check out her mother. That's what you'll get in twenty years. Noah had married Betsy in spite of her mother. How his mother-in-law had raised a warm, talented, loving daughter was beyond him. Betsy's passion for music must have lit a spark deep in her heart to overcome living with such a shrew. That was the only explanation he could come up with.

Did Paige share the same passion? Is that what kept her going?

Noah tapped on the door and was greeted with an icy glare. "Who are you and what are you doing here?"

Maybe she and Francine could share a room. Save a little money and finish each other's sentences.

He might as well use the same lie he'd used on his mother-in-law. "I'm Noah. Paige's…." He hesitated. Had Paige even taken piano? "Music teacher."

"Well, you can just turn around and head straight back out of here. You're not getting another penny out of me. Music, what a waste. I wish I had that money back. I'd be able to afford a nice apartment instead of this hellhole. I tried to tell Paige she'd be better off learning hair-dressing like me. But *nooo*, she had to have hoity-toity music lessons. A fat lot of good it's doing her now."

Not the response he'd expected, but he might as well run with it. If she was talking, he wanted to know what she had to say. "What do you mean? Paige is very talented."

"She's nothing but a slut, spreads her legs for anything in pants." If her first glare at Noah had been icy, this one burned lasers through him. "Are you one of them? Is that why you're here looking for her? A grown man like you, trying to take advantage of a girl half his age."

Noah held his hands up in a gesture of surrender. "No, Ma'am. I've never touched her. I've never even been in a room alone with her."

Estelle turned away from him with a shrug. "Doesn't matter now. You won't find her. I told her straight out, 'You want to run away from home, fine with me. Go. But once you head out that door, don't ever come back.' Good riddance, I say."

He already knew Paige had dropped out of high school, so discovering she ran away from home didn't exactly fall into the category of new information. The entire trip had been a waste of time. He'd only learned one thing.

No wonder Paige didn't want to talk about her mother.

Morning rush hour had passed and lunch traffic hadn't started. Noah took his eyes off the road long enough to enjoy the spring day. Not too warm, not too cold. He couldn't have ordered nicer weather. The sky was so blue it almost hurt to look at it.

When he caught himself comparing the clouds to meringue, he realized how hungry he was. Skipping breakfast to hit the road early had seemed like a good idea at the time, but not so smart now.

Could he afford the time to drive over to Mel's for the fried fish platter he'd missed with Rachelle and her family? Why not? He'd worked late every night. Let the office wonder where he was.

Traffic increased as he neared the mall and he congratulated himself once again on his choice of the heavy-duty pickup. The high frame gave him excellent visibility and the extended cab offered extra leg room. The lockbox in the back allowed him to carry a change of clothes along with his vest, fire extinguisher, and first aid kit plus other paraphernalia he'd either used or might use in the future.

The truck was his first brand-new ride and he was a little embarrassed how proud he was of it.

A warm feeling spread across his chest as he remembered how Betsy had ribbed him about his choice, asking what he was compensating for. "You treat this truck better than you treat me," she teased. "Nothing's too good for her: premium gas, hand wash, regular wax jobs. The way she gets whatever she wants, you ought to name her Lola after that character in *Damn Yankees*."

She might have been kidding, but Noah liked the joke and the name stuck.

But even Betsy admitted Lola was a comfortable ride and she loved the view from the higher cab.

For instance, he could see that stupid khaki-colored F-650 pickup with the oversized wheels speeding up behind him. What was that idiot doing? Traffic might have been thin five minutes ago, but it picked up fast as they passed Rayford-Sawdust Road.

He'd have switched lanes and let the road hog pass if he wasn't blocked in by an eighteen wheeler on his left struggling to maintain speed while climbing up the overpass. The way it belched black smoke, following it for only half a mile would be dangerous to his health.

Noah pressed on the accelerator, goosing his speed to

eighty-five, but the F-650 continued to close in. He pressed harder, and Lola responded with ninety, then ninety-two.

Just when he thought he might be able to pull ahead enough to change lanes, they topped the overpass and started down. The eighteen wheeler picked up speed and pulled even with him again.

And still the F-650 closed in, like Lola's bigger, meaner older brother.

A puke-yellow Honda with a *Baby on Board* sticker flipped on its blinker and pulled in front of him, probably aiming for the next exit a quarter mile away.

Yep. The Mom-mobile kept its signal on and brake lights flashed at him. He had no choice but to slow down.

The F-650 apparently didn't agree.

In a fraction of a second, the behemoth was riding his bumper. He was completely boxed in with cement construction barriers on one side, an eighteen wheeler on the other and the Honda in front. The F-650 inched even closer. Its heavily tinted windows and lowered sun visor obscured the driver's face.

The Honda was toast if he didn't slow drastically. When he did, the douchebag behind him tapped his tail gate. Lola leapt forward as if her mother had mated with a jack rabbit. She flew through the air long enough for Noah to appreciate the seriousness of his situation, then hit the ground with a jolt that lifted him off his seat. His head hit the roof until his seat belt yanked him back down so hard his breath expelled with an audible *ooph* and he bit his tongue.

At the last second, the Honda shot off onto the exit ramp and the giant behind him rammed into Lola like a big horn sheep head-butting a rival. Noah sideswiped a light pole, did a 180, and ended up half on the guard rail and half off. The air bag smacked him in the chest, knocking out the little breath he had regained while a hail storm of BB sized broken glass rained down on him from every direction.

Lola was still rocking when he wiped the blood from his eyes and looked around. The F-650 was nowhere in sight.

What the fuck had just happened? It wasn't road rage. He hadn't cut the guy off or blocked him. It wasn't an accident. The whole thing felt too deliberate.

Why now, and why him? That was the question, wasn't it?

He didn't know the answer, but he did know one thing. He was only working on one case at the moment.

Salsa music played in Conner's ear as he waited for a live human to answer his question. He caught himself boogieing to the beat and sat up straighter before anyone in the squad room noticed. Lefty Bob would never let him live it down.

The visitor's chair beside his desk emitted a groan as if protesting his dance moves instead of the substantial weight that had just plopped down onto its cracked plastic seat.

He jerked his head to the side and stared into Noah's battered face. Conner was so startled he fumbled the receiver trying to hang up. "What happened?" was all he managed to say.

Noah's left eye was swollen and turning black. A bandage covered the bridge of his nose. A trickle of dried blood showed at his hairline, and his left arm was in a sling. But the most disturbing thing was the look of utter desolation in his one good eye.

He tried to blink but only one eyelid cooperated. "Lola's dead."

In one practiced move, Conner sprang to his feet, yanked open his right-hand drawer and grabbed his weapon. His mind was whirling as he slipped his Glock into the holster at the small of his back.

Paige is under constant protection. How could someone get through? Was Lola the only one hurt? Should I have assigned more than one person on guard detail at a time?

Wait a minute. Wait a minute. Brian Mabry had the morning detail. *Who is Lola and why does that name sound so familiar?*

He willed his racing heart to slow down. "Please tell me you're not talking about your truck."

"Joe at Markham Motors won't be sure until he has her up on a rack, but the frame's probably bent. He tried to convince me he could straighten it good as new, but you know she'll never ride the same."

Conner eased into his chair, ignoring the Glock digging into his back. "What the God Damn Hell do you think you're doing? If you ever come in here and scare me like that again I'll come across this fucking desk and bend *your* frame until your asshole is staring back at your good eye. You think the speed limit is for peons and all those butt-heads should just get out of your way. Your business is more important than theirs. Well, here's a news flash, ass wipe. Accidents happen when you treat the freeway like your own personal racecourse."

He hated the profanity pouring from his mouth. Hated it. He tried to save it for exigent circumstances. Otherwise it would slip out when talking to witnesses, or Jeannie, or, God forbid, the baby. But if this didn't warrant strong language, he didn't know what did.

"Do you have any idea how many hours I've spent trying to get that jerk from the key manufacturing company to agree to speak to me? I wasted most of a day on the warrant alone. I drew Hard Ass Hargity and she made me resubmit twice due to 'Weak and circumstantial evidence.' Then the company kept foisting me off on numb nuts that only knew about sales or accounting. Finally, finally, I tracked down someone who knew about manufacturing and what did you do? Come in here bitching about a traffic accident."

"I wasn't speeding and this wasn't an accident. Some fuckhead intentionally ran me off the road."

Ah, hell. What had he done? Talking to Noah that way. Just because he'd been scared. There was no excuse for it. Noah would understand. Not hold it against him. But it shouldn't have happened. This case was frustrating and he was taking it out on his best friend.

And not simply his best friend. A friend who was teetering on the edge. Only two months ago he'd been worried Noah was contemplating doing something drastic. Not just contemplating. Had already taken steps to prepare. Had two garden hoses ready to attach to his truck's exhaust and pipe into his house.

Only to have someone try to beat him to it and cause him to pull back.

But anger at some lowlife wasn't enough. Noah needed to realize on his own that his life was worth living. Meeting Laurel Bledsoe might have helped, if they had worked out.

That's what this was about. He'd been walking on eggshells

for too long, weighing every word with Noah. Once the anger started flowing, he couldn't stop it. "You scared the tar out of me. Don't ever do it again or I'll kill you myself."

"I saw you dancing around in your chair as if this were any normal day. Indignation shot through me like a hot poker and I had to stop you. "

"Let's start back with when you walked in. What happened?"

Noah went through his story once, with Conner taking notes, and a second time while Conner peppered him with enough questions to make his head spin. Or was that slight dizzy sensation a result of banging his head on the truck roof?

"Did you see the driver's face? Can you describe him?"

"I can't even swear it was a man. When the truck first approached, the tinted windows and visor blocked my view, not to mention the sun glinting off the windshield. When it got closer, I was a little busy trying not to get killed."

"What about the license plate. Are you sure about the numbers you do have?"

"CWS, country western singer. And a seven. I never caught the rest, but you can probably lift them off my tail gate from when he rammed into me. Any closer and they'd have been imprinted on the back of my skull." This was too much. He realized witnesses had to go over their story multiple times to coax out every detail, but he was a professional, dammit. He knew what was important.

He closed his eyes and the scene played out in front of him. The smell of burning rubber and taste of blood from his cut lip were as real as when the wreck first happened. Especially the sensation of Lola flying onto the concrete barricade on two wheels before settling with a teeth-cracking jolt.

What if Betsy had been in something as heavy as Lola instead of her lime green bug? Would she still be here? She'd loved that little car. She'd resisted every time he tried to talk her into something bigger, sturdier. His eyes snapped open. He couldn't go there, not today. If the black funk swallowed him again, he'd never find the asshole who nearly killed him and might be after Paige.

"I'd like to go home now. I need to feed Sweet Pea and clean up before practice tonight." He wanted a nap, too, but he didn't see the need to share that with Conner.

"Are you crazy?" Conner gripped his pen so hard Noah worried it might shatter. Ink spewed over his dirty and bloody clothes wouldn't matter. But over Conner's suit and indigo silk tie would be a tragedy.

"Your cover's blown. You can't go back to the band like nothing happened." Conner's voice rose to drown out the hum of voices and telephones, causing inquiring glances from around the squad room.

"Why not?"

A look of incredulity passed over Conner's face. "Two reasons. First, the object of your assignment was to get information from the band. If they haven't told you anything yet, they're certainly not going to now. And second, are you out of your ever-lovin mind? Someone just tried to kill you and you want to stand up on a stage in front of thousands of people? That would give the nut bag two targets to shoot at. You do remember that someone in Paige's band was struck in a hit-and-run, also?"

That thought did cross my mind while I was flying through the air. "My assignment was always to protect Paige. Getting information that might help find our crazy nut bag was only a by-product. If no one in the band is our suspect, then they don't know what happened to me. If he is hiding behind one of those instruments, the closer I am to Paige, the better. You seem to forget I'm a trained peace officer. I don't need to be protected. I do the protecting."

Noah's breath came in short gasps. He'd been sitting too long. Every muscle in his body was cramping. A noose was pulled tight across his chest. Each time he exhaled, it tightened, making the next inhale that much harder. He'd broken at least two ribs, he knew it. But he hadn't told the doc and he didn't plan on telling Conner.

"What about your arm? It's in a sling. You can't play a guitar with only one arm." Conner was no longer shouting. He was using his *Keep calm and sound reasonable* voice. But that didn't work on Noah. He'd heard all Conner's ploys.

"My shoulder was dislocated. They popped it back into place and it's fine now. I can take the sling off whenever I want."

As long as whenever is sometime tomorrow.

Noah paused on his way out. Conner wouldn't leave any stone unturned in his search for the driver of the F-560. If it was the same guy who made his own hotel key and left no usable prints, Conner's chances of finding anything helpful were about equal to winning the Megabucks lottery.

He'd gone to visit Estelle Reimer in search of information Paige hadn't been willing to share. The old woman's memory was shot. Yet she'd sparked his interest just the same.

Noah swung around to face Conner. "I've got one more thing for you to check. It's probably nothing, but see what you can find."

CHAPTER
ELEVEN

THE SPACIOUS LIVING area offered Paige plenty of room to pace, and she took advantage of every inch. No matter how plush the carpet or how soft the luxurious sofa, the hotel suite was a prison. A prison with an exceptional view, a well-stocked bar, and room service at the touch of a button.

But a prison nevertheless.

She needed to run. She needed to breathe air that hadn't been conditioned and recirculated a dozen times. She needed to feel the beat of her feet against a gravel path. A beat that with every step traveled up the soles of her running shoes, through her body, and into her brain, obliterating the dark memories that threatened to once again overpower her.

A sweaty workout room treadmill didn't offer any of the things she needed.

A woman whose navy blue uniform must have been altered to fit her short but muscular frame came around the corner. "Can I get you anything, Miss Reimer?"

"Please, Tracy, you've seen me in my PJs, with bed-head and morning breath. Call me Paige. What if we didn't go to Memorial Park to run? What if we drove up to The Woodlands? I'll bet they have a lot of jogging trails. No one would expect to see us there."

"Detective Daugherty called and said not to let you leave the hotel. He was very specific. I'm sure he has a good reason."

Oh, yeah. She'd seen Noah at the nursing home. That shiny black truck with the extended cab was hard to miss among all the twenty-year-old gas-guzzlers. He was strutting in the main door while she and Tracy slipped out a side entrance. She'd told him her mother's memory was gone, but he hadn't listened to anything else she'd said. Why had she expected him to listen to that?

If only she knew what secrets the old woman had spilled.

It wasn't fair. As a child, her mother had never been an award winner, but she'd tried. She cooked meals, drove her to school, oversaw homework, all with kindness if not actual warmth. All the while trying to hide secrets of her own.

Then Paige had made the biggest mistake of her life. Well, the next-to-biggest mistake. She'd confided the things her father tried to do to her. Her mom had pulled up her big girl panties and kicked the bastard out, only to fall completely apart, blaming Paige for everything that went wrong from that day forward. And plenty had gone wrong.

Her mother's outer shell had cracked, leaving Paige to share a home with a bitter, venom-spewing witch just when she needed a mother the most.

She'd tried to run away, only to slink back home, tail between her legs. The shame heaped on her by a mother who worried more about the neighbors than her own daughter chafed more than the rules she'd lived under. No phone calls in or out. Stay away from the windows. Don't go outside except under cover of darkness. How she'd longed for sunshine, a friendly voice. Even now, she couldn't stand to be closed in.

How much worse if her mother had known the whole story.

In the last few years her mother had come back to her, only to be snatched away again by that insidious disease. Now her mother was a wild card. What did she remember and what had faded into the recesses of her constantly eroding mind?

Dammit. They were her secrets, to share or not share as she saw fit. They could hurt her career, sure, but more than that, they were painful reminders of things best left forgotten. It had taken her years to put them behind her and now Noah wanted to dredge them back up.

If she thought for one second they had anything to do with this crazy stalker, she'd spill everything. But they didn't. They were simply nuggets of white-hot lava, burning holes in her soul.

Let Noah deal with his own hurt and pain. Leave hers alone.

Noah had just fallen asleep—clothes on, stretched out on the sofa, Sweet Pea on his chest—when his phone rang. He jolted to a sitting position. Five pounds of fur with a zebra-striped bow tumbled onto his lap, earning him a glare of disapproval.

"Hello." *Dammit.* The crack in his voice might as well have been a neon sign.

"Did I wake you?"

"Just getting ready for tonight." *Shit*. He hurt worse than he had two hours ago.

"Yeah, right." Sarcasm dripped from Conner's words.

Best to ignore the jab. "Tell me you found the monstrosity that ran me off the road and nearly killed me."

"Don't be melodramatic. You didn't even break a bone."

Yes, he had. Two ribs. He'd have to be in traction before he admitted that to Conner.

The sound of papers rustling was audible over the phone. "The good news is we found the truck."

Why did he think he was about to hear a *but?*

"But it had been stolen sometime last night or early this morning."

"So this is another one of your good news-bad news things?" The little Yorkie had somehow morphed into a bull mastiff as Noah lifted her and struggled to his feet. Despite standing under a hot shower for twenty minutes, multiple shampoos, and a complete change of clothes, his body ached and light glinted off a layer of glass fragments left on the sofa.

He carried the dog outside and eased down on the back stoop while she began her rounds of the yard, checking for intruders.

"I'm afraid you haven't realized the really bad news."

What was Conner talking about? Really bad news? Noah let his mind work on the problem while he watched Sweet Pea investigate the spot where a neighbor's cat had been seen yesterday.

Conner broke into his contemplations. "Are you still there,

partner?"

"You're thinking he followed me from home, which means he knows my name and where I live, right?"

"Right."

"What if he was waiting at the nursing home? What if he was watching Estelle Reimer?"

Conner softened his voice. Noah had seen it a hundred times. It was a trick his partner used when he thought something was important and the person he was talking to needed to pay attention. "Are you sure you want to bet your life on that?"

No. But he wasn't willing to be taken off the case, either. Someone had the nerve to try and kill him. He wasn't about to let the ass hat get away with that, even if it meant he died trying.

A squirrel chattered from a safe perch on a pine tree and Sweet Pea yapped back at him. The squirrel waved his bushy tail in a catch-me-if-you-can motion and raced away. The dog continued her circle of the yard until she reached the side fence.

She came to an abrupt halt, sniffing the wooden gate. Her hair stood on end and her lips curled back. A deep growl built in her throat.

"Here, girl," Noah called, gently. The dog flicked a glance Noah's direction before burying her nose into the crack between the gate and the fence post. The volume of her growls inched up.

"What's that?" Conner asked.

"Just Sweet Pea objecting to the local tom cat that likes to use my flower bed for his private sandbox." An early morning shower had left the air sweet and clean, but the stoop damp. The wet began to seep into Noah's jeans, causing him to shift uncomfortably on the concrete step.

The answer must have satisfied Conner. "Are you ready to call it quits and give up the rock-n-roll lifestyle?"

"Not yet. Why don't you at least *attempt* to solve the car theft before you try to convince the Lieu to yank me off this case? Who owned the truck? Maybe they know something."

"I checked. A little old couple on their way to visit the grandkids. She wasn't any bigger than a minute, and he didn't top a minute and a half. I'll bet he had to sit on a cushion to see out the windshield. And they drove that monster here from Dallas? What a waste."

Was Conner actually worrying about saving the planet while someone was trying to kill him? "Anything left inside the truck that might help identify the SOB?"

"The guy didn't drop his wallet, if that's what you're asking. No prints, no discernable DNA. You said the driver wore a ball cap pulled low, so we were hoping for a few hairs to test, but it was the owner's hat and the guy took it with him. A Dallas Cowboy's cap, if you can believe it. That ought to stand out around here."

"Hell, with that cap on you don't need DNA. Just wait till some Texans fan beats him up. The nearest hospital will notify us. Where was the truck stolen, from, anyway?"

"The parking garage of Paige's hotel."

"There you go. Paige visited her mother first thing this morning. The nurse told me she came half an hour before I got there. I would have been pulling in about the time she left. He could have followed her, seen me, and waited for me to leave."

Noah retreated into the kitchen, closing the screen door before the mosquitoes followed. Sweet Pea's growls had turned into whines, but she never left her post at the gate. He found a liver treat and held it out the door. She didn't stop her quest to dig straight through the wood long enough to even consider the treat.

If he couldn't get her to slow down, she was going to rip off a nail and he didn't plan to face the emergency clinic vet ever again. He held the phone in place with one shoulder while he stepped outside and scooped her under his arm. "Call me when you find anything, *anything*, we can work with. Until then, I'm going to carry on as if nothing happened."

Conner grumbled for another minute but finally agreed. Noah returned the phone to his pocket so he could hold the little Yorkie with two hands. He stared into her face. "What's up with you? Is there something out there I should know about?"

Sweet Pea, now removed from the distraction, was only interested in the treat Noah had dropped into her bowl.

He lowered her to the floor and watched her scamper across the room to her feeding pad. She had never been particularly territorial when Betsy was alive, but now she guarded her terrain like the Secret Service watched over the President—every intruder was a possible threat.

The only problem was, she couldn't distinguish two-legged intruders from four-legged ones. Or at least she couldn't communicate that difference to Noah.

He tossed her another treat, grabbed his Glock from the top of the refrigerator, and slipped out the door while she was occupied.

The gate was six feet high and solid; impossible to see

through and even harder to jump over. And it was locked from the inside. The latch had been opened and closed so many times it had scratches, but none of them seemed new. He had fertilized last weekend so the grass was thick. If there were any footprints, he couldn't see them.

Was he turning into an old lady like Conner? Traipsing around his backyard with a gun? Two busted ribs that ached with each breath said he was only being sensible.

There was one thing his normally thorough partner hadn't thought of. And that wasn't like Conner unless baby-plans had distracted him. Or, even scarier, his partner was trying to keep the idea from him while making plans of his own to deal with it.

While Noah might not have been able to read all of his assailant's plate number, his was visible to the car-stealing son-of-a-bitch who rammed him. If the asshole didn't know his name and address before, he probably did now.

Years of practice allowed Conner to turn the normal clamor of the squad room into white noise releasing him to chew on a problem in peace. He glanced at the Lieu's office. The light was off, indicating Jansen was out. Good. There were times it was best not to involve the boss in a situation.

Noah was about to do something stupid. Conner could feel it in his bones. In their line of work, the minute you got angry and took something personally, you started to screw up.

The last time someone tried to kill Noah, the fool had used himself as bait. An ill-conceived plan that almost backfired. This time it was worse—they'd gone after his precious truck.

Conner drummed his pen against the top of his desk. If he had any idea who was behind this, there was a chance he could protect Noah. But he was completely in the dark. No closer to solving this case than when they walked into the Chief's office on Monday. He'd silently agreed when Noah claimed they'd have this case wrapped up and be back to working a simple, uncomplicated murder within twenty-four hours.

He'd run the name of every person who'd associated with Paige since she started her career. Nada. None were pristine, but none were what he'd call dirty. He needed to talk to that Kevin guy, get a few more names, but that would be tricky without blowing Noah's cover.

Who was he kidding? It was pretty obvious Noah's cover had already been blown, no matter what his partner tried to make him believe. Anyone capable of hacking into a hotel computer and making a room key, would find running down a plate number child's play.

If the guy was serious about taking Noah out of the picture, he'd likely be waiting at Noah's house by the time band practice was over.

Conner glanced at his watch. If he planned to confront Kevin and maybe get a feel for the rest of the band he needed to get a move on. Then he had to check out the long shot Noah gave him. Maybe that could wait for tomorrow.

First, he'd better call Jeannie and apologize. He had a long night ahead of him, and it didn't include shopping for a car seat.

CHAPTER TWELVE

NOAH STUDIED HIMSELF in the bathroom mirror. Not too bad. Ice packs had helped reduce the swelling in his eyes. With the bandage removed from his nose and the sling discarded, he almost looked normal.

For one brief moment he'd considered using some of Betsy's makeup to cover the bruising but decided against it… for so many reasons.

He popped three Tylenol and headed out the back door. The doc gave him a script for something stronger, but he'd wadded it up and tossed it in the trash before the man's white coat disappeared through his curtained cubicle. He couldn't do his job with a fuzzy head.

The sight of the two-tone, grape and rust, rent-a-heap loaner sitting in his driveway turned his stomach. He'd look like a giant eggplant, rolling down the street. Poor Lola. Would he ever see her again?

The struggle to keep the hunk-a-junk traveling in a straight line took all his concentration and kept his mind off his looks through the twenty-minute drive downtown and until he met Paige in the rehearsal hall.

"What the hell happened to you?" The expression on Paige's face told him he'd been wrong about the looking normal part.

"A close encounter with an impatient driver."

Her eyes, already wide, doubled in size. "Does it have anything to do with…you know?"

"Naw, just a fender bender. Surprising it doesn't happen more often with Houston traffic."

"Yeah, right," she muttered under her breath, but loud enough for Noah to hear before she turned her back on him.

She knew. The tight set of her shoulders gave her away. He'd tried to warn her after the first note, the fire alarm, the black rose. But she refused to admit the risk she was taking. He'd insisted she needed the truth. Needed to know about the danger. Needed to understand the importance of her cooperation.

Now she did know, and recognizing the fear in those blue eyes didn't make him feel any better.

He grabbed her arm and she swung toward him, her lips a tight white line. "Not now. Now is for rehearsing." Tears pooled and threatened to spill over. Only force of will could have kept that from happening.

"Okay, but later. We need to talk."

"Fine. Just don't say anything here. I still have to work with these people."

Not if one of them was the culprit.

Jeff and Craig got a good laugh out of his story about the NASCAR-eligible soccer mom on her way to the mall. Craig even wondered where the sale was and did they have time to go check it out.

Noah tried to join the fun at his expense, but wasn't sure he pulled it off. "The way she was driving, I hope she was headed to Sears for a new set of brakes."

Kevin's glance flicked from Noah to Paige and back, but he never cracked a smile.

Paige stepped in and got them back on track. "All right, guys. Let's quit indulging our reckless driver and see if he can still play and sing. We only have two more days to get ready and if he broke his nose, I may have to rethink our play list."

Any concern Noah had built for Paige evaporated at the thought of what was in store for him over the next four hours. She obviously didn't plan to show any sympathy for his poor, aching body.

At the break, Noah hurried into the bathroom in hopes of popping a couple more Tylenol without anyone noticing. Too late. The toke-em-if-you-got-em club was already underway. A haze hung in the room thick enough to give Noah the munchies. This might be their first hit for this break, but not for the evening.

A few puffs of weed hadn't mellowed Kevin one bit. "So what's the real story about that eye? And don't tell me it was a fender bender. Paige about freaked out when she saw you."

"She's worried I won't be able to perform. That's all."

"And what about that cop who was here before you dragged your sorry ass in twenty minutes late? He seemed to think Paige had some kind of problem. Somebody threatening her. You wouldn't know anything about that, would you?"

Fuck. He knew having Conner check out the band would lead to questions. "Is that why she seems jumpy? I'm just a temp. I don't know anything about that. You think I wasn't in a wreck? Come outside and look at the piece-of-crap rental I'm driving."

Jeff shook his head. "Nah. I guess we're all jumpy. We've invested too much time and energy into this thing. We can almost taste the payoff. If Paige pulls out now, and I don't just mean this festival, although it's a major step to the top, the whole thing could fall apart. And I for one am too old to start over with another newbie."

Good to know he was so concerned with Paige's welfare. *Jerk.*

Noah's cell rang before he made a comment he'd regret and he stepped into the hall before answering.

The sound of his partner's voice was comforting. Although he'd talked to the guy every day, and seen him several times, he hadn't realized how much he missed working next to his best friend.

"Just wanted to let you know I'll be heading to Dallas in a few minutes. That way I can do the interviews I need first thing in the morning and be back home by late afternoon. I'm not getting anywhere this way. Maybe if I look people in the eye I can shake something loose. What about you, anything new to report?"

"Your visit spooked the band guys, just like I warned you it would. They all looked at me suspiciously, but it didn't make one of them jump out and say, 'I did it.'" At least with Paige having real protection he could get home at a semi-decent

hour to feed Sweet Pea.

He'd only wanted to put the guy out of commission, not kill him, but the sight of the big guy going about his business, not even limping, was a shock. The cop, and there was no doubt now he was a cop, not a hired bodyguard, might have to go down permanently if he couldn't take a hint. Easy enough to do after a five minute search revealed his real name and address.

Only one problem. Remove a private citizen and the cops would run around in circles, flapping their arms and making noise. Take out one of their own, and they might actually try to solve the case.

He'd been careful. The plan had always been to swoop in at the last minute as Paige's savior, just like before. Protect her from herself and her own mistakes. Only this time he wouldn't let her forget how much he'd done for her.

Paige was supposed to call off the dogs once he showed her the error of her ways, before the cops had a chance to probe too deep. He chewed on a thumbnail as he tried to think back over every move he'd made. Nope, careful might not be good enough if he killed a cop. The Brothers-in-Blue wouldn't just turn over every stone, they'd inspect the sand underneath that stone.

Time for a change of plan. If he couldn't put away the cop, maybe he could go after someone the cop cared about. Someone close enough the cop wouldn't just change directions of his own accord, he'd be ordered to.

Someone who wouldn't necessarily point to *him*, yet would

take the entire department's mind off little-miss-country-singer, Paige Reimer.

Sweet Pea licked Noah's ear and he smiled, snuggling into his pillow and refusing to let go of the last remnants of sleep. He was dreaming of that final morning. A dream he cherished. One that came often those first months, but less and less as time passed. The room was just the way he liked it—AC set at seventy-two, with the ceiling fan moving the air in a gentle breeze. The bathroom light on but the door closed, offering enough illumination to get dressed in a hurry if he needed without waking Betsy.

When Sweet Pea licked him again, he wrinkled his nose and pushed the dog away. His phone hummed as it vibrated on his bedside table. *Shit.* He must have accidently lowered the volume.

At first, he didn't recognize the number. Then it all clicked. *Crawford, J.* What the hell was Conner doing calling from Jeannie's phone?

"Yeah," he said, instantly wide awake.

"Noah?" That wasn't the voice he was expecting. And wasn't Conner in Dallas?

"Jeannie, what's wrong?"

"I think someone's trying to get into my house."

"Hang up and call 911. I'm on my way." He juggled the phone with one hand and pulled on his jeans with the other, muscle memory taking over while his mind worked out the fastest route for this time of night.

"The noise has stopped now. Maybe it was a cat or tree

branch. What if I imagined it? I don't want the guys in the squad to think I'm jumping at shadows just because Conner's not home. Go back to sleep. It's probably nothing."

Odds were she was right—only a cat or a tree branch—but he certainly didn't plan to take that risk. "I'm almost out the door. You remember how to use that shotgun Conner keeps under the bed?"

"I remember, but I prefer my .9mm."

Noah pulled the portable bubble light from the floorboard and slapped it on the roof of his crappy rent car. He pealed out of the driveway, lights flashing, siren blaring. To hell with the neighbors

"Fine. Take both of them and lock yourself in the bathroom until I get there. And, for God's sake, don't shoot me by mistake. I'm calling 911 whether you like it or not."

He thumbed off his phone before keying in the radio to call for back-up.

The longest fifteen minutes of his life passed while he cursed his rent-a-heap and the shit-bag who ran Lola off the road. Jeannie wasn't one to imagine things, and she certainly didn't hide from shadows, but could pregnancy have made her more cautious, more protective?

He wouldn't know. He'd never had time to find out.

Noah screeched to a halt in front of the darkened house. Had Jeannie gone straight to the bathroom without stopping to turn on the lights? She must be frightened if she actually followed his directions.

He left the bubble light flashing to let her know he'd

arrived. Still, shadows covered the lawn, turning charcoal into ebony and slowing his footsteps. Anyone could be hiding, camouflaged, just out of sight.

His Glock bounced on his hip and he eased it out of its holster. Gripping the weapon in his right hand, he reached across his body with his left and felt in his pocket for the key Conner had given him. Even using his left hand, the key slid into the lock and the knob turned without a sound. Leave it to Conner to make sure everything worked smoothly.

Now, silent or full force?

Hell, he'd never been one to tiptoe around and his flashing lights gave him away. Full force it was. He slammed the door open and threw himself to one side.

"Police. Come out with your hands up." His voice reverberated through the house, then died away.

Silence.

He stood long enough to flip on the lights before dropping behind the sofa. Peering between the legs of an end table, he saw...nothing.

"Noah?" Jeannie called from down the hall, a slight tremor in her voice. "I don't think anyone's in here. I haven't heard anything for several minutes."

"Stay where you are until I make sure." No point in having her come out only to be grabbed by some creep hiding around the corner.

He took his time, switching on lights as he went. He searched every room, looking under beds and in closets, saving the room with the closed door for last.

The hinges creaked slightly as he eased his hand in far enough to flip the switch. One glance inside caused him to catch his breath.

The room was painted lemon-cookie yellow and a Noah's Ark mural decorated one wall. A stack of unopened boxes and shopping bags filled one corner. In the other, a high-chair and stroller stared back at him.

In the middle of the room lay a partially assembled crib and sheet of instructions, folded half open.

A lump formed in his throat. He flipped off the light and eased the door closed. He didn't belong in there. Neither did the ugliness he carried with him.

CHAPTER THIRTEEN

"JEANNIE?" NOAH STOOD to the side and tapped on the bathroom door. "Are you okay, what happened?"

She started slow, but picked up speed. "I was tossing around, trying to find a comfortable position when I heard something outside. At first I thought it was a cat, but then the doorknob rattled and a few minutes after that, there was a noise at the bathroom window. I almost shot him, Noah. I had my finger on the trigger and everything. Then I thought about that crib in the next room and how easily bullets can penetrate walls, and the Mahoney's bedroom is just on the other side of the driveway, I could hit them, and what if they shot a gun without thinking, and how would I feel if a bullet came into my house and hurt our baby and I couldn't do it."

Her voice broke with a sob. "After all the times Conner made me practice, did I endanger the baby because I couldn't pull the trigger?"

Jeannie opened the door and stood in front of him, her

eyes swollen and red. Her cheeks wet. Her hands shaking.

"No, honey. No. You did the right thing. You never shoot unless you know exactly what you're aiming at." He put his arms around her and pulled her close. Or at least as close as he could with that big bump between them. When had that happened? The last time he saw her—what was it, three weeks ago?—she hadn't been nearly this big.

Could she possibly be farther along than Conner had told him? If she kept growing at this rate, she could birth a truck. It took everything he had, but he managed not to look down at her stomach. Feeling it press against him was disturbing enough.

The wail of sirens came closer and doors slammed outside.

"Go put on something warm while I talk to the guys outside." Noah squeezed her arm and pulled away. She smelled of baby powder, or was that his imagination?

Jeannie nodded, her shaking already under control, and handed him the pistol she'd been gripping. "The shotgun is in the bathtub. When I heard a noise outside the window, I racked it and yelled, 'I've got a gun.' It sounded like someone ran away after that, but I could have just scared off a cat investigating the garbage can."

He waited while Jeannie waddled to her room and closed the door before heading out to greet the arriving officers, his badge held high in front of him. Two patrol cars had stopped in front of the house and four uniformed officers spilled onto the lawn.

Each car carried one rookie—obvious in their brand new uniforms—and one older, training officer. Fine if the rookies were eager to learn and the TOs were dedicated. Not so good if either one was marking time, waiting for something better, like retirement or promotion.

One of the TOs was older, out of shape, and overweight. He hesitated behind the half-open car door and eyed Noah's badge. The flashing lights hid his expression and turned his skin a sickly shade of green. The other TO was taller, slimmer, and closer in age to the rookies. His eyes scanned the yard, taking in everything. One out of four he could count on.

Not the best odds.

"Detective Noah Daugherty, Homicide." His voice seemed unusually loud in the still night air. Even the crickets had gone silent. He kept both hands in sight and didn't make any unnecessary moves until all four officers visibly relaxed. "This is the home of an HPD detective, out of town on a case. His pregnant wife reported a prowler outside her window. Let's get some light and search the perimeter of the house. See if we can find anything useful."

The two sets of partners grabbed Maglites from their cars and divided, one pair headed around the house to the right, and the other went to the left.

Noah waited on the porch, pacing. Should he go in and check on Jeannie? Did she need comfort or time to pull herself together? Somehow, he always seemed to pick the wrong response at times like these. He jerked around at the sound of footsteps on the wooden floor.

Jennie followed her extended belly down the hallway. Even her walk had morphed into an awkward, shuffling gate. How was this woman going to last another six weeks? Maybe her body had changed, but her attitude hadn't. "If it turns out I was hallucinating, having a hormone-induced fantasy, promise me you won't tell Conner or I'll shoot you myself."

Now what? He couldn't make a promise like that. Either way, his partner needed to know. His best bet was to change the subject. "Why don't you put on a pot of coffee? I know the officers would appreciate it."

"Already done. I've been married to a cop too many years not to realize the importance of caffeine, especially for the night shift. Don't think I didn't notice that little trick you just pulled. I'm serious. If Conner has to worry about me because a feral cat was scrounging in garbage cans, he won't have his complete attention on his job. And that's dangerous. For him and for you."

"Detective, can you come around here for a second?" a voice called from the side of the house.

Sure he could. And just in the nick of time. Noah had doubts he could convincingly lie to Jeannie. He'd never pulled it off before.

The sight of the older, heavier patrolman with his face inches from the ground surprised Noah. The guy looked up and motioned with his flashlight. "Make a wide circle and come up from that side. There're some stones you can step on."

As Noah worked his way closer, the man stood and aimed his light on the bathroom screen. "I can't tell if this screen has been loose for fifteen minutes or fifteen weeks. Maybe the tech boys can, but I sure can't. These footprints, on the other hand, appear to be new. See how soft the ground is here?" He poked one chubby finger into the mud.

Son-of-a-bitch. He'd treated Jeannie's call like an emergency because that's what you did when someone depended you, but he'd never truly believed it was anything more than a neighbor's cat.

The officer turned toward the rookie. "Norton, head back to the unit and call this in. We need Crime Scene out here."

The kid took a few steps forward from his post near the property line when the TO yelled at him. "Not that way, you idiot. Circle around so you don't tramp all over the evidence." He turned toward Noah. "I swear, these rookies get dumber every year."

Noah gave himself a mental head slap. He had to quit jumping to conclusions about people. Stupid with fellow officers, dangerous with suspects.

Was there anyone in this case he'd over or underestimated?

What about the perp? So far, they'd considered him some type of evil genius because of the trick with the hotel keys. Trying to run him off the road was a stupid, amateur move. Too many people could have seen him. And what was the purpose of coming after Jeannie? Did he actually think that would slow down the case?

He obviously hadn't done any research on Jeannie if he thought she was an easy target. Noah wouldn't take her on if he was wearing a vest and helmet with a fully equipped SWAT team backing him up. And that was while she was pregnant.

What if the guy was just your ordinary, sneaky, twisted, devious, run-of-the-mill ass wipe? Would he have treated this case any different?

He and Conner had wasted days worrying about hotel keys and hacking into computers and security cameras and Paige's fame. It always came down to the dark side of human nature—love, money, power, jealousy, greed.

They needed to get back to the basics. Generally, he liked

to follow the clues and worry about reasons later, but in this case they were woefully short of direct evidence.

So, who had a motive? Who would benefit?

Two hours later, the house was silent. Uniforms, crime scene techs, Lieutenant Jansen, half his squad including Earl Sparks and Lefty Bob, had all gone home. Only yellow crime scene tape remained, marking off one corner of the house.

Noah drained the last of his coffee and watched Jeannie cradle her herbal tea as if for warmth or searching for answers in the nonexistent tea leaves.

"Why don't you go back to bed while you can? It'll be daylight in a couple of hours. Until then, I'll sit here and fill out some of this paperwork. I talked Conner into staying to finish his interviews. There are too many *ifs* about this whole thing. You're not safe until we figure out what's going on and the fastest way to do that is to solve the case we're working on. If he uses lights and siren, and I'm betting he will, he should be back by 2:00 or 3:00. I'm not leaving before he gets here."

"I told you not to call him. He'll be itching for blood by the time he gets home. I'll let you be the one to deal with him." She carried her cup to the sink and rinsed it out.

Phoning Conner might have been the hardest thing he'd ever done. He knew what a blow getting a call like that could be. Like a sucker punch to the gut. He'd received life-altering phone calls twice. The last had been such a shock, he literally couldn't remember the details; just the feeling of darkness descending around his world. The sense of déjà vu. The first time, he'd been nineteen, sitting in his dorm room, listening to

Rachmaninoff, when his mother called about his father.

Such a gentle, peaceful man. Beaten to death on a city street over some pieces of wood, glue, catgut and tuning pegs.

What he'd done then was supposed to make him feel better, but it didn't. It ate a piece of his soul.

At least he didn't have to tell his sister when their mother passed. Rachelle had been beside him, holding his hand, as their mother slipped peacefully away only a year later. Leaving the two of them to cling to each other, the only family they had left.

Conner, Jeannie, even this unborn baby, were part of his family now and he didn't plan to let anything happen to them.

"Jeannie?"

She twisted to face him.

"You need to think about going to visit your parents until we get this wrapped up."

"We had this discussion last time. I'm not going anywhere. Solve the damn case." Without another word, she shuffled down the hall and closed her bedroom door.

CHAPTER
FOURTEEN

"**Y**OU LET HER go to work?" Disbelief bubbled up and Conner made no attempt to hide it. Tired as he was, he couldn't have hidden it if he'd wanted.

"What do you mean, *let her*? Have you ever tried to stop your wife from doing something she had her mind set on?"

Conner refused to blink and Noah finally looked away. So, the big guy felt guilty. Good. Not that it helped. Odds were he couldn't have stopped her either, but he certainly would have tried. She probably looked at Noah with those eyes and he caved.

At least Noah *sounded* apologetic. "I checked everything myself. Today's elementary schools may be the safest places in the country. The whole campus is locked down. No one gets in or out without a pass from the president. And I mean the U.S. President."

The muscles in the back of Conner's neck eased a negligible amount. Noah was right. Jeannie had complained about all the security. She worried the kids would feel like they were in prison instead of second grade.

"I escorted her to her classroom and she promised not to leave until one of us came to get her. Frankly, I think she's safer there than at home with all these windows."

"So, what's your opinion? Thief, peeper, or our guy?" Exhaustion wormed its way into Conner's bones, but he fought it back. There wasn't time to relax. He'd watched outside of Noah's house until well past midnight, not leaving before he was certain no one had followed his partner home from rehearsal or was lurking in the shadows.

Hell, he'd only been in Dallas half an hour when Noah phoned. It took everything he had not to turn around and drive back, but Jeannie was safe for the moment and the quicker he solved this case, the quicker she'd stay that way.

But what was he going to do tonight? He couldn't stay awake another night and Jeannie had to be his first priority.

Noah frowned when Conner yawned, that devious mind trying to figure out what he knew but wasn't telling. "I doubt a peeper. They're usually out earlier, when people are changing or showering. This is a safe neighborhood, but thieves can hit anywhere. Our guy? No way to know until we solve this thing. On that note, what did you find out?"

"The school principal and the guidance counselor both beamed and called Paige a wonderful girl. They always knew she'd be a success. Right. I doubt they could have picked her out from a line-up before she made a name for herself. The music-drama coach was a little better. He claimed Paige always had the talent and the drive but not the parental backing, so he was surprised with her success. Especially after she dropped out of school unexpectedly. And he had no idea why she disappeared or where she went."

Noah ran a hand through his hair. "That's all you got? Nothing more concrete, no names of friends?"

"The coach just laughed. Said anyone we asked would claim to have been her best buddy. He remembers her as a nice girl who didn't have any enemies, but not many friends either. A loner. I didn't want to stick around any longer, but he promised to get out a yearbook and see if he could find anyone worth calling."

Despite giving Noah the stink eye, his partner remained in the faded visitor's chair, drumming his fingers on the desk. Didn't he need to go somewhere, do something? Jeannie got off in one hour. That didn't leave much time to finish writing reports, much less follow new leads. Not that he had any solid ones.

They both jumped when Conner's phone rang. What were the chances it brought good news? The 682 area code was more Ft. Worth than Dallas but any distraction was welcome right now. "Homicide, Crawford."

"Detective Crawford?" The voice was young and definitely female. "Coach Benfield suggested I call you."

Conner flipped a button on his phone. "Yes. You're on speaker with me and my partner, Detective Noah Daugherty. Who am I speaking with?"

"This is Naomi Reasnor Henderson. I was a friend of Paige Reimer. Well, as close a friend as Paige ever had. We were next to each other alphabetically so she ended up sitting behind me in classes since sixth grade."

"What do you mean, as close a friend as she ever had?"

"Like I said, I knew Paige since we were eleven-years-old. Some people thought she was stuck up, but she wasn't. It's taken me years to figure this out, but I think she had a really bad home life. She didn't go to birthday parties or ask anyone over. She stayed to herself."

"Yet you consider her your friend."

"We sat next to each other at lunch when we had the same class and we would phone each other about an assignment if we needed to. We both loved choir and stayed after school to practice. With her voice, I was surprised and not surprised when she made a name for herself."

Conner grimaced when Noah leaned forward to jump into the conversation. The guy needed to stay back. Not rush the woman. Let her tell the story in her own way.

"Naomi, this is Detective Dougherty. Two questions. Why do you suppose Paige dropped out of school with only one semester to go, and was she hanging around with anyone new?"

"We didn't live in the best part of town. Dropping out wasn't exactly front page news. Even during senior year. At the time, I thought she'd had some type of fallout with her mother. That woman was a piece of work. Sour wouldn't melt in her mouth. When I called to ask if Paige was okay, the woman claimed she wouldn't have any idea. I should check the streets of Nashville."

Conner eased in, blocking Noah. This was his phone, his desk, his wife threatened. "Did that mean anything special to you?"

"The month before Christmas break, Paige started talking about going to Nashville. That was going to be the answer to all her prayers. She would take the city by storm. Which brings me to your second question."

Now they were getting somewhere. "The someone new in her life part?"

"There was a guy. I had totally forgotten about him. Talk about a loser. He should have had an L tattooed on his forehead. I had to go through the yearbook page by page to find him and I couldn't tell you for the life of me what's happened to him now."

Noah opened his mouth, but Conner shook his head and waited.

"Finlay Brown. Scrawny, ugly, a funny scar through his eyebrow and a mean streak a mile wide, but he did have a car."

Noah was already entering Finlay's name into the computer when Conner asked the next question. "So, Paige dropped out of school to go to Nashville with Finlay Brown?"

"But that's just it. She didn't."

Now what? Whenever they seemed to get close, *bam*, wrong answer. He didn't have time to waste if this woman didn't know anything. He needed this settled, *now*. He wanted his life back.

Naomi's voice floated down the wire. "I was gone most of that summer, then off to A&M, so I didn't see Paige again until homecoming. She was singing lead for some band at a party. She sounded good but looked awful. Skinny, bags under her eyes, home bleach job on her hair. When they took a break I went up and hugged her. I said I thought she'd gone to Nashville with Finlay Brown."

"Did she give you an answer?"

"She rolled her eyes and said, 'That jerk? He wouldn't

have had gas money to get us to Plano.' She'd been working at a burger joint across town and singing for whoever would listen. Sleeping on people's couches. I've always regretted what I did next. That's why I want to help you find the creep who's trying to hurt her."

The sadness in her voice broke Conner's heart. "What was that?"

"I slipped her forty dollars. She looked embarrassed and promised to pay me back as soon as she could. I've never been able to decide if I regret giving her money or not giving her more."

~

"Bingo! We have a winner of a loser." Noah swung his computer screen to face Conner. He might be able to babysit for Rachelle after all.

Conner leaned forward and studied the screen. "You're sure this is the right Finlay Brown?"

"Right age, from the Dallas area, and get a load of the scar through his left eyebrow. Your friend was right. He ought to have a big L tattooed on his forehead. His rap sheet is two pages long and that's not counting his sealed juvenile record. No felonies, but the entire alphabet of misdemeanors: A, B, and C. God, what a *putz*. He ought to be locked up for his own good."

"Is he? Locked up?"

"Not at the moment." Laughter bubbled up from deep in Noah's chest. He thought he'd seen everything. Some of these were new, even to him. "He walked into a house the owner admits was unlocked. Ate all the leftovers and fell asleep on the sofa watching TV with the bag of goodies he planned to steal on the floor by the door. They couldn't get him for anything but trespassing. Plead it down to a B. He got six months but with time counted at three to one, he only served a little over two in county. He can't even do a smash and grab right. Broke into a car to grab a package, but it wasn't worth but fifteen bucks. Another B. Another two months"

Noah tapped the next line. "Look at this one. He stuck his hand through a doggy door and surprise, surprise. The dog grabbed his wrist and wouldn't let go until the owner came home from work four hours later. During that time, he must have needed to go to the bathroom. He managed to pull his zipper down with one hand, but got his dick caught when he tried to zip up. The cops felt so sorry for him they dropped him at the hospital and never came back."

Conner's eyes squenched. "Aren't we looking for some kind of Einstein? Someone good with computers? Someone who can get into hotel rooms without a trace? This fool can't even break into an empty house without getting caught."

Leave it to Conner to bring him down just when things were falling into place. "I've been thinking about that and I'm not so sure. Half the people who check out of a hotel don't return the key. After that, it's just a matter of recoding. I'm not sure how you do it, but there must be a way."

Conner pulled at his lower lip. "Could someone who's good at sleight of hand reach over the counter when the clerk's distracted?"

Now his partner was actually helping. "Brown's six-three. He'd have the reach for it."

"That still leaves the computer and finding the room

number."

"Shit, Conner. Any decent thief knows how to look over your shoulder when the clerk hands you the room key, or follow without being noticed. Failing that, people are all too willing to talk about seeing a celebrity or police checking a room."

"I still think it's more likely someone she's crossed paths with lately than ten years ago, but you're right. We've been going about this all wrong. How about I get the ball rolling on finding Brown while you see where the hotels keep their key coding machine?"

There went any chance of going home for an hour before practice. Only one more day if he had any hope of solving this thing before Paige stood on the stage and made a target of herself for anyone holding a grudge.

CHAPTER FIFTEEN

NOAH GLARED ACROSS the hotel registration desk at the red-haired pixie guarding her territory like a miniature pit bull. Was she worried about letting him in on tightly held secrets or was she so clueless she honestly didn't know the answer? His badge usually opened doors for him, but she acted like he'd bought the gold shield at a dollar store.

"You'll need to step aside, sir. I have guests waiting to check in."

Behind him, a man cleared his throat and a child whined. Noah moved back, but mentally kicked himself for giving in so easily. Why had he let twelve pounds of dynamite in a two pound can push him around? Fuck it. He'd go over her head.

Locating the general manager's office turned out to be harder than he expected in a maze of restaurants and upscale boutiques. The main lobby alone was so expansive it sported two separate jewelry stores for the woman who hadn't brought just the right earrings or the businessman who needed to smooth things over with his neglected wife.

Band practice started in an hour. At this rate he'd be late and have to face Paige's wrath. What was it with women trampling all over him these days? First Paige, then Jeannie, now the little pit bull at the front desk, and, if he didn't solve this case before Saturday night, his sister.

He slipped through an unmarked door and found himself in a narrow corridor obviously not meant for public use. The floor and walls were dingy and the lighting left a lot to be desired. The scent of old food and machinery lingered in the air.

A fireplug-shaped man in a charcoal gray suit stepped into the hallway. A security badge hung from his lapel. "Daugherty, were you looking for me?"

No, but finding him was a stroke of luck. "Hey, Garcia. I hoped you were on duty tonight. I'm having trouble figuring out how your key card system works."

The ex-cop nodded and led him into a room with a bank of video monitors. A young security guard sat with his feet propped on a long, low table and munched on takeout fries, never lifting his eyes from the screens. An extra-large milkshake cup and a discarded hamburger wrapper were pushed to the side.

Garcia swept the remnants of his own brown-bag meal into a nearby trash can and parked one hip on his desk. "It's brand new, top of the line. SecureTech came out with a machine about eight, nine months ago that's only half the size of the old model and ties directly into the computer system. You don't have to punch the number in manually. The clerk checks in the guest on the computer like always, taps the key card against the machine, and *Bingo,* your room key is ready. Talk I heard is they made downtown Houston their test market and gave all the hotels in this area an offer they couldn't refuse."

Now he was getting somewhere. He should have come to Garcia in the first place. "Could you just use an old key? People go home with them sometimes."

"Sure they do. Happens all the time. Company even makes special commemorative keys to double as souvenirs. Like this oil well convention. Keys are printed with an oil derrick on one side. For the women writers convention they had pictures of men with their shirt off. Doesn't do any good. Key's automatically deactivated on your check-out date. Can't be used again."

Damn. He'd had high hopes for that idea. He was back where he started.

The pit bull at the desk might not have volunteered any information, but he could see the machine was kept on a ledge under the counter. At the other two hotels he'd checked, one also stowed theirs on a lower shelf, and the other on the counter next to the computer. No matter how long Brown's arms, he couldn't reach that far, plus the computer would have to be on the correct screen with the right guest information pulled up.

"What about you guys, or housekeeping, or maintenance. Don't you have master keys? Who issues those?" Conner checked the first day, and accounted for all the keys, but they came from somewhere.

"Maintenance issues them. Each key has an I.D. number that traces back to its owner and the big computer in the sky knows exactly who opened a door and at what time."

Yeah, that tallied with what Conner had learned. The keys that opened Paige's door in one hotel and the room across from her in the other had no I.D. number. So where did they come from?

"Hey, Garcia, look at this." The young security guard pointed to a grainy, black and white image of the interior of an elevator in which a man kissed and fondled a woman in a revealing dress. "Pro?" he asked.

"Naw, that's his wife. See the ring?" Garcia rolled his eyes and glanced at Noah. "I have to get back to work, but you might check with the Chief Engineer. He'll know more about this than I would."

Five more minutes of wandering back hallways and he was facing a giant of a man with hands the size of a catcher's mitt and fingers that twisted several directions. This man wasn't doing much actual engineering himself these days, not with such unmistakable signs of rheumatoid arthritis. His own hands ached just looking at the guy.

Noah didn't have a warrant, but luckily the engineer didn't mind helping. Having a stalker break into one of the rooms reflected harshly on him and the hotel. "It's my job to make the master for new employees, and I take that very seriously. Once I plug in the code and their I.D, they have a key that opens any door and never expires. Before that happens, the company runs a thorough background check and I talk to them myself."

Conner checked all the employees the first day. And not much got by Conner. There had to be something. "Where do you keep the machine? Can anyone else get to it?"

"When not in use, it's stored in a locked cabinet." The engineer nodded toward a metal locker bolted to the wall.

"And this room is never left unsecured."

Noah was running out of time and ideas. "I'd like to look at the machine, if you don't mind." Maybe that would jog something loose in his increasingly frustrated brain.

The engineer fumbled with the oversized key ring on his belt and finally swung the door to the cabinet open. Not an easy feat with those hands. Did he sometimes take a shortcut and leave things unlocked? No, the guy was too conscientious.

The machine was flat black, about twice the size of a deck of cards, with a slightly rounded, cloth covered area at the top. Inconspicuous if you didn't know what you were looking for. Invaluable if you did.

Noah glanced at a digital clock on the wall. Each tick of the red numerals counted down the seconds he had left to solve this case. "Anyone else know the code?"

"My assistant, but he's a happily married man. No way he's running around town chasing after some singer, no matter how pretty she is. We got the machine with the code already set. It can't be changed by anyone here. It's just the street address to the hotel, but that doesn't matter.

Nobody's getting to this machine. They'd have to come through me first. That covers all I know. If you have any other questions, you might try calling their home office."

"Where's that?"

"I think the machines are manufactured in Italy, but when the top brass went to the demonstration, they traveled to Dallas."

Noah wasn't much for coincidences. They might happen occasionally, but this wasn't one of those times.

Rush hour traffic was heavy, so Noah waited until he reached the parking lot of the rehearsal hall to phone Conner. The sun had dipped below the skyline, leaving his car deep in shadow. He lowered the window, enjoying the evening air, and punched in the familiar number.

When his partner answered on the first ring, Noah jumped right in. "You know how I didn't believe this mess had to do with Paige's past, that it felt more current? I was wrong."

"Happy as I am for you to grow a pair and admit you were mistaken, could you be more specific?"

Movement near the corner of his eye caused Noah to jerk his head to the left. Kevin strolled through the darkening lot toward the stage entrance. The guitarist never glanced his direction. Either his ugly purple car was better camouflaged than he thought or Kevin was avoiding him. Damn, he had trouble believing the guy didn't have something to do with this.

Noah waited until the heavy metal door clanged shut before resuming his conversation. No reason to attract unwanted attention. There were enough questions pointing his direction as it was. "The company that sells the key coding machine for all the major hotels in the downtown area has its home office in Dallas." He leaned back, satisfied.

"That's it? Two hours and that's your big discovery?"

"We still have to track down the connection, but it's too much of a coincidence not to be important." Fuck. It had sounded so good in his head, "Do you have anything better?"

"I'm not arguing you haven't found something interesting, but a place like that would do a background check before they hired so much as a janitor. Brown has a record that goes from here to last Tuesday. They'd never hire him. He dropped out of high school and has spent half his adult life behind bars. Where would he get the skills? You were right when you said to forget the mechanics, go after the person. Brown's the one we need to find."

Hell, even when he was right, he was wrong. This case was driving him nuts. The dashboard clock in the pile of junk he'd rented showed two minutes till six. Time to get moving. Let Conner take over the leg work. "So find him."

"I'd love to, but it's not that easy. He's in the wind. His parole officer doesn't know where he is. However, I checked, and his last cell mate was a major degenerate from Houston. That guy started with B&E and moved on to crashing through store windows to steal the ATM. Surprisingly, he doesn't feel the need to check in with his PO, either. "

Noah closed his window, shutting off the refreshing breeze and allowing the rent car to resume its normal aroma of half-eaten meals and dirty socks. "None of this means Brown is in Houston, but it does mean he could be and from here on out, we have to assume he is."

That was it. He'd give Paige a couple of hours to run through their set. After that, it was back to the hotel for her. No dinner at a local dive, no margaritas in the bar. A room service meal and a long talk.

Like it or not, tonight she'd tell him everything she knew about Finlay Brown.

Weeds struggled to find purchase in the hard packed

dirt surrounding the two room structure. Once a watchman's office, the building remained sturdy, although neglected. In other places, bluebonnets covered the hills and roadside. Not here. And he liked it that way. It fit his mood.

Things didn't have to be this way. Not what he'd planned at all. She was supposed to be worried, nervous, and turn to him for help. Just like she had before. He'd swoop in, make arrangements, be her savior. Set her on the road to real success.

But she'd done the one thing he couldn't forgive. She'd forgotten him entirely. Forgotten everything he'd done for her.

She'd turned to that cop instead.

He'd been naive. That had been his first mistake. Thought if he sidelined the cop, took him out of the picture temporarily, she'd realize who she could actually count on. But the cop was tougher than he looked.

No, that was another mistake. The cop *looked* plenty tough. But how tough a guy could be who studied music, played and sang for kids, had a dog that wore a pink hair bow and wasn't any bigger than a shoebox? Well, he'd found out the hard way.

Then he made miscalculation number three. The pregnant bitch. Weren't women in that condition supposed to be soft, dependent? She'd pulled a gun on him! And he'd run like a scared rabbit. He pitied any kid who grew up in that family.

Now he had to start from scratch with a new plan. This one would be a lot harder to pull off.

The key he'd been given hung in the rusty lock and he jiggled it several times before the door swung open revealing just how far he'd sunk. The room was much smaller than he'd envisioned. The only window was in the door, and he could cover that.

He glanced around and a wave of depression washed over him. This place was dirty, dreary, and foul smelling. On the other hand, it was cheap and isolated. His two main criteria.

Still, if he planned to keep Paige here for any length of time, it needed to be spotless. A vase of flowers would help cover the odor of the nearby refineries and a colorful spread might offer a spot of cheer. He had enough set aside to rent this shack for two months, although he could get more. He needed to get more. And he needed to do it before he took Paige.

There would certainly be times he'd have to leave her alone, but those should be kept to a minimum and not during the first days or weeks. He'd dole out little bits of freedom as she began to trust him and depend on him. He'd read about this. It was called the Stockholm Syndrome.

Soon she would defer every decision to him. And he wouldn't let her down.

Once he took over, all she had to do was sing and write her music. He'd take care of everything else: the money, the promotion, the scheduling. No more two-bit venues. She'd paid her dues. She was ready for the big time.

There were other changes he planned to make and the first would be her band. The world was full of decent musicians. He'd hire only those whose loyalty lay with him, not her. When they weren't playing or practicing, she wouldn't socialize with them either.

She'd spend her off time with him and him alone. He'd earned that right. She'd forgotten for now, but he'd remind her.

He glanced at his watch and rolled up his sleeves. Only two hours until he had to leave and he still had a list of things he needed to buy: a bed, chair, hot plate, and mini-fridge for starters. Tomorrow he'd stop by the hardware store for a sturdy length of chain and a padlock. With all these expenses, he might have to forgo the vase and colorful spread.

Right now, he'd start with the bathroom. Women always appreciated a clean bathroom.

As soon as she realized how much work he'd done for her, she'd come to her senses. After that, the stars were the limit. For both of them.

Then he could see about payback to those who'd thwarted him. The cop, the pregnant, gun-toting bitch, and that fucking barking rat with a hair bow. Maybe a cut brake line? A house fire? How fun to think and plan.

He'd have plenty of opportunities. Paige would do concerts in Houston for years to come. And he knew how to wait. Bide his time. He'd proven that.

CHAPTER
SIXTEEN

N OAH HAD TO send Paige half a dozen dirty looks before
she cut practice short by twenty minutes. Either
he was slipping or she was bullet proof. Hardened
criminals had folded under that glare.

She simply ignored him.

"Let's call it a night, guys," she finally said, unhooking the
monogramed guitar strap around her shoulder. "Go out. Have
fun. Burn off some steam. Tomorrow we meet an hour earlier
and run through the set twice. Get a good night's rest. I want
you fresh as a spring flower for Saturday."

She didn't have to ask twice. Band members had their
instruments packed away and headed toward the stage door
before her words faded from the air. Only Kevin offered a less-
than-sincere request she join them.

Arrangements for Paige's safe return to the hotel had been
made well in advance. Noah would drive her up to the front
door where one of the hotel security guards would be waiting

to escort her to her room. Whoever had night duty would be waiting inside for the handoff. That way, neither Paige nor her room would ever be left unguarded.

Tonight, Noah planned to valet his car and walk her to the room himself. Like so many of his well thought out plans, this one hit a snag almost immediately.

Paige eyed his rusty hunk-of-junk and came to a screeching halt. "You've got to be kidding me. I don't know how you get into that thing, much less add me and both our guitars."

"There's room in the back for the guitars." Well, he hoped so. There sure wasn't room in the front for her to hold one in her lap. Not and let him shift.

Luckily, the drive to the hotel was short, because it certainly was silent. Paige seemed buried in her own thoughts which gave him time to work out his approach to questioning her about Finlay Brown. If he put her on the defensive, she'd clam up.

A light mist began to fall and he tried his wipers for the first time. At high speed, they left streaks of dirt in an arc pattern across the windshield. At low speed, they couldn't keep up with the increasing drizzle. At any speed, they made a grinding sound that hurt his teeth.

Ten-thirty on a Thursday evening and the streets were deserted. Even the restaurants were closed for the night, leaving only the reflection of neon signs on wet sidewalks.

Downtown Houston had pulled up the covers and gone to sleep.

He turned the corner a block from Paige's hotel and saw a white pickup sideways across both lanes of the street. Had the truck spun out on the rainy road? Noah slowed to give the driver time to recover.

Instead of straightening, the truck shifted into reverse and slammed into the glass storefront of one of the hotel shops.

"Oh my God," Paige screamed. "Are they hurt? Should we call an ambulance?"

Two men dressed all in black with ski masks over their faces flew out of the truck while the glass was still falling. The men hurtled over jagged shards of glass and twisted rebar and bounded into the shop.

"They're not hurt, they're robbing the place. Call the police." Noah shifted, but his wheels spun on the slick pavement. The left wheel found traction before the other three and the car fishtailed down the road.

Noah swung under the porte-cochere by the front door. Fifteen feet away, he could see the men breaking display cases and grabbing the contents. Diamond rings, necklaces, and watches glittered as they disappeared into black duffel bags.

"Get out," he yelled at Paige. She wouldn't like that. He'd have to make it up to her later. "Hurry. A security guard is waiting by the door. He'll see you safe to your room. I have to stop these guys." If they were the same ones Conner had complained about, they'd already killed one person.

If he let them get away, and they killed someone else, it would be on his head. Even if he was the only one who thought so.

Paige jumped out, but left the door open as she lowered the seat back and reached for her guitar.

"Leave it," he yelled. He had to stop yelling if he ever expected to get back in her good graces and find out about Finlay Brown.

"I can't. It cost everything I have. It's worth more to me than all of that jewelry. If anything happens to it, I'm finished."

The pickup driver honked twice and the men raced out of the shop, vaulted over the crumpled tailgate and into the bed of the truck. One man slapped the back window and the driver pealed out. Two wheels jumped the opposite curb as the driver fought to make the tight turn.

The instant Paige's door closed, he slammed his foot on the accelerator. The car leapt forward and died. *Shit. Fucking stick shift.*

Two tries later, the engine caught. He forced himself to ease forward, building speed gradually as he pulled onto the street. In the rearview mirror he could see Paige, standing on the flagstones, guitar in hand, eyes wide in either fear or shock. He sent a silent message to the unknown security guard: *Get your ass outside and grab her.*

Running up on the curb had slowed the pickup. It was only half a block ahead when the driver noticed Noah following him. The truck picked up speed. Noah tried to keep pace, but his rental didn't have the necessary juice. After a mile or two, he began to lag behind.

One of the men in the back pulled something from his duffle. It looked like a gun, but Noah couldn't be sure in the dark. Two seconds later, his windshield spider-webbed and he knew the answer. Fuck, would his insurance cover this?

And how many people could try to kill him in the same week? One was usually his limit.

Had anyone called for backup? At this speed, he couldn't operate the radio and maintain control of the car on slick streets. He eased back on the gas and the distance between him and the pickup increased. The black-clad man stood in the bed of the pickup and aimed at Noah chugging behind him.

Noah took one hand off the wheel and groped around his ankle for his backup piece. His fingers brushed the telltale bulge. The cramped space made it impossible to pull the weapon free.

Ahead, the pickup took a corner on two wheels and began to rock as it struggled to right itself. The driver overcompensated, veered across the road and smacked the curb. The truck flipped onto its side—throwing the two masked men to the pavement—and skidded down a shallow embankment. The truck came to rest with its headlights buried in the mud and its tires still spinning.

Noah pulled his Glock and approached the overturned truck cautiously. These men were dangerous, and dangerous men were deadly when cornered. One man lay in the street, his body a crumpled mass that seemed, to Noah, inconsistent with life. He checked for a pulse, but found none. Now he only had to worry about the other two.

He pivoted toward the truck when his foot skidded on wet grass, sending him sliding down the embankment into six inches of icy ditch water. His sore ribs managed to find every rock along the way.

In the cab of the truck, the driver wailed and begged for help. "My arm's broken. Get me out of here."

Noah clawed his way up the slope, one leg covered in mud, the other soaking wet and clinging to his skin. Ignoring the man moaning in the truck cab, he limped around to the far side, muddy water sloshing out of his shoe with each step. The shooter lay with his legs pinned under the truck. One hand groped for the gun, just inches from his fingertips. Noah had only played soccer one year, when he was eight, but he remembered how to deliver a kick.

His foot connected with the shooter's hand, breaking bones and sending the gun skittering away. Mud splattered the man's face as Noah's leg continued its arc.

The satisfaction of hearing those bones crunch was worth every single form he'd have to fill out.

Both duffels lay on their sides, contents scattered. Loose diamonds mixed with broken glass under his headlight beams, turning the wet cement into a magical sparkling pathway.

Sirens screamed in the distance and the glow of flashing lights grew stronger.

Let someone else straighten this out. He was done.

A thin band of dirty gray struggled to overtake the starless sky. The time caught somewhere between morning and night.

The crime scene techs had ordered Noah's rental towed in as evidence, leaving him stranded for an hour longer than necessary. More expense. Would he have to pay for Lola, this rental, and another rental? Something to discuss with his insurance company later, when his head was clearer.

He had to beg Conner to drop him in front of the hotel door.

"Between Jeannie and the smash and grabbers, you've been running for almost forty-eight hours straight. You need to go home and get some rest. I'll phone Paige later today and bring her up-to-date."

Could he do that, drop this whole thing on Conner? If he could prop his feet up and rest for fifteen minutes, he'd feel human again.

No, he owed it to Paige to tell her in person. And he owed it to himself to bring this whole sorry mess to its less-than-satisfying conclusion. "Go home, partner. Take care of Jeannie. She needs you. And I need to close this case, wrap it up with a bow, and send it back to Nashville."

He stepped out of the car and waved as Conner drove away. To his left, invisible workmen had already covered the jewelry store window with plywood and swept away any sign of glass or debris.

Wouldn't do to let the guests know what happened. They might decide they were safer at another establishment.

If Noah had any doubts about how bad he looked, the expression on the receptionist's face pushed them away.

Cold, wet, and exhausted. Not to mention a black eye and swollen nose from Wednesday's encounter. Good thing the broken ribs weren't visible. That might have pushed the poor woman over the edge.

He flashed his badge, unwilling to face any argument about entering the hotel in his condition at such a late—or was it early—hour. In the lobby, the diner was still closed, but lights flickered on as he passed. A barista rolled out a coffee stand near the reception desk and started the process of setting up. What he'd give for a cup of coffee and some dry clothes. Both would have to wait.

Not one person spoke to him as his long strides took him across the lobby, to the elevators, and up to the top floor. He hesitated at Paige's door. He hated to wake her at this hour.

She hadn't answered the text he'd sent warning to expect him in fifteen minutes, but light spilling under the threshold and through the peep hole said someone was up.

He gave a soft tap and waited. Who was working tonight? Someone who knew him? When a shadow crossed over the peephole, he held up his badge.

A uniformed officer- opened the door.

"Hi, Detective Daugherty. I'm Tracy Barrows. I think we met on the Macdonald case. The wife who shot her husband, thinking he was a burglar."

"I remember. You helped canvass the neighborhood. You were also at my house a couple of months ago when Ryan Howell tried to kill me." God, he'd hated that. Not the nearly getting killed part. He didn't like it, but it came with the job. But having his house searched wasn't. People he knew and didn't know, touching Betsy's things. Pawing through his life. Seeing how he lived. Intruding in his private world.

Judging him.

Tracy avoided his eyes as she held the door open. "Paige told me you were coming. She jumped in the shower. I put the coffee on. Would you like a cup?"

"Thanks Tracy. That's the best thing I've heard in the last five hours." Rain tapped at the sliding glass door. The sky lightened imperceptibly, but anything past the balcony railing remained invisible. Noah's eyelids felt as heavy as the air outside.

He was too wet to sit on anything upholstered, so he pulled out a dining room chair and dropped into it. His extra clothes and rain gear were still in Lola's lockbox. Conner and Earl Sparks were first on the scene, but they were too skinny to lend him a jacket. Lefty Bob had one he could borrow. The jacket fit over his arms and shoulders, but the zipper was broken and it didn't have a hood.

Tracy handed him a cup and he cradled it in both hands, sipping the magic potion even though it was so hot it burned his throat on the way down.

A dishtowel landed in his lap. "You look like you could use this," Tracy said from the kitchenette. Noah ran the towel over the back of his neck and through his dripping hair.

By the time Paige came from the bedroom, he felt alive, if not normal.

"I've been worried about you," she said, sinking into the nearest armchair. "The way you took off after those guys. Then, a few minutes later, all the sirens. Are you okay?"

"I'm fine. Tired and wet. What about you? Did security get you to the room without any trouble?"

A look of surprise crossed her face. "I didn't see any security. Everyone ran toward the jewelry store like they were giving away free samples. I stood outside until you rounded the corner, then took the elevator up by myself. I tried to watch from the balcony, but it was too far away to see anything."

Son-of-a-bitch. He'd never trust outside back-up again. If they'd given him Lefty Bob, like he asked, she wouldn't have been left alone no matter what else happened.

But it was the same old story: money and manpower and to hell with safety.

He bit back his anger. Now wasn't the time. Not with what he had to tell her.

"Tracy, you want to take a break? They were just opening the coffee shop downstairs. I'll stay here with Paige until you get back. No need to hurry."

The officer might be young, but she understood she was being dismissed.

Noah waited until the door clicked behind her before putting his elbows on his knees and leaning closer to Paige. "I hate to be the one to tell you this, but your friend, Finlay Brown, was killed tonight as part of that robbery of the jewelry store downstairs."

Paige's eyes went wide and her mouth formed a perfect O. One tear escaped and crept down her cheek. "Did you kill him? I thought I heard gunfire, but I wasn't sure."

"No, no. I didn't kill him." *Well, I might have played a part, chasing them through downtown in the rain.* "He was thrown out of the pickup when the truck skidded on wet pavement and flipped over. He landed on his head. It was fast. He wouldn't have had any idea what was happening."

More tears followed the first. "He never caught a break, his entire life."

Now they were getting somewhere. She hadn't denied knowing him. "You want to tell me about him?"

"We had a lot in common. His mother left. My father left. We both had only one parent and not much of one at that. My mom either ignored me or yelled at me, but I always knew, deep down, she loved me and wanted the best for me. Finlay's dad was a different story altogether. The guy blamed him for his mother leaving and slapped him around for kicks. That's how he got the scar." She tapped her left eyebrow.

"What's he been up to lately, besides robbing jewelry stores?"

The tears had stopped. Paige lifted her face toward him, her eyes clear. "I don't have any idea. I haven't seen or heard from him since Christmas vacation, senior year of high school."

Noah fought the urge to tumble deep into those startling blue eyes. *Watch yourself. You're tired and more likely to make a serious mistake.* "Your boyfriend never contacted you once in all these years? Not even after you got famous? I always heard every distant relative, ex-lover, and wanna-be friend crawled out of the woodwork the minute you got famous."

Paige studied the coffee pot sitting on the bar. "First, I'm not famous. I have one, semi-popular song with hopes for more. Second, I don't have any relatives that I know of. My mom and dad were both only children and my dad died years ago in California. A few people I don't remember from school have contacted me, but not the ones I'd like to hear from. And Finlay Brown was never my boyfriend, just a casual acquaintance who sat next to me in World History."

Now it started. The lies. The cover-up. She might honestly believe her father was dead. With the number of names he'd used over the years, he'd been hard enough to track down. At present, he was a guest of the state of Florida, under his real name. Not the one he'd used when he married Estelle Reimer. Probably the reason Paige's mother could never get social security benefits for her dead "husband."

Iron bars, three missing toes, and the need for dialysis three times a week meant he wasn't running around hotels making threats. Although the expense of keeping him might convince Florida to cut him loose early.

It wouldn't be fair to Paige to withhold that information, but he didn't have to give it to her yet. She had enough to deal with now.

Finlay Brown was something else entirely.

"Then why did a casual acquaintance have newspaper clippings and photos of you papering the walls of his rented room along with a schedule of your appearances?"

Paige quit studying the coffee pot and turned her attention to the balcony door. The sky was clearing by the minute and buildings across the street were fading into view. "You said it yourself. Wanna-be friends come out of the woodwork."

"That's not exactly what Finlay told his partners-in-crime. He said you had been lovers and he'd taken a hit for you. He claimed you owed him big time and he'd worked out a plan to collect. Said when he finished with you, you'd be throwing money his direction. You'd be afraid not to. Everything points to him as your stalker. He even drives an old Ford Taurus, the same type of car that hit your bandmate, Harvey. Want to tell me why he had it in for you?"

Paige twisted to face him, her eyes now as fierce as a summer thunderstorm. "I think I want to speak to my lawyer."

CHAPTER SEVENTEEN

NOAH PACED THE penthouse suite. Body heat had dried his clothes—except for one shoe which still squished with each step. Hot coffee and an apple from the hotel provided fruit basket had revived him, but he still wanted to finish this case and get home. Paige had been on the bedroom phone for almost fifteen minutes. How many people knew a lawyer they could call this early?

Okay, it was an hour later in Nashville, and she probably had someone that took care of her contracts. The real question was: why did she need an attorney's permission to tell him about her relationship with Finlay Brown?

He'd started out believing this whole thing was a publicity stunt, but quickly changed his mind after getting to know her. Had he been duped by her looks and talent? Was he that lonely and hard up?

There'd be plenty of time to kick himself later. Now he needed to man up and get to the bottom of this.

The bedroom door opened and Paige marched out. Her eyes were dry and her back straight. She grabbed a coffee cup from the counter, filled it, and sat at the dining room table, facing him. "Finlay and I became good friends our senior year of high school. I guess you could say we dated."

She didn't mention the *lovers* part, but he could live with that. She'd admitted they were close. That was progress. Her lawyer must have reassured her she could talk.

"Whenever his father got drunk, which was a regular occurrence, he'd beat Finlay and throw him out of the house. Finlay would sleep on a friend's sofa, or in an abandoned building, or a construction pipe. After a couple of days, he'd go home as if nothing had happened. We both had one dream— to get the hell out of Dodge."

Paige took a slow sip of coffee and sat the cup down as if it were the finest china instead of a ceramic mug. "Anyplace was fine with Finlay, as long as he felt safe. I had my eye on the prize—Nashville. I had already figured out Finlay was bad news the last day I saw him, but he was my only real friend."

She looked at Noah, her eyes wide. "Do you remember how awful high school was for anyone who didn't fit in?"

No, not really. His music labeled him one of the odd ones, but he found kindred souls in choir or band. Plus, he played football. That made him, while not part of the popular crowd, accepted anywhere. Yet he'd watched his sister suffer. As an exceptionally tall orphaned child of a murder victim, Rachelle struggled to find her place. Volleyball had been her savior.

Noah nodded in agreement. What else could he do?

"Finlay showed up at my door over Christmas break. He'd had another run in with his father. He was cut and bleeding.

Apparently, he'd decided to fight back for the first time. That was a big mistake. He didn't have anywhere to go. He'd overstayed his welcome with the few friends he had and it was too cold and rainy to stay outside. He wanted to leave and take me with him. We could be in Nashville by the next day."

Paige played with her cup, adjusted her chair, ran her fingers through her hair. She was stalling. She must be getting to the good part of the story. Fine, he could wait. He'd already arranged for Mrs. Powell to come over from next door to take care of Sweet Pea last night and this morning. All that had cost him was the promise of pastries from the hotel coffee shop. Once he'd tried offering her one of Rachelle's casseroles. He'd never make that mistake again.

"My mother came in from work in time to hear the last part. She started yelling at me. Go if I wanted, but don't come back. I was an ungrateful little bitch after all she'd given up for me. Oh, and Finlay was bleeding all over her clean kitchen. I grabbed my backpack, stuffed a few things in it, and we left."

She cleared her throat and swallowed twice. Her eyes had a damp look, but she didn't cry. "We had only reached Plano when he stopped for gas. He asked if I had any money, but I didn't even answer. I was already regretting letting my mother push me into something I wasn't ready for. He shrugged and went into the station. We were parked in front of the plate glass window and I watched him out of boredom, I guess. How was he going to handle this? Did he have his dad's credit card?"

Noah held his breath. Whatever she said next was the key.

"He poked around for a minute, waiting for a shopper to leave, then pulled a gun. I couldn't believe it. I didn't have any idea he owned a gun. But he couldn't even do that right. A customer came out of the restroom and bashed him over the head with a six-pack of beer. I panicked. I didn't want to go to jail for something I didn't do."

The tears finally came, but she kept going. "A city bus belched its way down the road so I grabbed my backpack, ran to the street, and flagged it down. I only had enough money to make it part way so I walked the last mile. My mother was horrified when I dragged in. I'd only been gone four hours and she'd already told anyone who'd listen I'd had a call from a Nashville producer who was interested in my music. The humiliation of admitting that was a lie would be worse than when my father abandoned us. I could only come back if I agreed not to show my face for at least two months. I promise you, I haven't seen or heard from Finlay Brown in all the years since."

It was a good story, and most of it was true, but there'd been a little hiccup somewhere in the middle. She'd left something out. He didn't know *what,* but it had to be something she considered important. As her lawyer undoubtedly told her, even if she'd known what Finlay was up to, or had encouraged him, the statute of limitations was long over.

He'd be more comfortable if he knew what she was hiding.

She'd done it. Paige took a long swallow of her cold coffee. She'd gotten through the main portion—the only part that mattered now. It was funny. She'd never told that piece of the story to a living soul, not even her mother. Now Noah knew half the story and her mother knew half—if she remembered— but no one knew it all. Not even Finlay.

She'd tried to forget it herself. The rest was up to Noah. He could do with the story whatever he wanted. Her lawyer swore she couldn't be held criminally liable for anything at this late date. There was some possibility Finlay could have sued her in civil court, if he had lived. But he didn't.

Had Noah believed her? His eyes still held questions. "Why do you think Finlay went to all that trouble to frighten you? Breaking into your hotel room, pulling the fire alarm. That's serious stuff."

"I'm completely baffled. I can understand bragging to his friends that he knew me, or planning to hit me up for money. That sounds like something Finlay would do. Hell, if he'd called me I would have tried to help him. Given him a little cash, found him a job, something. But the sneaking around, what did that accomplish? It breaks my heart to learn he held a grudge all this time. I never hated him for what he did." *Maybe a little, the first few years.*

She rushed on, before Noah could question her. "I certainly didn't think so at the time, but those months closeted away with my mother were the best thing that ever happened to us. Mother bought me a second hand computer with a cracked screen at a garage sale and I got my GED. I realized for the first time the toll standing on her feet all day had taken on her. She had arthritis so severe her back ached by closing time and she developed a limp. I didn't have anything to do all day so I volunteered to clean the house, do the laundry, and cook the meals. She would come home exhausted from work to find a tidy house and dinner waiting. The change in her attitude was amazing. We'd have supper on a TV tray and watch one of those talent shows. Every time, she'd tell me I sang better than whoever was on and I should try out. That was the first time anyone had ever encouraged me."

Noah watched her but hadn't said anything. He probably didn't understand. How could he? He'd come from a loving family that valued education and music. While she'd been told over and over again that she needed to quit wasting her time and learn something useful.

"I realize now that as much blame as I heaped on my mother, I was a resentful, hard to love teenager. My mother worried about my future. She wanted me to be able to support myself. Not depend on someone else like she had. Once the worst had happened and we survived it, we grew close. Until I lost her again. That's why I wrote the song for her."

He sat up straight. "You wrote *Dreaming of You* for your mother? I thought it was for an ex-love."

"Everyone does, and I let them. The real reason is too personal. Anyway, it sells better as a love song."

A sheepish look crossed Noah's face. "I was sure you wrote it for Finlay Brown."

"Hardly." Paige couldn't help the laugh that escaped. Was she a terrible person to think that was funny after all that had happened?

She and Noah twisted toward the door when a key sounded in the lock. Finlay might be dead, but they were both still jumpy.

Tracy Barrows slipped inside carrying a to-go box from the coffee shop. "I hear congratulations are in order. You got the guy."

"Where'd you hear that?" Noah's cup clattered against the table.

"My boss called and pulled me off the case. With your stalker dead and the smash-and-grab case wrapped up, all overtime is immediately cancelled. That includes you."

Noah watched, dumbfounded, as Tracy gathered her things. Paige hugged her and they exchanged email addresses like they were long lost friends.

"Pleasure working with you, Detective. Hope we can do it again sometime," Tracy said over her shoulder.

"Same here, Tracy. I'll be sure to ask for you when something comes up," but the door clicked shut before he finished. He and Paige stood in the silent penthouse, each waiting for the other to go first.

When Paige finally spoke, it was with a chuckle. "Not sure why I feel so deserted. After all, I was the one who fought against allowing someone in my room. Yet I don't know when I've been so relaxed. Part of it was feeling safe, but the other part was the companionship. I've never had many true friends. Most people want something from me: to give them a job, to listen to their music, to introduce them to people who can help them. Guess I've always been afraid to let anyone get too close."

Paige was right; she was hard to get to know. She had built a wall around her like Fort Knox, but scaling that wall was worth the trouble. Inside was a person of value. Someone you wanted to know. Someone *he* wanted to know better.

"I'm glad having an officer here helped you feel safe. I wish she could have stayed another night."

Paige's eyes grew big. "You don't think it's over? Am I still in danger?"

Damn. He hadn't meant to frighten her. "No, not at all. Finlay was our prime suspect. Everything points to him. I don't know how he managed to pull off the key part yet, but we'll figure it out."

"Finlay wasn't bright, like a rocket scientist or a mathematician, but he was…clever…street smart… manipulative. He could have slipped that key out of someone's pocket or talked them into loaning it to him. He knew what you needed to hear to make you help him. He certainly did that with me."

That probably explained it. Still, he'd feel better when Conner called to say he was satisfied with the evidence. Conner didn't mark a case closed until he'd checked and rechecked every possibility.

"Paige, it's been a pleasure working with you. You've pushed me, tried my patience, and driven me to the edge, but I've learned more about music from you than in two years at Julliard. I know you'll be a big hit Saturday, and I look forward to following your career. You have my card, and if anything frightens you or doesn't pass the smell test, give me a call. I'll look into it. I'm going to head home now. You need your rest and I have to see about Sweet Pea. Good luck with the festival." Why was that speech so difficult? He should be relieved this assignment was finished and he could get back to doing his real job.

He held out his hand but Paige glared at him.

"You fucking well better be kidding me. You can't bail out on me now."

His hand dropped to his side. "You heard Tracy. This case

is closed. You don't need me anymore. You're perfectly safe."

"I'm not talking about the case." Frost formed on every word. "You agreed to play with us on Saturday. We've practiced all week so you'd fit in. I can't find anyone else at this late date."

"The Musicians Guild has plenty of guitar players who could wipe the floor with me. They can find you someone in fifteen minutes."

"You're not listening to me. I can't just plug in someone we haven't worked with before. It takes time to get used to a new player. And for the new player to get used to us. Don't you remember the first few practices? This is a big show for us."

"I can't. I have to babysit my sister's kids Saturday night. It's her anniversary."

A sense of sadness filled Paige's voice. "You knew this whole time you wouldn't make the show? I thought you were a professional. That you were someone I could count on."

Ah shit. She's right. "I'll call my sister. She's not going to take this well. But we should be finished by seven. Maybe she can change their reservation to eight."

"What if I invite her to the show? I'll get V.I.P. tickets for the whole bunch. They can watch from the roped-off area in front of the stage. Hell, I'll even bring her kids up and dance with them. How old are they?"

"Five and seven." Was that right? Iris had a birthday recently.

"Perfect. I'll introduce her from the stage. Make a big deal of it. She'll have the time of her life. You can even use your real name."

"Naw, I'll stick with the name I've been using. I don't need anyone to know who I am." Maybe it would be fun. If Rachelle went along with it.

Noah started for the door, but stopped, his hand on the cold knob. "Shit. Lola's in the shop and the crime lab towed my rental in for tests. Conner dropped me here. I don't have any way to get home."

Paige blinked twice. "Who's Lola?"

"My truck. Remember, Finlay ran me off the road?" Was it Finlay? No prints had been found to say for certain. Noah closed his eyes, picturing the shadow behind the wheel of Lola's assassin. The driver seemed shorter than Finlay, but who knew how the seat was positioned or if his mind had decided to play tricks on him.

"Take my car. I'm not leaving the hotel. I have a massage scheduled for eleven and a long nap planned after that. You can pick me up in time for rehearsal. In fact, if you'll drive me back and forth, you can keep it for the weekend. I'll be more relaxed Saturday if I don't have to face Houston traffic again."

"I can't do that. I'll just call a taxi." A taxi to his house would cost a good thirty bucks. Then he'd have to come back for rehearsal. He could check on Saturday to see if his insurance company would cover a second rental. If they were open on weekends. The Lieu would probably okay a pool car, but that would have to wait until Saturday, too.

Paige had already disappeared into the bedroom. When she came back, a key with an oversized rental tag dangled from one finger. The key *clinked* against the tag in time with each step. He didn't object as she pressed the key into his hand, the metal tag warm from her fingers. "I'll be waiting downstairs at five-thirty. Don't forget me."

As if that would happen.

CHAPTER
EIGHTEEN

A THREE HOUR NAP and a brisk walk with Sweet Pea revived Noah to the point of feeling almost human. The day had cleared off, last night's rain only noticeable in how fresh the air smelled and how bright the colors seemed.

Paige's rental wasn't a luxury car, but felt like one after the purple clunker he'd been driving for the last two days. The legroom alone was heaven.

Friday afternoon traffic was a bitch, but most of it was headed away from the downtown area while he driving toward it. The case was solved. Paige could stand on stage without any fear. Jeannie and the baby were safe, even Rachelle had forgiven him.

So what nagged at the pit of his stomach?

Paige paced, guitar in hand, as he pulled under the porte-cochere. She tossed her instrument onto the back seat and jumped in without a word, nodding to him as she fastened her seatbelt. The echo of his tires against artificial cobblestones the only sound as he drove away.

Well, hello to you, too.

Neither spoke until they reached a block from the rehearsal hall. Paige twisted toward him. "I need a cup of coffee, bad. Could we stop somewhere?"

"I can't think of any drive-thrus in this part of town. Aren't you worried about being late?"

"Fuck that. It's my band. I'll be late if I want to."

He wasn't sure which startled him more, her language or her disregard for the time. She must really be jonesing for a caffeine fix.

The side streets were deserted so he hooked a left at the corner and parked in front of a diner. The place, which overflowed for breakfast and lunch, was nearly vacant once downtown cleared out. Even empty, the aroma of pancakes and bacon remained. Probably seeped deep into the walls.

They slid into a booth near the back and Noah held up two fingers. A waitress magically appeared, carrying two steaming mugs. The heavy ceramic kind that kept the contents good and hot, just the way he liked. How many times had he come here with Conner after pulling an all-nighter?

Paige added sweetener and stirred, then added a touch of cream and stirred some more. One more drop of cream and more stirring. She pulled her mug closer, then pushed it back again. She must not have liked the way the mug was positioned because she adjusted the handle, first one direction, then another.

She did everything except actually drink the coffee.

Her head still lowered, she glanced up at him. "I need to talk to you."

About damn time.

"There's something about Finlay I didn't tell you." She held up her hand, eyes wide. "It doesn't change anything about the case. Finlay didn't even know."

Yeah, he was beginning to figure out what that was.

"Mother kept me hidden in the house for two months while she told the neighbors I was in Nashville cutting a record. About the time she deemed it safe to cut me free, I realized I was pregnant."

Now it was Noah's turn to play with his coffee mug.

"I stayed, locked in that house, curtains drawn, the whole time. Mother bought me prenatal vitamins at the health food store. I found a block of wood in the garage and used it as a stair stepper for exercise. She waited until my water broke and drove me to a hospital on the far side of town where no one would recognize us. The next morning, I signed some papers and walked away, without the baby."

Noah lifted his mug only to discover it empty. When had that happened? He didn't dare signal for a refill. He needed Paige to keep talking.

She reached across the table and took his hand. "It wasn't just my career. My mother insisted. I was seventeen. How was I going to take care of a baby? We could barely feed ourselves. I was groggy when I signed the papers, but I had sixty days to change my mind and I didn't. I wanted a good family for that baby. My mother and I and Finlay Brown weren't it."

Noah opened and closed his mouth twice, like a fish gasping for air, but words didn't come. Weren't women supposed to have girlfriends they talked to about this sort of thing?

"I only saw her once, when they cut the cord. Her face was red, but her tiny ears and fingers were perfect, like the delicate angels in paintings or Valentine cards. At the time, she had a dusting of fuzzy blonde hair. Of course, that could have changed by now. Not a soul in the world knows except my mother and she's forgotten." She gripped his hand so hard she stopped the circulation, but he didn't pull away.

"I did the right thing, I'm sure of it, but I worry about the baby all the time. Did I endanger her by not going to the doctor? Did she end up with a good family? One that loves her? It's like I can't rest until I know she's safe. I'm sorry to drop this on you, but I needed to talk to someone. Keeping this secret was eating me up inside. I trust you. Anyone else I told might sell it to the tabloids. I'd live over it, but would the publicity harm her?"

He knew the feeling. He had secrets he'd never told anyone but Betsy. At the time, her love and acceptance had washed him clean. But she was gone now. And not being able to share weighed on him like a physical presence.

"My wife and I were married for three years. We started trying for a baby almost from the beginning. We were already checking into adoption when she died." That day. That damned day. He'd pulled Betsy onto the bed and they'd made love. Which made Betsy late for work. And put her directly in the path of an eighteen-wheeler driven by a man who hadn't slept in thirty-six hours.

The last time he ever had or wanted to touch a woman in that way.

Rachelle had guessed a small portion of his sins the day she insisted he clear out some of Betsy's things. She'd discovered the violin the mugger had stolen from their father, hidden in the back of his closet. They never discussed where he found it, or how he got it back, but she realized the implication and demanded he destroy the incriminating evidence. The loss broke his heart, but he'd done what she asked.

Noah studied Paige, conflicted. She was someone he'd grown to care for. Yet she'd given birth to a daughter and handed her over to a stranger like a piece of unwanted clothing. No, that wasn't fair. What she'd done had actually been best for the baby. And for couples like him and Betsy, who desperately wanted a child to love.

He cleared his throat and started over. "Placing a baby for adoption isn't a sign of weakness. It's a sign of strength and generosity. You put aside your own feelings and did the right thing for the child. And in the process, you gave a couple immeasurable happiness."

A happiness he was never likely to experience. He understood he had much to atone for, but why had Betsy been the one to pay the price for his sins?

Jeff and Craig shot Noah dirty looks when he and Paige strolled in late. Kevin merely smirked, as if he were privy to some secret.

Jerks.

Noah ignored them as he unclasped his case and lifted his guitar.

Paige clapped for attention. "Okay, guys. Let's take it from the top. No breaks."

They were on the second song when his phone vibrated in the pocket of his jeans. He ignored it. By the time they finished the next song, he'd had three more phone calls and two texts.

His hip was almost numb and they had one more song to go before Paige would give them a break. Whatever this was, it better be important; not Iris and Emma wanting him to talk their mother into letting them stay up late.

Whoever wanted him so badly must be catching on. His phone only vibrated once during the last number.

As they hit the final note of the fourth song, Noah jammed his hand into his pocket, only to withdraw it again. He couldn't do this here. The bathroom was out of the question with Kevin and his merry men toking up a storm.

Paige spun toward them. Her face was flush with excitement. Her hair gleamed under the stage lights. "That was good, guys, but see if you can do it better next time. Noah, you were late on the downbeat on *Dreaming of You.* That's my signature number. We can't afford to mess it up."

You'd have been late, too, if your pants were jumping all over the place.

"Craig, back it down a bit on *Angel Eyes.* If you overpower me again, I'll come back there and cram those sticks down your throat. Okay, five minutes and five minutes only. I want to finish this early so everyone can get a good night's rest."

Noah leaned his guitar against his case and double-timed it toward the exit. He could hear Paige's voice in the background calling, "Noah?" as he slammed the ball of his hand on the release bar, causing the door to fly open and crash against the outside wall.

He didn't wait for his eyes to adjust to the darkness,

clicking *unlock* on the key to the rental while digging in his pocket for his still vibrating phone. He slid into the driver's seat and pulled the door closed to shut off the street noises before glancing at the screen.

Conner.

Three missed calls and three texts. He went for the texts first. They would give him an idea what was going on.

The first text read simply: *Call me*

The second read: *911*

The third got his attention: *!!!!*

That wasn't like the always-under-control Conner he knew.

He didn't waste time listening to the voice messages. Conner would fill him in. He punched his partner's number and waited. He didn't have to wait long.

Conner answered on the first ring. "What took you so long? Don't you know what 911 means?"

"If I could have answered, I would have. Now, quit bitching and tell me what's wrong." Noah's heart rate crept up to an unacceptable level.

"It wasn't Finlay Brown."

"But I saw him." Or had he? He'd certainly seen *somebody*. The guy who flew out of the pickup had landed on his face. There was definitely a cursory resemblance to the mug shots he'd studied, but not even Finlay's mother could have positively identified that mound of ground hamburger as Finlay. "The other guys called him by name. He had Finlay's driver's license in his pocket. Sure, the ME's office is waiting to get the fingerprint reports back, but if you wanted to steal someone's identity, why in the world would you pick a loser like Finlay Brown?"

"I didn't mean the dead guy wasn't Finlay—he most definitely was—I meant Finlay wasn't the one who broke into Paige's hotel room."

"So he had an accomplice?" Talk about crazy. Two stalkers working together? He'd never heard of that.

"Forget Finlay. He was just a poor slob who got killed robbing a jewelry store. He had nothing to do with Paige's problems."

Noah shifted in his seat and banged his bad knee against the steering wheel. "But he had photos and clippings about Paige. He bragged that she was going to help him out."

Exasperation filled Conner's voice. "I didn't say he wasn't above a little petty larceny. I said he didn't have anything to do with her current troubles. He was in jail. Been there since Monday. Got out yesterday, just in time to get back to work robbing stores. I don't know if it will make his family feel any better, but he was locked up when the gang shot the security guard. So he wasn't a murderer, just your common variety crook."

"I don't understand." But he did.

They were back to square one. Not a single lead. Paige had to stand on that stage tomorrow and they had no clue who wanted to hurt her.

And her protection detail had been disbanded.

CHAPTER
NINETEEN

THE CLOYING SCENT of pot drifted through the ceiling vents into the ladies' room as Paige washed her hands. Not again. What was wrong with those guys? She'd have to get on them about it.

She didn't care what they did to relax on their off time. Hell, she'd been known to indulge herself on occasion.

But this wasn't their off time.

This was crunch time.

Too much was at stake to blow things now. This careless attitude was her fault. She hadn't been paying enough attention. She'd been distracted by all the stalker nonsense. Now the guys weren't taking this gig seriously. She'd keep working till midnight if that's what it took to get them on the right track.

Who could have guessed a mistake made ten years ago would come back to haunt her now?

That wasn't true. She'd always known someday she'd have to pay the piper.

Only half her nightmares were worries about the baby's welfare. The other half concerned Finlay Brown. She kept expecting him to show up on her doorstep, making demands. *Where is my baby?* or, *How could you leave me to face those cops alone?* or, *You stole my life, my youth. I'll make you pay.*

Then there were the replays of her fights with her mother. Of all the other bad choices she'd made in her life.

Karma was a bitch alright.

Finlay was dead, would he still haunt her from the grave? Talking to Noah had eased her mind about the baby, but was that enough? Was it too late to go back and fix her past mistakes?

Only time would tell, and she didn't have much of it at the moment.

Voices drifted through the door of the men's room. Did they even know what five minutes meant? She hurried down the hallway to the stage.

Good. Noah was already there. He was the one person she could count on.

She looked again. What was he doing? His guitar seemed to be put away and he was placing hers in its case. "Wait, stop. I need that."

"We have to leave. Now. If you see the guys, tell them to do a run through on their own. Or tell them to go back to their hotel and rest. I don't care, but we're leaving."

What did he mean, tell them to do a run through on their own? They couldn't even go to the bathroom without screwing up.

Noah shoved her guitar case into her hands and grabbed her arm. "You know what? Don't tell them anything. Let's get out of here before they come back."

She stumbled after him for a few steps. "I can't leave. We're working."

He twisted to face her. "Please, Paige, just this once, do what I ask and I'll explain in the car. We need to get moving before anyone sees us." He tugged on her arm and she followed him, unsure why.

He didn't speak as he drove out of the parking lot, his eyes flicking from the road to the side mirrors, the rearview mirror, and back again. What was he afraid of? Wasn't everything settled?

"We're in the car. Tell me."

"Conner called. It wasn't Finlay."

Had she heard him right? "He isn't dead?" Relief flooded her, then dread, then relief again. She didn't want Finlay dead. But it did make life simpler.

"No, no. He's dead. He just wasn't the one after you."

"So, who *is* after me?" This was like living on a rollercoaster. And she hated rollercoasters.

"I was hoping you could tell me."

Not that again. "I. Don't. Know." And she didn't. This was all too far beyond anything she'd expected. The fire alarm. The dead rose. Those weren't done by someone timid and shy, withdrawn. Those were the work of a crazy person. A reckless person. Someone she didn't know.

Tears threatened and she was too exhausted to stop them. She'd been fighting all her life. Holding the world together by force of will. She couldn't do it any longer.

"Let's find someplace safe, then we'll worry about who's behind this."

Noah made a right from the center lane without benefit of a turn signal and her heart skipped a beat. This was déjà vu all over again. She hadn't liked it the night of the fire and didn't like it any better now. But he hadn't killed her then, so she had to trust him.

"Can't I go to my hotel?" She wanted her yoga pants, her toothbrush. Her life back.

"Whoever this is traced you down twice and broke in to your room once. Your security detail has been cancelled. Are you comfortable with that? Because I'm not."

Thanks. You've made me feel so much better. "Are we going to your house?"

"The guy recognized me and ran me off the road. By now, he almost certainly knows who I am and where I live."

Was she relieved he'd admitted his "accident" wasn't one? No. She'd been clinging to that slightest bit of doubt.

"So where are we going?"

"That's the question, isn't it?"

Noah drove aimlessly for forty-five minutes, doubling back, scooting through yellow signals, and making U-turns. Thank goodness he'd given in and allowed Mrs. Powell to keep Sweet Pea until this was over.

A schematic of a gas pump glowed red on the dashboard. Damn. How long had that been lit up? The needle rested on the big E, daring him to keep driving.

Where the hell were they? He'd driven through Alvin a few miles back. They weren't anywhere that had an actual name. Or much in the way of creature comforts. They needed to find a gas station. Soon.

A canary yellow light beckoned in the distance with the promise of civilization. Hopefully, a Shell station, or at least a McDonald's, waited a mile up the road. He hadn't realized how hungry he was.

Paige rested her head against the back of the seat. Thinking or sleeping? Neither of them had spoken for the last fifteen minutes. He'd been running every possible scenario through his mind. Was she doing the same?

The yellow haze formed into a Shell sign and within two minutes, he pulled under the canopy and next to a pump. Good thing. The red warning light had started blinking.

His seatbelt unfastened with a sharp *snap*, and Paige twisted her head toward him. "I stand by everything I said."

What was she talking about?

"It's not that I'm such a nice person, or that I wouldn't have if I needed to, but I didn't step on, or cheat anyone on my way up. I didn't ask Finlay to take me to Nashville. He begged me. I didn't fire any band members. The weak ones quit on their own when they couldn't keep up. I didn't desert the band. That National Anthem gig was pure dumb luck. Being in the right place at the right time. The band could have come with me but didn't think it was worth $25 split five ways. And in Nashville, I simply worked my butt off. Finding good people to help was another stroke of luck."

Luck was a fickle lady. In his experience, the luckiest people were those who just happened to be prepared when an opportunity came around. "I've come to the same conclusion."

"Where does that leave us?"

In the middle of nowhere, driving on fumes? "A nut job is

the only thing I can think of." The hardest type of case to solve. The most difficult to protect from.

He slid out of the car and stood in front of the gas pump. He froze with his hand on his wallet. Shit. They were screwed. He tapped on the passenger window, the glass cold on his knuckles. "Paige, how much money do you have?"

"Here, use my Visa," she said, her voice muffled from inside the car as she dug into her pocket.

"No, cash. If we're hiding, we shouldn't use credit cards."

"Do you really think he could find us from that?"

Hell, he didn't know. On cop shows they knew within five minutes, but that was TV. They also had DNA results by the next day. And enough money in the budget to track down every lead. "We aren't sure who this guy is. Does he have an in with some agency? Is he a computer genius, or a relentless idiot? That's the problem; we're completely in the dark. If we're going to spend the next twelve hours hiding, then we're going to do it right."

Paige shook her head. "I don't have any cash. When we're rehearsing, I slip a credit card and my room key in my back pocket. That's it."

He opened his wallet, a five and two ones. He'd spent the rest on hotel pastries for Mrs. Powell, intending to stop at the ATM on his way home. In the back of his billfold, creased into quarters, and hiding behind his insurance card, was his emergency hundred. Whenever he pulled it out to pay for his share of the coffee, the guys threw wadded balls of paper at him. It had become the office joke.

Not a joke now.

He held the bills in front of Paige. "This is all we have to pay for gas, food, and a place to stay. We have to choose which is most important. And we can't drive far with what's left in the tank."

Paige opened her door and swung out a cowboy-booted foot. "We can use my card here, then drive to the other side of town before he knows where we were. You fill up. I'll go inside to pay and find us some snacks. I'm getting hungry."

Had she always been this smart? Why hadn't he noticed? "One more thing. Turn off your phone." That should show if she was ready to take this situation seriously.

She reached into her pocket for her phone and thumbed the power switch. He did the same. When was the last time he'd been so completely off the grid? The sense of isolation should have made him nervous. It didn't.

He stood in the middle of nowhere, surrounded by a mixture of exhaust and gas fumes, his stomach emitting audible *feed me* signals. He was out of money and out of touch.

Nearly a year had passed since he'd felt this alive.

Where the hell were they?

One minute they were rehearsing. The next, *poof.* Vanished.

Paige, that cop, and both their guitars, gone. Along with Paige's rental car.

The band members didn't have any idea what happened. They were sitting around with their thumbs up their asses, waiting for a sign from Heaven. Morons.

He'd spent an hour circling all the logical places they could have gone.

The cop hadn't taken her to any nearby restaurant. Not

even the dive where they dawdled over this morning's coffee—another sign of how far Paige had slipped. She was lucky he'd be taking over before she ruined her reputation.

They hadn't gone back to Paige's hotel, or any hotel in the downtown area. In fact, all of Paige's belonging still waited in her fancy-schmancy penthouse suite.

They weren't at the cop's house. Or at the other cop's house.

He still had a score to settle with the second cop's wife—pointing a rifle at him was a *big* mistake—but he could take care of that later. Houston was a major concert market. He'd schedule Paige to return when the money was right. Kill two birds with one stone as it were, or one airline ticket.

Might as well add that barking mutt to the list while he was at it. Maybe he should wait on the dog. Not set off any alarm bells. Now he had two reasons to come back to Houston. So far, the cop was only doing his job. If he continued as paid protection only, and didn't overstep his bounds, he was safe. Anything else, and he could go down with his annoying pooch.

For now, his priority was to find Paige.

Every contact he'd reached out to had come up dry. And after all the money he'd spent greasing the way. Fucking useless shits! He powered down the car window, ready to hurl his phone across the crowded parking lot. He halted, his arm halfway out the window, at the sound of laughter. Just a foursome exiting a nearby bar, one too many margaritas under their belts.

His frustration level had reached critical mass. He needed to cool down before he did something to attract attention to himself. Let them play their games. He knew where she'd be on

Saturday evening. That's all that mattered.

He'd already proved waiting was only one of the many things at which he excelled.

CHAPTER TWENTY

S PEEDING THROUGH THE night, dashboard lights or an occasional passing billboard the only illumination, increased the sense of isolation and dependency. Their own little dome of secrecy.

Even without seeing Noah's face, Paige could feel him relax. They chatted easily about amusing incidents from their childhood. She entertained him with stories of life on the road. The life he might have had if he'd chosen a different path.

She began to catch glimpses of the man who'd hidden from her for the last week. The man who masked himself behind hard work and dedication and responsibility. As if that could keep his life from falling apart.

Hell, he probably thought the same about her. She'd certainly put up as many walls as he had. And the effort of keeping those barriers in good repair, rushing to mend cracks, exhausted her.

She studied the flimsy gas station sack in her lap. "Not

the most well balanced meal I've ever had, but not the worst, either."

He glanced at the cookies and chips. "When have you had worse?"

"When I first got to Nashville. I ordered a cup of hot water for tea, put the tea bag and a couple of sugars in my purse for later and emptied the ketchup packet into the water. Voila. Tomato soup. Add the free crackers and I had a meal."

Noah took his eyes off the road for a moment to glance her direction. "Really? I thought that was just an urban legend."

"It ought to be. That stuff was *nasty*. I only did it the once before I found a job. You know, I kept the tea bag for a long time to remind myself to work harder."

"I've never been desperate enough to try that trick, but I've had some odd meals. I've eaten bread hard enough to use as a Frisbee, then covered it with cheese so old I had to trim off the mold."

"When was that?"

"Last week."

This was a side of him she'd never have guessed. Funny, self-deprecating, companionable. If he was trying to put her at ease, make her feel safe, it was working.

They'd left the gas station behind almost an hour ago when he exited I-59 toward Humble and studied the surroundings. "We need a place that uses real keys, not electronic ones, so watch for an older motel, probably one story. A mom-and-pop type. They usually have names similar to one of the national chains, but not quite. Think Comfortable Inn, or La Quota."

A chuckle bubbled out. "Like Motel 9 or Come Right Inn?"

Street lights allowed her to see his smile. "You've got the

idea."

"How about Hollywood Inn?"

"Yep, that's a good one."

"No, really. Over there. Hollywood Inn."

She pointed to the left and he squinted, making out a sign in the distance. "Perfect."

Up close, the place was less than inviting. Half the overhead lights weren't working, but she could still make out new cracks in the adobe siding and patches over the old ones. Waist high weeds covered a vacant lot next door.

Across the street and down the block, neon signs flickered over a neighborhood bar, giving the entire area a faint red cast.

When Noah opened the car door and slid out, she followed close behind him. He glanced her direction. "What? I'm not sitting out here by myself." She hadn't let him drag her all over town to keep her safe, only to desert her in the riskiest place they'd been so far.

"You realize they're going to think we're here for... nefarious purposes."

For some reason, that made her grin. After all the work she'd put into keeping her reputation spotless, this might be fun.

Despite an *Open* sign, glowing in the window, the place appeared empty. Noah swung the door wide to let her pass and a buzzer sounded from deep behind the front desk.

Aged photos of Hollywood legends, all now gone, filled the walls. John Wayne, Paul Newman, Lana Turner, Marilyn Monroe, and James Cagney smiled down at them, but didn't make the room any more cheerful. In fact, the whole place felt like a mausoleum.

While the portraits caught the stars in their prime, the yellowed paper hinted at what the passage of time would do to their bodies.

She and Noah crossed the lobby and waited at the empty reception desk. A forlorn bell with pieces of chrome flaking off sat on the counter. He reached over and tapped it with the palm of his hand. A woman appeared from behind a glass-beaded doorway before the *ding* died away. She smoothed her turquoise sari. Wisps of graying hair stood out among jet black tresses escaping from the bun at the back of her neck. Even the red bindi on her forehead seemed sad and faded.

Sounds from a TV turned to a foreign language station followed her into the room, along with the sharp aroma of *curry*, and other spices Paige couldn't identify. Better than the musty smell when they first opened the door.

"May I help you?"

"We're looking for a room," Noah said. He glanced her direction. "A double, please."

The woman called over her shoulder. "Ramesh, turn down that TV. I can't hear a thing."

The volume might have lowered half a decibel.

"One facing the back," Noah added.

"Did you fix the sink in Thirty-six, liked I asked you?" The woman's voice grated, like Paige's mother when she got home late from school or forgot her homework.

"I still need a new stopper. I'll get it from Ace tomorrow." Ramesh sounded as thrilled as Paige had when her mother berated her.

"Fat lot of good that'll do us tonight," the woman muttered. She thumbed through a peg-board of keys, only a few of which were missing. "What about Thirty-two?"

Ramesh didn't answer.

The woman made a sound Paige couldn't identify. It might have been a groan or a fart, she wasn't sure. "I don't suppose you had time in your busy schedule to repair the lock on Eighteen?"

The TV volume swelled.

"Number Twenty-eight. Around back on the left." She handed Noah a key big enough to open a bank vault, attached to a one pound block of wood sanded, varnished and hand painted with a two and an eight.

No one would accidently slip off with that key.

"That'll be $59.99 plus tax." Her eyes went cold when Noah pulled out his well creased hundred. She lifted the bill to the light, rubbed it between her fingers, and sniffed it before it disappeared into the folds of her sari.

Noah held out his hand for change, but she shook her head. "There's a deposit required for cash."

Paige could feel Noah aching to flash his badge. "Not now," she whispered. "You can report her later. After this is all over."

Noah still fumed as they climbed into the car and drove behind the main building, but she couldn't stop laughing.

"What's so funny?" He tried to keep his voice gruff, but couldn't hide the amusement underneath.

"When you said look for a mom-and-pop establishment, that wasn't the couple I envisioned."

Room Twenty-eight wasn't exactly what Noah expected. The entire room sported a western theme, from the cowhide lampshade, to the saddle-shaped chair, to the deer antler chandelier.

Some movie star cowboy he didn't recognize—Tom Mix? Roy Rogers?—stared down at him from atop a white horse. The photo, enclosed in a lighted, shadow box frame, hung over the wagon-wheel spokes of the king sized bed.

Maybe the double beds were in number Eighteen, with the broken lock.

The size of the bed didn't matter, he'd be sitting up all night, but he sure wished the single chair looked more comfortable.

For the time being, he positioned the chair against the front of the door and engaged the deadbolt.

Paige acted as if she didn't notice. She made a quick run for the bathroom, turning on the faucet to drown out any sound. When she returned, she plopped onto the mattress and opened the plastic bag she'd guarded since the city of Alvin was a mere reflection in their rearview mirror.

"Ready for supper?"

Man, was he.

The sodas were long gone and they were left with four bottles of water, two cans of deviled ham, a box of saltines, a package of Goldfish, sour cream potato chips, two individual packages of Oreos, and a bag of jellybeans

An absolute feast.

She'd picked up napkins, but no cutlery, so they alternated using his Swiss Army Knife to spread the deviled ham on the crackers. For a moment, he feared she'd use the knife on him when she finished off her ham spread before he did.

When they emptied the chips and started on the Goldfish, she leaned back against the wagon-spoked headboard and turned on the TV, flipping from one channel to another until she'd gone around twice. "I thought they advertised *Cable* on the sign."

"They did. Without it, you wouldn't be able to get even those five channels. They never mentioned HBO or anything like that."

She flipped around again, landing on *The Voice*. "I'm good at this," she said. "I can spot a winner with my eyes closed."

"Wanna bet?" He would never admit in public he watched a reality show, but he'd seen the program a time or two. Maybe more. And he wasn't any slouch at recognizing a talented performer.

"Oh, you're on, mister. Show me what you got."

They sat with their backs facing the screen and Noah muted the sound while the announcer introduced the singer and told their background. He could see enough of a reflection in the cowboy photo to realize when the singing started and he'd turn on the sound.

The first one to slap their pillow indicated they wanted that performer on their team. Paige beat him out on the first singer and they both declined the second.

When Noah pummeled his make-shift buzzer for the third act, Paige snorted at him. "Are you kidding me? He's pitchy and weak."

"He's a she and she has a good range. The rest can be taught."

They finished the Goldfish and were on to the Oreos by the first commercial. By the next break, he had eaten his last Oreo and eyed the one she held carelessly between two fingers. She must have felt him staring, because she moved it back and forth, taunting him.

He leaned forward to chomp when she yanked the cookie out of the way. "Go ahead, take it," she said. "I'd rather have jellybeans anyway."

By the end of the program, they each had one contestant on their team, and one they agreed to share. The judges had argued over one singer they both felt was overrated.

When the season ended, would they still be in touch? Could they call back and forth to discuss the judges' choices?

He'd had fun tonight. All the things he'd recently claimed to Conner were fun, were merely pleasant. He hadn't lied. He just hadn't realized the difference until now.

Paige swung around and they watched the news. Her photo was displayed and she was listed as one of the performers at tomorrow's Shadow of Spring Festival. No mention was made of her disappearance. Thank you, Conner.

Would the motel owner recognize her? Odds were against it. They were tuned to a different program.

She stretched out and turned off her light. "You can keep watching if you want. I need to get some sleep. I have a big day tomorrow."

She couldn't possibly be planning on singing tomorrow? Standing on a stage when they had no idea who was after her or what the creep wanted? No point talking to her about it tonight.

A miracle could happen and Conner might solve this thing by then.

Yeah, right. They'd had such good luck so far.

He reached across her for the bag of jellybeans and switched off the TV and his light. He wouldn't bother her and this was 100% more comfortable than that damn saddle chair.

He ate one jellybean and wrinkled his nose. Licorice. He tried again. Another licorice. He rooted around to the bottom of the bag and pulled out one more. Still licorice. What the...

Ignoring Paige, he switched on his light and peered into the bag. All black.

Paige rose onto her elbows. "What is it?"

"You ate all the good jellybeans."

"I don't like the black ones."

"Neither do I."

"Well, some people do. I didn't know."

"So you were just being considerate in case I liked licorice?" He tossed a jellybean her direction.

"It could happen." She bit her lip, holding back a smile.

He lobbed another jellybean at her.

"So that's the way you want to play." She tossed one back and it bounced off his forehead.

"Oh, no. You're the one who likes jellybeans. You should take them all." He grabbed several and pushed them into her mouth when she opened it to laugh.

She chewed for a moment, then gave him an evil grin, full of black teeth.

He didn't resist when she leaned close and covered his mouth with hers.

Licorice never tasted so good.

Shit. "Paige, I can't do this."

"Why not?"

A couple of reasons. Best to go with the one she'd understand. "It's against regs. I'm on duty. I'm supposed to be protecting you."

"No, you're not."

"What?" She didn't believe he was protecting her?

"You were fired, remember? Your boss called off my protection and cancelled all overtime. You're on your own dime here."

She was right. *Fuck, no expense account. I'll never get my hundred back.* Only one reason left. Too much time had passed, too many things had happened. He didn't know if he was capable anymore. His body had forgotten what to do.

She kissed him again and he didn't hold back. Something inside him crumbled. His hands tangled in her hair and his tongue searched for hers. He shifted his hips against hers and lost himself in the sensation.

He dove into her as if his life depended on her touch. Maybe it did.

Turned out he did remember how after all.

CHAPTER TWENTY-ONE

S UNLIGHT SLIPPED THROUGH a crack in the curtains and hit
Noah directly in the eye. He tried to move but a weight
held his arm steady. A weight that sighed and snuggled
closer. Blond hair tickled his nose.

The air conditioner clicked on and blew cool air over bare
skin.

Shit. What had he done? Let down everyone who depended
on him. Again.

One glance at the door showed the dead bolt still engaged
and the saddle-chair firmly hooked under the knob. They were
safe. No thanks to him.

That didn't change the fact he'd betrayed Betsy by taking
advantage of Paige while she was in a vulnerable state.

He slid his arm loose and shook it. Pins and needles
exploded. If someone broke in now, he wasn't even capable of
lifting his gun.

Where the hell *was* his gun? He twisted and found his

Smith and Wesson, sitting on the nightstand beside him.

Okay, so he wasn't a complete fuck up. He'd secured the room and kept his weapon handy. He hadn't taken advantage of Paige any more than she'd taken advantage of him. As to Betsy....

He'd been faithful from the day he first set eyes on her until eight months after her death. He still loved her, thought of her every day, took care of her dog and her mother and honored her memory.

Paige groaned and pulled a pillow over her face. Her breasts rose and fell with each breath. The sun highlighted all her curves and planes, every nook and cranny. Her skin begged to be touched.

He needed to make a decision. Live or die. Pick one and get on with it.

At the moment, he leaned toward living.

A hard knot dug into Paige's hip. She scooted up an inch but that didn't help. She rolled onto her back only to have the knot press against her butt.

What was this, *The Princess and the Pea?* She tried to open her eyes, but one little crack in the curtains allowed daylight to hit her directly in the face.

The far side of the bed shifted and, to hell with the sun, her eyes flew open. Noah leaned against the wagon-wheel headboard, in all his naked glory, using a threadbare motel washcloth to clean his gun.

"You're not going to shoot me with that, are you?"

"I thought about it a few times this week when you

wouldn't do what I told you, but I think you're safe for now."

"Have you ever killed anyone with it?" Was that okay to ask? He was a policeman, but….

"With this little thing? No."

What kind of answer was that? "With anything."

He buffed an invisible spot off the handle.

Holy crap. She hadn't expected that. No answer was definitely an answer. Here sat a man much more complex than she'd realized.

She sat up, but that pesky little knot dug in deeper. "What *is* this?" She shifted to one hip and felt behind her.

"A jellybean," Noah said. "They're all over the bed."

Black smudges stained the sheets and pieces of smashed licorice littered the bed. "I don't think we're going to get our deposit back."

He sat the gun down and stretched out beside her. "Serves them right. They gave us the room where the curtain doesn't close all the way. They were going to keep the money anyway. Want to make them earn it?"

She did and they did and it was even better than the first time. Hell, it was even better than the second time.

As he lay back with his arms around her, she realized the little bits of candy didn't seem as uncomfortable as they had before.

"What's this?" she asked, her hand tracing a string of numbers tattooed above Noah's heart.

He didn't answer.

"Come on, give. I told you my secrets. Time to spill some of yours."

He opened his mouth, closed it, and tried again. Whatever

this was, it was hard for him to talk about.

"The date of Betsy's death."

She had a knack, didn't she? First she asked if he'd killed anyone and now about his dead wife.

"You're the only one who knows. Well, the guy who put it on and one other person saw it, but they don't know what it represents."

Yep, a top rated homicide detective who studied at Julliard, sang opera at Carnegie Hall, raised his little sister after their father was murdered, had killed someone, adored his late wife, and lived with a dog the size of a can of Spam.

Why had she thought he was just a simple cop she could use to help fill her lonely nights?

Noah sopped up the last bite of egg with the final remnants of his toast. Having the meal come out even seemed like a good omen. He'd get this mess cleaned up today and everything would work out as it should.

Whatever that meant.

Paige's plate, on the other hand, was a frigging disaster. She'd poured warm maple syrup on her pancakes, cut them into pieces, and moved things around. Blueberries left a purple trail on the white dish, bacon floated in a puddle of now cooled syrup, and one egg stared up at him with its yellow eye. She'd done everything but eat.

The sight of her mutilated food left him with the irrational fear the day would turn out as big a shambles as her breakfast. When had he turned superstitious?

That was easy. It happened when, for the first time in a

long while, he had something to lose.

"I thought you were hungry." He reached across the table and snagged a slice of bacon. Did that make him responsible for the condition of her food, now? Had he just jinxed their chance for success?

"I can't eat. I guess it was all that candy." She glanced at his clean plate. "It doesn't seem to have bothered you any."

"I didn't actually *get* any of the candy." If she'd had a jellybean left, she'd have thrown it at him. He could see it in her eyes. "Are you sure there isn't something else on your mind?"

He held his breath. Did she regret anything that happened last night, or again this morning? He certainly didn't.

"Are you sure we're safe here, sitting out in public like this? We can't pay for this meal without using a credit card." She dragged her fork through the syrup and blueberry stain, making an abstract design.

This was a change. Now she was the one worried about covering their tracks and he felt an unrealistic sense of calm. "We're five miles away from the no-tell-motel and we won't use the card until we're ready to walk out the door. Not even the FBI could find us that fast. When we leave here, I'll drive a ways and find an ATM. Then we won't have to keep using the card. Is there anything you need?"

"I know I showered before we left, but that place didn't leave me feeling squeaky clean. I'd kill for a toothbrush or a hairbrush." She leaned her head down and took a deep sniff. "And maybe a clean shirt."

"Eat up. I want to call Conner before we hit the road. Maybe he has this case solved by now and we can all go home. If not, there's a Dollar Store on every corner. I've got a five dollar bill with your name on it."

Conner studied the instructions for assembling the baby bed. The thing had more pieces than a jigsaw puzzle. While the directions purported to be in English, it wasn't any form of the language he'd ever seen. The translation had obviously been done by a non-native speaker.

Add to that a couple of missing pieces, and others that didn't seem to belong. Maybe this was an IQ test to see if he was smart enough to raise a child. If so, he was failing miserably.

He glanced at his phone on the floor beside him. If his disappearing partner ever decided to surface, he didn't want the call to wake Jeannie. She'd been up half the night with leg cramps and he'd convinced her to go back to bed after breakfast.

The crib teetered at a precarious angle as he inserted a pivotal screw when his cell rang. It figured. He'd tried to contact his missing partner half the night and again this morning, to no avail.

Yet the moment he had his hands full was the time Noah picked to return his calls. If he let go now, the whole thing would crash to the floor.

He took two quick turns on the screw and reached for the phone. A photo of Noah in a clown costume at the children's hospital identified the caller.

"About time you checked in. The big Kahunas are having a cow. The Chief himself arranged for a safe house and extra protection. I had to lie about your whereabouts. And you know how I feel about lying. Especially to our boss."

"And a good morning to you, too. Paige and I are fine, thank you for asking."

Why did Noah sound so happy? He should be shitting a brick by now. Something wasn't right.

"Have you found the stalker? Is it safe for us to show our faces?"

Not hardly. "Things have escalated. The creep broke into Paige's suite and left a message not long after the two of you disappeared." He refused to ask. He didn't want to know where they went or what they'd been doing for the last fifteen hours.

"What kind of message?" Noah's tone suddenly turned serious.

Man, he hated to say it out loud. "The perp took a knife from the kitchen and stabbed it through a pile of Paige's underwear into the middle of her bed. She needs to get off the street so we can protect her." *And we need to put him away now so I know Jeannie's safe.*

"The fuck you say. He's found her three times when you thought you had her hidden. I'm keeping her with me until you catch him. This isn't a joke any longer."

Conner wanted to argue. He hadn't actually been the one to decide where to stash Paige, but he had been in charge of checking the location and making the reservations. Which made Noah's accusations valid.

"It was never a joke and if we treated it that way, I'm sorry. Now you need to bring her in and let's do this thing right. She can't be out running around with you all night. It's not proper procedure."

"That won't be a problem. I'm not working."

What the hell did he mean by that? Not working? Conner

let go of the crib to rub a hand across his face and the rail slipped off, allowing the whole bed to fall apart and crash to the floor. Jeannie would be in any minute.

"I'm off duty. Fired as bodyguard. The brass let all of her protection go when Finlay died."

Surely he couldn't mean… That was crazy. Noah would never… Not with a citizen he'd been assigned to protect. "Not any more. Half the department is searching for her. You're back on the job."

"I didn't hear that and you didn't say it. Now, let's figure out what we're going to do. We can't just watch over her for the next twenty-four hours and stick her on a plane to Nashville with a wave and a smile. If this guy wants her so bad, he'll be at the concert. Do we have a policewoman who can pose as her until then?"

There went the rest of his weekend. At least he had an excuse to hire someone to put the bed together. Jeannie was due at her sister's for a baby shower, so she should be safe all day. "I'll run it by the brass. They'll love it. Before you know it, they'll be claiming it was their idea in the first place. Meanwhile, you keep Paige hidden. You can't be part of the take-down and she can't be anywhere near the concert. Got that?"

"Don't worry. Just do your part. I'll take care of Paige."

Now, why didn't that make him feel any better about the situation?

CHAPTER
TWENTY-TWO

"WHAT DO YOU mean, you'll take care of me?"

Noah glanced up, sheepishly. Wonderful. Paige had come back from the restroom while he was talking. She must have heard what he said to Conner.

"I'm back on the job. Protecting you."

She rolled her eyes. "Did anything happen besides learning Finlay wasn't my stalker?"

"There's evidence the guy broke into your room again. Probably looking for you." He rushed on, before she had time to ask questions. "That's a good thing. Means he doesn't know where you are. So you're safe."

"For now. Until I step onto that stage at 6:00. I must have had a dozen texts from the guys. I assured them I'd be there on time."

Hoo boy. Here it came. The part where she threw a fit. "You're not going out on that stage or anyplace near the park.

A trained police woman will act as decoy and when he makes his move, we'll grab him."

"What fool came up with that idiotic idea? "

Um, I did? Best not say that out loud.

"You actually believe you can dupe someone who's followed me for days, studied my schedule, knows what I look like, sound like? How far are you going to take this? If you don't find him, is she planning to get up on stage with my band, sing my songs? Does she even *know* my songs? How about my guitar. Does she want to borrow it along with my identity?"

Time to wrap this up. Diners were starting to look their direction. "I've already paid the bill. We've both used our phones. We need to turn them off and get out of here." Hopefully, she'd cool down on the way to the car.

He'd parked a block away so anyone who spotted their car wouldn't know exactly where they were. He motioned Paige to stay put while he scanned the neighborhood.

Nothing. A few dog walkers. A mom with a stroller and a Starbucks coffee. A train of six bike riders in matching Lycra shorts and shirts zipping through an intersection without slowing down. A normal spring Saturday morning.

He nodded to Paige. They hurried across the street to an ATM and each withdrew $200, then they double-timed it to the car. Once inside, he drove under the freeway to a different area and stopped at a park. A kid's soccer match was in full swing and he slid the rental between two not-so-mini vans, out of easy sight.

They had several hours to kill. Might as well do it someplace pleasant.

One section of the park was used a playground and they found a bench in the sun facing a jungle gym constructed in a medley of primary colors. Kids climbed up the green steps and scooted down the blue slide or across the red bridge. Yellow swings and orange tunnels provided additional adventures. The ground was padded with a spongy material.

Noah had brought Emma and Iris to parks like this on other Saturday mornings.

Paige watched the children run and squeal with the joy of being free. "My daughter would be almost ten now. Do you think she'd be too old for this?"

"Probably. She'd more likely be over there, playing soccer."

Paige's eyes drifted across the parking lot to the sports field. A cheer went up as some kid made a goal. Or blocked one. It was hard to imagine Paige as a soccer mom, but if things had been different, who knew?

"My baby would be too young. Still an infant." *Fuck.* What made him say that?

Paige snapped her head around to look at him.

"Betsy was pregnant when she died. We only learned that morning." He'd never told anyone, not even Conner. Yet, here he was, spilling his guts to this woman like his soul had sprung a leak.

"Do you want to move?" she asked.

"No. I like it here. It makes me happy." In the last twelve hours he'd revealed Betsy's pregnancy, the significance of his tattoo, and admitted to killing someone. All secrets he'd hoarded like his life depended on it.

And with each admission, a small portion of the weight he carried, lifted.

"I haven't changed my mind," Paige said.

"What?" Noah pulled himself back to the present.

"I still plan to be up on that stage this evening, singing my heart out."

He'd been wrong to gloss over the perp's last break-in. "The thing is…" He didn't want to scare her, but she needed to realize the danger. "This time he's escalated. He destroyed some of your underwear."

"*Damn!* Do you know I've worn Wal-Mart undies all my life? That's all we could afford growing up and I sure didn't have any extra money once I went out on my own. I was nervous about this gig so I went to Victoria's Secret and splurged. Knowing I had the fancy stuff on underneath gave me an added boost to my confidence."

Whatever she'd had on last night and this morning looked pretty good to him, no matter where she bought it.

She kicked at a pine cone, missed and sent a shower of dust over her boot. "That tears it. I've got a credit card bill to pay off and new underwear to buy. I'm not backing out now."

"You're crazy. You can't put yourself in danger over new panties. It's time to leave this to the professionals." He knew when he said it he'd made a mistake. Telling her about the break-in was supposed to make her more reasonable, not more stubborn.

"Just because you had your way with me last night—"

"—and this morning."

"Doesn't mean you can tell me what to do today." She laid her hand on his arm. "Noah, I trust you—in my bed, in my band, and in charge of my safety—but I'm in charge of my career. You may parade your decoy around the grounds all you want, but when the lights go up on that stage, I *will* be the one standing behind that microphone."

He slammed his hand against the metal bed frame and shock waves traveled up his arm, setting his teeth on edge. That bitch. Where had she gone? He'd spent all night and a full tank of gas searching, leaving him exhausted. And broke. He couldn't afford for things to fall apart now, not after pouring everything into preparing this dump.

A swift kick at the chains waiting beside the bed filled the room with the screech of metal on metal, but did nothing to steady the whirlwind churning through his chest.

Only one thing held him together. He knew exactly where she'd be at 6:00 p.m. Until then, he needed to rest and reassess his plan. He took a calming breath, stretched out on the new flowered bedspread—more money wasted because of her, but best not to think about that now—and stared at the ceiling, going over the events of last night.

Why had she run? Had the cop, Daugherty, talked her into it? She was definitely leaning on him too much. That had to stop. Somehow, she needed to be convinced *he* was the one she should trust.

Throwing a tantrum in Paige's hotel room had been a major blunder, but he couldn't stand to be overlooked, ignored. He'd had enough of that growing up when his mother obviously preferred his sister. Not until he helped her fill out Social Security forms did the reason become clear. She'd been four months pregnant when she married his jerk of a father.

From the day he was born, she'd treated him like dirt under

her feet. His father had been worse. Two resentful people, trapped in a loveless marriage they both blamed on him.

As a child, so little attention was paid to him he actually began to believe he was invisible. When his little sister screamed at him for breaking her doll, he realized his mistake.

He wasn't invisible, just unimportant.

Invisible was better, so he learned to blend in. Act like everybody else. Dress like everybody else. Don't call attention to yourself.

With an average build, average hair, he could go anywhere, do anything, and no one remembered seeing him. As long as he kept his mouth shut.

You could tell a lot about a person by his closet. Business suits for weekdays and pressed slacks and golf shirts for weekends. Or sturdy work clothes and steel-toed boots. Or an assortment of ragged jeans and T-shirts. Not him. His closet kept his secrets, full of clothes to disappear in.

Getting a tattoo was a big mistake. He'd wanted to join in, be accepted. It hadn't worked. Now his sleeves stayed down, his collar buttoned and *presto*, invisible again.

Just like his childhood. Paige saw him, but didn't see him.

Was it any wonder his frustrations sometimes boiled over? The question now was how to turn this calamity to his advantage. Ideas swirled through his mind until one took root.

After his last stunt, Paige would be more frightened than ever. The trick was to convince her the police were useless. They couldn't protect her. *Whoever* was after her must have an in with the department. How else had the guy found her and waltzed into her room whenever he wanted?

She didn't have to know how easy it was. There were only

a few hotels in the downtown area the city would use. And he'd installed the key imprinter in each of them. No one had even run a background check because he didn't actually work for SecureTech. The electrician did all the wiring. His only job was to follow the guy around and hand him the equipment. An anonymous pack mule. When everything was finished, he plugged in the box and checked that it worked. Something a tenth-grader could do. A piece of cake after years of hooking up audio/visual equipment, microphones, speakers.

The brilliant part was planning ahead and giving each hotel an easy-to-remember code. He'd been breaking into rooms and lifting a little here, a little there, for years. Rich people never seemed to notice if he didn't take too much.

Mornings were best. All he had to do was wait until the guests were packed and stuffing themselves at the breakfast buffet, then duck into their room and slip something out of the suitcase.

Stealing one earring was his favorite. Women always seemed to think they'd lost the mate. They'd call from Dallas or New York and ask housekeeping to look for it, but nothing ever happened.

The adrenaline rush was almost better than the cash. Almost. But he couldn't keep it up forever. Sooner or later, he'd get caught. Besides, he deserved better. He'd been the one to discover Paige. He had a right to his share.

So how to get it? Back to Plan A. He'd be her savior, just like before. She'd been tired, hungry, unknown. He'd recognized her potential, her beauty. He'd given her the opportunity to shine. His mistake had been not making sure she realized he was behind her good fortune. That he was the one who presented her talent to the entire world, not just a few fans as she thought.

He wouldn't make that omission again.

First, he had to turn this shed into her sanctuary instead of her prison. A place where she was out of danger until he gave the all clear and drove her back to Nashville. From today on, she would depend on him for everything. Food, water, her life. She just wouldn't realize it.

He jumped off the bed and dug a key from his pocket. If she caught sight of the chains, his idea would backfire. He'd hide them in the trunk of his car for now. There was always the chance she wouldn't cooperate.

Until then, she couldn't realize he'd fixed this place just for her. She had to think it was his. He yanked the flowered spread off the bed and threw it in the trunk with the chains. No point obsessing over the money wasted. She'd pay for it all, one way or another.

All the feminine products—hand lotion, deodorant, tampons—went into the trash. The flowers almost followed, but he thought of a better use for them.

For this scheme to work, she had to be more than nervous or anxious. She had to be terrified.

That meant an escalation in his plan, but he could manage. No pain, no gain, as the saying went. He was fine with that.

As long as it was someone else's pain and his gain.

CHAPTER TWENTY-THREE

"WHAT TIME WILL it be safe to go back to my hotel and get dressed?"

Noah twisted toward Paige. Hadn't she been listening? "We're not going back to your hotel. Period."

"Well, we have a problem, because I've got to fix my hair and makeup and I'm certainly not going on stage wearing *this*." She tugged at a blouse that looked perfectly good to him. "That goes for you, too."

He glanced down. His shirt did look pretty bad. Black jellybean stains appeared almost, but not quite, like part of the design.

"You shouldn't go on that stage at all. Not unless Conner calls and says they've caught the guy."

"And how will that happen with our phones turned off?" They had walked half way around the jogging trail and now faced the playground equipment from the other direction.

He'd learned not to be surprised when she pointed out

holes in his carefully constructed plans. "There are still a few pay phones around, or I can flip my phone on briefly to check for messages."

"Whether I decide I'm going to perform or not—and make no mistake, that is still my decision—I can't wait 'til the last minute to get ready."

Was it just yesterday he'd told her it had been a pleasure working with her? Was it too late to take that statement back? Dealing with her was like riding a seesaw. He never knew if he was up or down.

Suddenly the hours he'd wondered how they would fill, seemed like not enough time. "Guess we're headed to the mall."

Noah hadn't been to a mall in over a year. He'd never cared for shopping and only went when absolutely necessary. If Betsy said she wanted him to go with her, he considered it absolutely necessary. Otherwise, he did without.

He thought about taking Paige to The Galleria. She should be able to find anything she wanted in its three stories of overpriced greed surrounding an ice skating rink atrium. But her photo had been in the paper. The shoppers at Neiman's or Saks might actually recognize her. While at a neighborhood mall, they'd never expect to see her.

Deerbrook Mall was bustling on a Saturday afternoon. He parked amid a lot full of nondescript cars and ushered her into Dillard's. No one looked twice at a slightly rumpled couple.

Paige took her time, pulling out dresses and blouses, holding them in front of her, and replacing them with a dismissive shrug. Noah tried to hurry her by raving over one or two she clearly found inappropriate. "That print would never work on stage and this one for an outside venue? Any amount of wind would have the skirt blowing in my face. I have to be able to move."

Noah learned his lesson and kept his mouth shut.

Finally, she took an armful of outfits and headed for the dressing room. Now what? He couldn't go in there with her.

He found a chair near the entrance and scrutinized every woman who went in, earning several withering glares. What could Paige be doing in there for so long? After fifteen minutes he stood at the edge of the curtained doorway and called in, "Paige?"

"Almost ready," her voice floated from behind the magic curtain.

Ten minutes later she emerged, a dress hanging over one arm. The saleslady *oohed* and *ahhed* over her choice, but Noah was too busy studying other customers to notice.

When Paige stopped in the lingerie section, he broke out in a sweat. After the looks he received in the dress department, he was afraid he might be reported as a pervert watching women pick out bras and panties.

At least he could keep her in sight in the shoe section, where she tried on every shoe available but bought nothing. "I better stick with the ones I'm wearing. Giving a concert in new shoes probably isn't a good idea. These aren't perfect, but I know I can stand for an hour in them."

He put his foot down when she stopped in the men's department. "We've been here too long and you've used your credit card several times. We need to get moving."

"Not until I find you a decent shirt." She dug through the bins and found a dusty blue button-down he actually liked. Not too dressy, not too casual. It could pass for western in the right circumstances, but didn't look like it belonged at the rodeo.

She tried to pay for it, but he refused. "It's my shirt. I'll get it. Do you have everything you need? Can we leave now?" He'd been watching a guy who seemed to be eyeing Paige.

"Hardly. I still need the two most important things. My makeup and hair."

"Not in this store. We have to move somewhere else." If creepy guy followed them, he'd know for sure. Otherwise, he was just a guy ogling a pretty woman.

They strolled to Macy's with Paige lingering at every shop window. While he wished she would hurry, the reflective windows gave him a change to watch the people behind them. No sign of creepy guy or anyone else paying them too much attention.

At Macy's, Paige headed straight for the cosmetic counter. "I'm interested in a new blush," she told the woman in a black lab coat. "And is there any chance I could get a makeover?"

Noah had never seen a woman's face light up that fast. Had she not had any clients that day?

The cosmetic counter was situated next to the perfume counter. Sitting on the extra stool, watching Paige, he was overcome with the scent of various fragrances tested liberally by customers as they strolled past. Combined with the aroma of an entire tray of cosmetics the makeup artist pulled out, Noah felt almost lightheaded. How did these women work here all day?

Paige knew exactly what she wanted and stopped the cosmetician before she started. "I'm not here for a muted, daytime look. I'm going to be on stage in front of a large group of people. I need dramatic eyes and bright or dark colors that will show up or I'll seem pale and washed out."

He had to hand it to Paige. The more he was around her, the more he realized a career in music wasn't only about singing. This was a business and Paige was up on every aspect of it.

When the make-up artist finished, Paige looked stunning. Yet somehow, he liked her better with little or no makeup. She bought extra blush and lipstick and tipped the lady generously. He thought they were finished. Wrong.

"Can you work on my friend here? He needs something heavy to cover that black eye."

He'd allowed his precocious nieces, Emma and Iris, to paint his toenails and put bows in his hair, but he'd never sat in public and had makeup applied. If anyone he knew came by, he was in for a lifetime of heckling.

Next came a hair salon down the mall. Again, he was impressed as she told the stylist exactly what she wanted and why. When she finished, the woman put half a can of hair spray in a cloud around Paige's head.

Paige had enough sense to close her eyes. Noah didn't. He nearly choked and his eyes watered. Between the perfume and the hairspray, he smelled like a French whore house. Surely they could leave now.

He checked his watch. They'd been in this mall close to two hours. Way too long in one place. They had to leave. Now. His neck ached from constantly swiveling it from one side to the other and his gut was in such knots he was bound to get an ulcer.

Paige took her time paying and leaving a tip, so he darted

into the mall to use his phone. Maybe Conner had good news for him.

With Paige refusing to listen to reason, his only hope was that his partner had pulled off a miracle.

Paige sailed out of the Blow Dry Bar with a smile on her face. She could handle this. She was satisfied with her hair and makeup. The new outfit was better than the one she had intended to wear. She'd prefer to have the boots she'd brought with her, but the ones she had on would do.

Despite everything life had thrown at her over the last week, she was ready.

Then she saw Noah's face. He slipped his phone into his pocket and stared toward the food court.

"See the guy in the Texan's shirt and ball cap?"

Texan's shirt and ball cap? This was Houston. He was going to have to be more specific than that. "Where?"

"By the Cinnabon. Does he look familiar?"

"No. Should he?"

"I've seen him three times today."

Her heart skipped a beat and she froze, unable to move her feet. Was that him? The guy who broke into her room and left a dead rose? He didn't look dangerous. Guess Noah's phone call didn't solve the problem.

Noah took her arm. "Let's go see who he is."

What? Go over there? No. "Aren't you supposed to protect me from him?"

"If we slip out another door we'll lose him."

Wasn't that the idea?

Noah never took his eyes off the guy, but managed to grab her arm and tug her along. "We're better off knowing who he is and what he wants. Otherwise, he could be out there, anywhere."

"Should I wait in one of these stores?" Two minutes ago she'd been floating on air, ready for anything. Now, her chest tightened and she found it hard to swallow. The sudden jump from one emotion to another stunned her. Had she been too cavalier about this whole situation?

"I don't want you more than two feet from me at any time, but I do want you to hold the packages. I need my hands free."

The man glanced up, saw Paige, and smiled. Then he registered Noah's expression and nearly dropped his sticky-bun.

Noah swept her behind his back and faced the guy. "Who are you and why the hell are you following us?"

"I…I'm a fan of Miss Reamer's. I'm taking my girl to the concert tonight and thought maybe I could get an autograph for her." Coffee sloshed over the edge of his cup.

Noah flashed his badge. "Let me see some I.D."

Ten minutes later Noah had vetted him through Conner and offered a weak apology.

Paige grabbed a napkin and scribbled her name. Her hand shook so she tore a hole in the paper. "Tell your girl I said *Hi* and enjoy the concert."

The guy may have been a fan before, but he sure wasn't now. She watched as he wadded the napkin and dropped it on the floor before stomping away. Noah's overreaction had lost her an admirer. Plus undone all the reassurance a day of shopping had accomplished.

Was this what she had to look forward to for the rest of her life, worrying about every stranger who approached her? Could any ordinary guy pose a real danger? How could she stand on that stage knowing a pervert waited out there to do her harm?

Even if they caught him, was another waiting in the wings?

Maybe Noah was right. She shouldn't go on stage tonight.

CHAPTER
TWENTY-FOUR

"I CAN'T BELIEVE YOU stopped for a Cinnabon."

"Why not? We were right there and we never had lunch. I'm surprised you didn't want one for yourself." Noah licked icing from his fingers, but still managed to get it on the steering wheel. He'd never have done that in Lola.

Did he not care because this was a rental, and not his rental at that, or because he was too involved in this case? As soon as he had this stalker locked away and figured out what-the-hell he was doing with Paige, he had to call about Lola.

He couldn't even pretend he didn't know why he kept putting off checking on his truck. He was afraid of the answer. What he didn't know couldn't hurt him—any more than it had already. He took a deep breath and his two broken ribs protested.

Paige handed him an extra napkin. "I can't eat much before a performance. A little yogurt is usually all I can manage."

For one glorious moment when he confronted fan-guy, he thought she might have changed her mind. That she would listen to him and not climb onstage. His relief lasted about five minutes. By the time they reached the car, she was back in performance mode.

Conner had argued with her for ten minutes, but didn't have any better luck changing her mind than he had. So far, his brilliant plan for a decoy hadn't worked, either. Now what?

Much as he'd like to, he couldn't physically stop her from performing.

The dashboard clock already showed ten after four and they still needed to change. He didn't have time to shop for yogurt. Would his sister have any? Probably.

He parked in front of Rachelle's and checked the neighborhood. Her house should be safe long enough for them to get ready. Seeing Fred's car in the drive was a surprise. He'd assumed they would already have left for the concert.

At the door, he knocked instead of using his key as he'd planned. Emma and Iris tumbled over each other, trying to be the first to greet him.

"Hi, Uncle Noah," they crooned, almost in unison. They stopped and stared at Paige. Four eyes grew large and round.

"Momma," Iris called. "Uncle Noah's here, with a strange lady."

"Who is *she*?" Emma stuck her thumb in her mouth.

This was why he'd hoped they had already left. An interrogation from his sister was bad enough, but no telling what his nieces were likely to say.

"Girls, mind your manners." Rachelle appeared down the hall. "Invite your uncle and his friend inside."

"But you said not to let strangers in the house." If possible, Emma's eyes grew even bigger.

"I also said don't answer the door unless you know who's on the other side. You didn't let that stop you." Rachelle reached the door and swung it open wider. "Come in. Come in. What are you doing here? Shouldn't you be getting ready for tonight?"

"That's what we're doing." Noah held up the shopping bags. "We needed someplace to change and a yogurt if you have one. Paige, this is my sister, Rachelle. Rachelle, this is Paige Reimer."

"Of course, I recognize you. Girls, this is the lady we're going to see sing tonight."

Emma and Iris hung back and studied Paige as if trying to decide whether she was friend or foe. Might she steal some part of their Uncle Noah's affections from them?

Paige entered with a thousand watt smile. "Rachelle, it's so nice to finally meet you. And you girls…" She knelt in front of them. "You must be Emma and Iris. I've heard so much about you."

She had? When had that happened? He might have mentioned them when she was at his house or when he worried about not babysitting for Rachelle's anniversary. But she actually remembered their names?

Paige rubbed her chin as if thinking. "Now, let's see if I can figure out who is who." She made a circular motion the size of a pizza with one finger and tapped Iris on the head. "You're Iris, so you must be Emma." She moved her finger to Emma, and made two friends for life. Three, counting Rachelle.

How had she done that? Must have been the photo in the

hall. He twisted toward his sister. "I'm sorry to drop in on you with no notice."

"You're always welcome. I'm sorry the place is such a mess."

Noah glanced around. The house was as spotless as any human living with Fred and two young girls could possibly make it. He didn't want to live that way, but if controlling her environment made Rachelle feel safer, he understood.

He chose to carry a gun. Was that any better?

Paige grabbed two little hands. "May I borrow your room to change for tonight? I might need some help with the buttons."

The three females scampered down the hall. Rachelle eyed him with suspicion. "What's up? Doesn't she have a hotel?"

No point in lying. He couldn't get by with it. "Too happening at her hotel right now. We'll head straight for the park from here." That was close to the truth.

"What's going on, big brother? You're obviously not telling me the whole story."

Fuck. Maybe he could get the department to hire her as a human lie detector. She was miles better than the fool and his machine they used now.

"There's been a little trouble with an overzealous fan."

Rachelle didn't say a word. She just waited.

He was such a pussy. "Okay, she has a stalker. He broke into her room at two different hotels and left threatening messages. After a week of searching, we don't have any idea who he is."

"Are we safe to go tonight? What about the girls?"

How could he have been so stupid? The guy was after Paige, but what if he panicked and started shooting? What if the crowd stampeded? He'd spent so much time worrying about Paige, he'd forgotten his own sister and nieces. That's why doctors didn't operate on their family and cops didn't work cases involving people they cared about. It was too easy to get distracted.

And he'd been *way* too distracted with Paige.

Noah dug out his wallet and found the hundred he'd taken from the ATM a few hours ago. "You and Fred take the girls out to eat instead. I'll give you a raincheck on the babysitting."

Rachelle rolled her eyes. "Use my room to change. I'll get an organic acai yogurt for your friend."

Putting himself on the front line was one thing. That was his job and he'd been trained to do it. Rachelle and the girls were something else. He couldn't live with himself if something happened to them.

If he let Paige go on stage, and other people got hurt, could he live with that?

Noah flipped off his phone. Conner was on his side, but fat lot of good that did. The Chief wouldn't tell Paige not to perform at the concert. He drove another block before breaking the silence.

"I know you don't want to hear it, but I'm going to say it one more time. Then I'll shut up. I don't think you should go on tonight. The Chief believes it will be a black eye for the department if he says we can't guarantee your safety, but you still have the right to decline. We could announce you fell ill. Hell, I'll even take you by the hospital so it'll seem real."

"I can't do that. If the Chief had ordered me not to go on,

that's one thing, but I can't just up and say *No*."

Of course she couldn't. She wouldn't get paid.

"It's not about the money."

Right. It sure seems like it's about the money.

"I've given this a lot of thought and come up with two possible outcomes if I back out. Either Jake will hunt me down somewhere else when you're not around, which will put me in more danger—"

Horns blared as Noah nearly ran into the car in front of him. "Who's Jake? Did you figure out who was behind this?"

"No. I had to give him a name. I couldn't think of him as "the guy." Calling him Jake makes him all the more real to me. So, you see, I am taking this seriously."

Okay, that was kind of a dumb idea, but she had a point.

"—Or, I don't show up and he takes his anger out on people in the audience. Innocent people could get hurt."

"The plainclothes cops will still be there, mingling with the crowd."

"I've checked out the venue. The park's a big place. They wouldn't have any idea where Jake might be if he's not looking for me."

A whiff of perfume drifted across the seat. The setting sun glinted off large, hoop earrings and a wide silver necklace. The girls must have borrowed some of their mother's things while helping Paige dress. He couldn't afford to be distracted now. They were closing in on the park. He only had a few minutes left to talk her out of this. "He never bothered you before. He might not follow you when you leave town." That sounded lame, even to him.

"So, I could never come to Houston again? Who'd look

after my mother? If Houston isn't safe, what about Austin? Dallas? How far away do I have to stay?"

Crap. He wasn't going to win this argument.

Her touch on his arm was so light he thought he imagined it. "You can't think of every scenario, Noah. There's no guarantee I'll be safe if I stay off that stage. The world is full of things you didn't plan on. You can waste your life in a constant atmosphere of coulda, woulda, shoulda, but you can't change fate."

That's exactly what he'd been doing for the last eight months. No wonder he was exhausted. One truth was plain. He had no idea how to break the cycle.

CHAPTER TWENTY-FIVE

"Wait." Noah held up a hand to stop Paige from opening the door while he studied the backstage parking area, looking for a place her stalker could hide.

And there were plenty of places that fit that bill.

Workers' cars, trucks filled with supplies or equipment, tents, and concession stands surrounded them. Add a nearby tree line, bicyclists, joggers and cars zipping past on Allen Parkway, and there was no way he could protect her.

Paige should know the drill by now. Wherever they went, he inspected the surroundings before he let her get out of the car. She might be used to it, but this time, instead of looking annoyed, she seemed unnerved. At least she was taking this seriously.

Noah lifted his phone from the cup holder and texted Conner. *We're here*

I C U All clear

He nodded and she opened the door.

"I've got something for you." He popped the trunk and headed to the back. The scent of fresh cut grass and mulch from the newly landscaped flower beds drifted across the park.

"Now what?" She followed him around the car.

If she didn't like him scouting the area, she sure wasn't going to like his next defensive measure.

He reached into the trunk and pulled out a bulletproof vest. "You need to wear this."

Her eyes iced over. "I don't think so. Do you remember how long I searched for just the right outfit after you wouldn't let me go back for the one I planned to wear? Not that black isn't a fashionable color, but it doesn't match my dress or my boots."

"You'll wear it under your clothes."

"It'll show through, plus I certainly don't want to make my big debut looking *fat*."

"Fasten your top button and no one will see it. And I brought you something to help disguise the bulk." He held out a blue jean jacket he'd borrowed from Rachelle. They were about the same size and he knew it was stylish. It had a Neiman's label. She probably bought it with the gift certificate he'd given her for her birthday.

"Besides, no one will think you're fat once they catch a glimpse of those legs."

Paige eyed the vest and jacket. She didn't exactly agree, but she quit arguing.

He could kick himself for not thinking of the vest sooner, but would she have given in this easily if fan-guy hadn't scared the shit out of them both? It wasn't until Rachelle insisted he wear his vest that the subject even crossed his mind. He'd nodded, but having Paige wear it was more important.

She was the target.

A security golf cart appeared and Noah checked the driver's bona fides before letting Paige slip into the front seat. His eyes swept the area one more time before he slid in behind her. They bumped down the jogging path and under the freeway toward the stage, Noah on alert every inch of the way.

He could feel hundreds of eyes watching them. He just didn't know which ones were up to no good.

Paige let Noah carry the bulky package and lead the way to the stage, while she tucked in close behind him. They'd been out and about all day and she hadn't been nervous, but walking across this open space, knowing Jake was out there somewhere....

She took her first full breath when they stepped behind a tent flap, although canvas was certainly no protection from a bullet. A roadie showed them to a curtained dressing area and Noah stepped in behind her, filling the miniscule space with his maleness. Feet the size of gunboats had her stumbling for a place to stand. Broad shoulders left no room to turn around.

How was she supposed to concentrate with him taking up all the oxygen?

His elbow pushed against the flowered divider—a shower curtain?—as he emptied the shopping bag. His closeness set her on edge. How could this man, who she'd slept with, kissed so passionately, only hours earlier, now seem so removed? So methodical. His only interest in seeing her suited up in that ridiculous vest.

She hadn't made any promises. If the vest was too bulky or

heavy, she could still refuse to wear it.

Her hands shook as she fumbled with the tiny, cloth-covered buttons. Once undone, she let the dress fall to her waist. Noah stood behind her, tightening the straps on the vest.

Good. She didn't want to look him in the eye.

Her skin prickled and her nerves twitched as she waited for him to drop the garment over her shoulders.

Instead, he let one hand caress her arm as he planted a kiss, soft as rose petals, on her shoulder. "You can do this. It's no different than any of a hundred other times you've sung in public. If anything happens, I'll protect you."

He was right. She had done this countless times. So what if the venue was larger? She'd just concentrate on the people in the front rows until she felt comfortable. With Noah close beside her, and the vest protecting her, she could relax and focus on the music.

She ran through a series of scales, hardly noticing as he slipped the vest over her head and adjusted the fit.

As Noah swung her around and fastened her buttons, she even imagined the guys tuning their instruments. No. Wait. That *was* the guys getting ready. She had to get out there with them and warm up her voice. They must be frantic, wondering where she was.

She shrugged once, letting the vest settle. That would have to do. She didn't have time to mess around.

The show started in ten minutes.

Fresh air rushed into the minute dressing room as Noah threw open the shower-curtain-divider, causing the metal rings to scrape against the bar with a harsh sound that sent chills down his back. Paige rushed out and he followed as close behind as he could.

She never moved that fast when he wanted her to.

When they stepped onto the stage, Craig's face lit up and Jeff beat a riff on the drum.

Only Kevin didn't look relieved. His eyes darted between Noah and Paige and he glowered Noah's direction. "About time you two love birds showed up. We were beginning to think we'd have to go on without you. You disappear in the middle of rehearsal and can't be bothered to return a call or text for twenty-four hours?"

What the fuck? It wasn't what the guy thought. Well, it was, but that wasn't why they disappeared.

Paige carried on without catching the vibe racing around the stage. "Hi, guys. Sorry I'm late. I've...." She snapped her mouth closed and glanced at Noah.

What did she expect him to say? He put on his innocent face and grabbed his guitar. "Is everybody ready?"

No one acknowledged him, but they all took their places. He leaned close to Paige's ear. "I'll be two steps behind you and slightly to the right. Tug on your ear if you see anything that worries you."

She nodded twice and took hold of the mic. When she strode to the front of the stage, she was in full performance mode.

He'd rehearsed with her all week. He knew her voice, her range, her inflections. He knew every note of the song she was singing. But he'd never seen her perform. And that was another story altogether.

She might have been a little tight for the first few chords, but after that, she blossomed. Her voice soared, crystal clear.

The crowd was captivated. They sang along with her. They danced. Daddies carried kids on their shoulders. Moms swayed with babies on their hips. Women in tank tops and Daisy Dukes gyrated. Men held their Koozie-disguised beer high.

His mother always claimed performing fed her soul. For the first time, he understood what she meant.

If he hadn't been worried about Paige's safety, he'd have enjoyed the experience. Except for sick kids, he hadn't sung in public for years and those were stiff, formal occasions.

The band segued straight into the second song without a stop. When that song finished, Paige took a few minutes to thank the audience for coming and related several anecdotes about her life and the music business. Noah used the time to hunt for danger. No alarm bells went off as he searched the crowd for anyone who didn't seem to fit in or acted suspicious.

The stage was situated at the bottom of a bowl at the east end of the park. Friends and family stood in the roped off VIP area in front of the stage with a few early arrivals close behind. Others wandered from one arena to another or picked up refreshments and brought them back to their friends. The rest of the audience stood or sat on the grass in tiers up the side of a hill.

In possession of the high ground. Not something Noah found comforting.

He couldn't see Conner, but he and the rest of his squad were there. Not like hotel security that could be distracted when needed the most. Not with a friend of the Mayor's in danger. Not with one of their own in the front line. He didn't have to see them to trust they were in position.

But it would have been nice.

CHAPTER
TWENTY-SIX

THE STIFFNESS BETWEEN Noah's shoulders eased with the last notes of the third song. They were going to make it through this okay. Creepy stalker guy was just another coward who got his kicks from frightening women.

He didn't have the balls to show his face in public.

Paige took a moment to introduce the band and Noah managed a genuine smile when the crowd applauded him. If he hadn't been so uptight, this would have been fun. The only problem now was the ribbing he'd get from the squad on Monday morning.

But he could live with that as long as he got to spend one more night with Paige before she went home to Nashville. Planes flew between the two cities every day. He had some weekends off and she had a mother here she needed to keep tabs on. Couples managed long distance relationships.

He took a deep breath of night air, roasted turkey legs, and cotton candy. Maybe living didn't suck after all.

Dreaming of You was the last song and he positioned his fingers for the opening chord. Paige turned to take a swallow from the water bottle on the stand next to Noah.

She leaned over and pulled on one ear. "There's a guy near the front with a tattoo on his neck. He looks kind of familiar but it's too dark to tell for sure."

Damn. That should teach him. Whenever things went smoothly, whenever he thought he had life under control, *wham,* the fates kicked him in the nuts and reminded him he was fallible. He'd been thinking with his dick and put Paige in danger. Just like Betsy.

Paige swung around and started into her signature song before he could answer. He was so flustered he missed the first chord, earning him a steely glare from Kevin.

He fumbled until he caught up, then studied the crowd. There, on the right. Wearing a shirt the color of the azaleas in his front yard. Evan. The oil well safety equipment guy from the first hotel. He'd let the salesman's baby face fool him.

An intricate tattoo decorated one side of his neck. No wonder the guy always kept his collar buttoned.

Noah stepped next to the mic and turned the chorus into an impromptu duet with Paige then pulled her arm so they both stepped back and let the band play a bridge. He ignored the daggers the band members sent his way and whispered in her ear. "Stay on the stage and milk the applause as long as you can, then exit left. Earl Sparks is waiting at the bottom of the stairs. He's a tall, skinny black guy with a deep voice. Sounds like Marvin Gaye. He'll get you someplace safe while I check out this guy."

He released her arm and gave her a gentle push toward

the mic. She picked up the song where they left off without missing a note. How did she do that? He had a tongue like cardboard and not enough spit to douse a candle. He'd come across a lot of strong women in his years on the force, but not one who could have managed that feat.

Yet Paige smiled and looked sexy while doing it.

Paige's voice soared on the last stanza. When she let it fade away, the crowd clapped and cheered and waved light from their phones. She bowed and motioned to the band.

Noah took several steps back as he bowed. His foot hit the keyboard stand and he twisted to lean his guitar against the instrument. He eased toward the right, still clapping as Paige took another bow, and slipped behind the side curtain.

Craig hissed and he looked over his shoulder as the keyboardist shot him the finger. "Hey, asshole. Where do you think you're going? You too busy to finish the set?"

He only knew one way to shut the guy up without calling attention to himself. He shot the finger right back then raced down the right-hand stairs.

The applause had died down and people milled around, heading for the concession stands or another venue. Soon, the next ensemble would want the stage. Paige couldn't stall much longer.

Noah wasn't anywhere in sight and the guy she'd sent him after had blended in with the crowd. Shouts, laughter, the general hum of a large group of people stirring mingled with the sound of instruments being shut down.

She couldn't point the guy out to Noah if he asked or hear

his voice if he shouted a warning. Amidst all these people, she'd never felt so alone in her life. She had to get off this stage before she broke down.

The members of the band glanced at her for instructions. "Good show, guys. Thanks for all your hard work. Let's pack up and blow this joint." She stowed her guitar in its case and two feet to the right, Kevin did the same. Craig stood and stretched and gathered his sheet music.

She put one hand on Kevin's shoulder. "Will you watch the roadies and make sure they get all our equipment into the van without breaking anything?"

"How about we let Jeff do that? His drums are the most difficult to pack."

Jeff beat a *ba dump dump* and nodded. "Same old story. *Pick on the drummer.* One well packed van, coming up. But Kevin buys the first beer."

Somehow, Kevin had already disappeared.

Noah's guitar, leaning against the keyboard caught her eye. She couldn't carry it with her. Not and keep an eye out for Jake or whatever his name was.

"Craig, can you take care of Noah's guitar until he gets back? I don't want it to get on the van by accident." How would she return to him? She didn't even know if she'd see him again after today. They hadn't made any plans.

"When the fuck will that be? The guy barely showed up in time for the first chord and lit out of here like his hair was on fire before the last song ended. You really think he'll be back? There's a reason he doesn't have a steady gig. My guess is he didn't just fall off the wagon, the whole train pulled away without him. Did you catch how bad he screwed up that last song? Something's either gone up his nose or down his gullet."

Now what? Was it safe to admit what had been going on or should she continue to keep his secret? "Just do it, okay? I'll owe you one."

"Yes, ma'am, Boss Lady."

Somehow, she'd managed to play the best set of her life, yet offend every member of the band.

All she wanted now was to find a tall, skinny black guy with a Marvin Gaye voice and let him take her someplace safe so she could ditch fifteen pounds of Kevlar that made her sweat like a fat girl in Spanx.

Tomorrow morning she was boarding a plane for Nashville, stalker or no stalker. If Noah wanted to see her again, he could come find her.

Always leave them wanting more.

Any fool knew that.

Yet there was Paige, dawdling on stage like a kid who was afraid of missing out on something. All the confirmation he needed.

She was great at writing and performing, but had no idea about the marketing end of the business. That would be his job.

He'd already proven his worth. He just needed to remind her how much he'd already done for her. He'd plucked her out of obscurity once, he could do it again.

It all came down to time.

Getting her away from all these people so he had time alone with her, time to convince her, time to show her what he was capable of, that was the key.

Managing to spirit her away would be tricky, no doubt about that. He had to be in position before she left the stage.

All that mattered was the one thing he'd mastered. Timing.

Noah wove his way through the crowd while Paige waved and thanked the audience. By the time she'd put her instrument away, he'd spotted Evan, strolling in the opposite direction and offering less-than-enthusiastic applause.

She was still on stage when Noah reached the guy's side and clamped a death grip on his upper arm. For a man who gave an overall impression of softness, Evan's bicep felt like a slab of unyielding concrete. Noah squeezed harder, but felt no give. "Why don't we step over here to the side where we can talk?"

Evan's eyes narrowed and his pupils contracted. 'Hey, sorry if I gave you the wrong impression, but I'm with someone. I just wanted to get any inside scoop on Paige Reimer. I'm a huge fan."

Noah held his badge cupped in one hand so only Evan could see it. "Let's get the scoop on you first, mister. If you resist I'll have you on the ground and slap on the cuffs before your next breath. You wouldn't want that to happen in front of all these nice people, would you? Especially not if some of the guys you work with might still be around."

He was in trouble if the guy did resist. He didn't have his cuffs with him, like a fool he hadn't called for backup, and he couldn't fire a gun in a crowded park. Worst of all, he'd underestimated the man's strength.

Evan took a few steps then dug his feet in. Noah tugged on his arm, but he didn't budge. "I haven't broken any law and I'm not moving unless you have a warrant or I'm under arrest. Am I under arrest?"

CHAPTER TWENTY-SEVEN

A WOMAN STOOD DIRECTLY in his path, wiping remnants of blue slushy from a kid's face and hands. He wanted to gag. Kids were disgusting, always filthy or sticky. He detoured around her only to encounter a mom settling a child in a stroller more intricate than the cockpit of a Black Hawk helicopter and twice the size. Add costly to that list.

Seemed like rich bitches always stood in his way. That part of his life was about to end.

He shouldered past her and she stumbled. The woman shouted, "Hey," at his back, but he didn't slow down. He couldn't afford the time or the attention.

All this interference delayed him. He should have started sooner. Who knew crossing twenty feet of grass would be so full of land mines and interruptions? He slid under the rope marking the VIP section without missing a step.

At the corner of the stage, he bent down as if tying his shoe. His hand snaked out and grabbed the bouquet of flowers he'd hidden under the stage. Two more steps took him to the edge of the stairs, only to run into a tall guy with graying hair and a gun poorly hidden under his shirt tail.

"Sorry, sir. You'll have to stop there. I can't allow you to come any closer."

Cop? Security? Didn't matter. The guy was in his way. "It's okay, sir. I'm with Ms. Reimer's group. I need to get back on the stage so I can present these flowers to her before she finishes." The flowers were worth the last of his money after all, though they did look somewhat bedraggled. Into the cabin, out of the cabin, and under the stage for several hours hadn't done them any favors.

"Not happening, mister. If Ms. Reimer wants to talk to you, she'll let me know when she gets down here. Until then, please wait behind the rope."

Hard to believe the guy could be a cop. He was so skinny a good wind would blow him over and his voice was so deep and mellow he'd be more likely to put a perp to sleep than to scare him into cooperating.

What did some teacher always warn him? *You catch more flies with honey....* Although why anyone wanted flies was beyond him. "Yes, sir. I'll wait over here, but would you please tell her where I am? She'll be waiting for me."

"Will do, son." The guy actually smiled before he turned away.

Big mistake.

Lefty Bob materialized from out of the crowd and slapped a hand on Evan's shoulder. "You want to be arrested? That can be arranged."

Noah tried not to smile. Lefty Bob obviously thought he had dressed to blend in, but the sight of a 250 pound man in gym shorts, a dirty Astros T-shirt with the sleeves ripped off, dress shoes with black socks, dangling a pair of handcuffs from one finger was too much. The aroma of beer, which he'd apparently dabbed behind each ear and down the front of his shirt like *eau du cologne,* completed the ultimate disguise.

It must have been too much for Evan, also. He deflated like a balloon from yesterday's birthday party and followed Noah and Lefty Bob to the far side of the park, where it was quieter.

Noah struggled to remain calm. "What the fuck do you have against Paige Reimer?"

"Hey, I don't want to hurt her. I just need to talk to her about something personal."

"Oh, well. I didn't know it was *personal.*" Noah glanced at Lefty Bob. "We should probably let him go then. Doncha' think?"

Lefty Bob scratched his chin. "Hell, no. I love *personal.* My life's so dull, *personal's* all the fun I have. Come on. Give. What's this about?"

"Her daughter. I mean my daughter. Josie."

Confusion coated Lefty Bob's face, but Noah knew exactly what he meant.

"My partner and I adopted Josie when she was four days old. She's starting to ask questions now. She wants to know about her mother."

"Isn't that information supposed to be secret? How'd you find out?"

Evan hung his head. "My partner worked in the social

services department of the hospital. We'd been trying to adopt for years. One of the papers he gave her to sign listed me as the friend she wanted to adopt her baby. We still had to go through all kinds of scrutiny, but the letter got us in the door."

Anguish filled his eyes. "Please, I'm begging you, don't do anything to take her from us. We're the only family she's ever known."

"Is that why you tried to scare Paige? Sticking notes under her door and cutting up her clothes?"

"What? Why would I do a thing like that? I need her to like me, not be afraid of me."

"You're too late for that. She was frightened when she recognized you from the stage."

"That's impossible. Except for publicity photos, I've never see her in my life."

"Then why were you stalking me at her hotel?" None of this made any sense.

"I wasn't. When I heard she had a performance scheduled in Houston, I traded vacation days to be assigned this convention. I didn't know we'd be at the same hotel, but I saw the two of you when I checked in. Okay, I might have tried to pump you for information, but I only wanted to know what she was like before I let Josie contact her."

The handcuffs disappeared somewhere in Lefty Bob's pocket. Where he kept his gun and badge in that outfit was anybody's guess. Noah didn't plan to look close enough to find out.

"Want me to take him in for you? I live to fill out paperwork on a Saturday night." Lefty Bob scratched his belly and the outline of a gun appeared under his black nylon shorts.

"Nah. Keep an eye on him until I give the all clear. Be sure to get his contact information. She'll want to talk to him, but not tonight. He's not the one we're after."

If he wasn't the one, who was? Noah pivoted and shot across the grass toward the stage, weaving through families on blankets and teenagers waving sparklers in the darkening night.

At this point, he didn't care who the pervert was, as long as Paige was safe. He trusted Earl, but he trusted himself more.

He glanced at the stage, thirty yards away. Paige had finished talking to the band guys and headed across the stage toward danger. He picked up the pace until a lanky figure stepped in front of him. Without looking up, he dodged to one side.

The figure followed his move.

"What the hell do you think you're doing?" Kevin asked.

"I'm in a hurry. I need to check on Paige."

"No, you don't. She's my responsibility and I'm the one who should see about her. You, on the other hand, need to stay out of our way. We were fine before you got here and we'll be fine after you go back where you belong."

Now here was an interesting development, and just when he was ready to write this guy off.

The guitar player took a step closer, his fists clenched. "She's been jumpy since the day you showed up. She almost missed the performance, for fucks sake I don't know what going on between you two, and I don't care. I've got too much invested in this band to watch her screw it away. Your job's over. Run along home and leave the rest to the professionals."

Noah flashed his badge. It had been out of his pocked

more times tonight than in. Maybe it was time to leave it out and to hell with this undercover shit. "I *am* a professional, dickhead. Let's talk about your relationship with Paige and why you think she's your responsibility."

CHAPTER
TWENTY-EIGHT

P AIGE RUSHED FROM the comparative safety of the stage, searching for anyone who fit Noah's description of Earl Sparks. Only one person waited in the backstage area and it sure wasn't a tall, skinny black man.

Aldo Rodgers. The weird audio/visual kid no one noticed in high school. The man with the neck tattoo she'd warned Noah about. The one person she hoped to avoid.

How had he gotten back here? Where was her protection?

"Hi, Paige. It's nice to see you again." He thrust a raggedy-ass bouquet of flowers her direction, half the stems broken and the blossoms dropping petals like tears at a funeral.

She was too well brought up not to accept the flowers, but she avoided touching his hand.

There was no doubt he was strange, offbeat. Hell, some kids had even called him weird Al. And not always behind his back.

After school he'd become the minor league gofer who

helped arrange for her to sing the National Anthem and post it to YouTube. Some of his other ideas for publicity were way out there and she'd ignored them. But he wasn't frightening, evil. Just trying too hard to impress her.

He'd never hurt her. Would he?

No wonder she hadn't recognized him. He hadn't aged well. And who'd believe such a dweeb would get a neck tattoo?

"Thank you, Aldo. I thought that was you in the audience, but I didn't have my contacts in so I wasn't sure. You living in Houston now?"

"Yeah. I've been here three years. I work for an electronics company. It's a great job, but I miss the excitement of being in the thick of things. Making arrangements, escorting big wigs, keeping the players happy. I plan to get back into the entertainment field. That's where I shine."

In the thick of things my ass. You were low man on the totem pole. Barely above the peanut vendor. Still, he'd been a help to her when she needed it and she didn't want to hurt his feelings.

"It's a pleasant surprise to see you again, Aldo. I wish I had time to talk, but I'm waiting for my driver. He has to take me back to my hotel so I can pack and head to the airport. He was supposed to be waiting right here. I don't know where he could be. Maybe he's up on the stage. I'd better go see."

But Noah was gone and so were Kevin and Craig. Only Jeff was still onstage and he didn't weigh one-thirty with bricks in his pocket. A hell of a drummer, but not much help if someone was lurking in wait for her.

Paige was lying. Her missing driver was a cop—he should

know, he'd taken the guy's gun and badge—and she wasn't due to fly out until tomorrow.

He never expected this to be easy. Nothing in his life ever had been.

"Yeah. That's why I was standing here. I couldn't believe the concert promoter didn't have a guard waiting by the steps to keep rowdy fans from hassling you. I always took care of you when you sang at the ball games."

"You sure did, Aldo, and I appreciated it."

Angry voices spilled around the corner of the stage. He glanced over his shoulder. The cop and the guitarist were in a shouting match. He didn't have much time.

"There's some kind of fight brewing out there. I don't think it's safe for you to stay here. My car's parked in the next lot. Why don't I take you back to your hotel?"

Paige had known Aldo—sort of—since high school. He'd always been odd, but more in a nerdy way than creepy. His job at the ball park had been to see her safely on and off the field. She'd even been in his car.

So why was she hesitating now?

Because she may have known him for ten years, but she hadn't spent three hours total in his company. And she hadn't seen or spoken to him since she moved to Nashville five years ago.

Something had happened to him during that time. He'd moved closer to the creepy end of the spectrum. One thing hadn't changed: his interest in the entertainment business.

Apparently he still envisioned himself as a mover and

shaker.

As if he could negotiate contracts or promote exclusive events with that lisp.

The noise level rose and Paige's breath caught in her chest. Where the hell was Noah or the guy he sent to protect her? The man made promises but where was he when she needed him?

What were her options? Go back on stage where she'd be out in the open for whomever had it in for her, wait in this trash strewn alleyway for someone she didn't know and might never show up, or let Aldo drive her home.

Seemed like a no-brainer to her. She knew how to handle Aldo.

Noah cursed under his breath. He'd wasted precious time on those two. Evan wanted something from Paige, but he had to stay on her good side to get it.

Kevin wanted something, too, but he needed Paige in good shape.

That must be what it was like to be famous. Everybody wanted something from you. And Paige was just starting out. No wonder his parents had no desire to go to New York and try for stardom.

He never should have gotten so far away from Paige. She was his job, not some bozo nut case. He raced toward the stage, passing vendors and food trucks. The aroma of sausage on a stick enveloped him long enough to remind him how long it had been since he ate. Just as quickly it was gone only to be replaced by funnel cakes, fried Twinkies, and popcorn as he rushed down the hill.

If Paige didn't like him buying a Cinnabon while they were at the mall, she probably wouldn't appreciate him showing up to protect her carrying a burrito.

As he neared the stage, he saw Jeff issuing instructions to three men wearing black T-shirts with *STAFF* emblazoned on the back. Paige wasn't on the stage, nor, as he rounded the corner, in the service alley.

Good. Earl had done his job and whisked her out of sight.

Noah pulled out his cell to text Conner. He'd know where Earl had taken Paige. A low moan stopped him. A moment later he heard a solid thump, as if something had been dropped or hit.

Every nerve went on high alert. He executed a slow 360, looking for anything out of order. Near the stage, an area of gravel showed drag marks. His hand went to the pistol strapped to his ankle.

Another moan, followed by a string of profanity that would make a sailor do a double take. It was like hearing the Dalai Lama curse.

"Earl. Earl. Is that you?" *By all that's holy, no. Don't let it be Earl.*

"Over here." The voice was weak, but still deep and smooth as river stones.

Noah knelt beside the end of the drag marks and lifted the skirt surrounding the stage bottom. Earl Sparks lay on his back, one hand cradling his head.

Where the hell was Paige? Was she under there, too?

Noah tried to crab-walk under the stage but hit his head with a *thump* that sounded just like the one that had first alerted him to trouble. "Give me your hand. I'll pull you out."

"Hell, no. This is gravel. My back already feels like shredded pork."

"Wait right there. I'll get something to help." Noah bounded up the stairs and onto the stage. The boards had been covered with a patchwork of imitation Asian rugs. He grabbed the corner of the nearest rug and started toward the steps.

One of the roadies shouted, "Hey," and Jeff snapped his head around with a dumbfounded expression, but Noah didn't take time to explain. Let 'em wonder…or come help.

He jumped down the four steps, pulling the rug behind him, and shoved it as far under the stage as he could.

Earl snaked himself forward. When his knees were on the carpet, Noah steadied his feet against the stage, grabbed the rug with two hands, and pulled. The rug and Earl moved forward eight inches. He adjusted his grip and tugged a second time. For a skinny guy, Earl wasn't a lightweight.

Noah scooted back two feet and dug his heels into the hard packed ground. He braced himself and heaved with all he had. The top of Earl's head appeared from under the white skirt.

His forehead had a golf ball-sized lump—probably from trying to sit up under the stage—but it was the back of his head that worried Noah. Salt and pepper hair was matted with both drying and fresh blood. His face had an unnatural gray cast.

Earl pulled himself the rest of the way out and sat up. He swayed unsteadily and placed one hand on the ground for balance. "The son-of-a-bitch blindsided me."

In all the years they'd worked together, Noah had never heard Earl curse. Wasn't even sure the man knew the meaning of most of the words. "Who was it?"

"Don't know. Said he was one of the band."

Shit. Just when he had one suspect crossed off the list, he popped back up again.

Earl adjusted his glasses and studied Noah's face. He pointed to one eye. "Your makeup's running, hoss. You look like a clown."

The old coot would survive.

Kevin rounded the corner, his fists clenched. He got in Noah's face and shouted, "What do you mean, you're the least of Paige's problems? What the hell problems *does* she have?"

Noah glanced at Earl. "That the guy?"

"Nah. Never seen him before."

"So what'd he look like?" Craig was who-knows-where and Jeff could have slipped around back.

Kevin's voice rose. "What the hell is going on here? Where's Paige?"

"Shut the fuck up. We're working." The guy was seriously getting on his nerves. Like a wasp buzzing around his head. How could he concentrate with so many distractions?

A fresh trickle of blood rolled down Earl's neck. "The guy was good-sized. Not huge but substantial. Not even his mother would ever call him pretty, and he had a funny way of talking. Like a lisp, but worse. So he sort of showered you when he talked."

Damn. Not Evan. Not anybody in the band. Somebody entirely new. Someone they knew nothing about. What was he supposed to do now?

"Kevin, this is Earl. Keep an eye on him until help gets here." Noah started toward the parking lot. He'd have passed them if they came out front. He dug his cell from his pocket and hit Conner's number, hopeful he was still watching from the police van at the top of the hill. His partner answered before the first ring died.

Noah didn't wait for a greeting. "We're in big trouble. Earl's hurt and the douchebag got Paige."

Conner never failed him with useless recriminations. "I'll send an ambulance. Where's Earl?"

"On the pathway beside the stage. Do you have eyes on Paige?" He continued to jog toward the back parking lot. Logic said that's where they'd head.

"Give me a minute." Conner set the phone down, but Noah could hear him breathing. After long enough for Noah to start worrying, Conner was back. "I see you, and I see what must be them. Woman is wearing a pinkish dress, blue jean jacket, and cowboy boots. Guy has on khakis and a blue plaid sport shirt."

"Sounds like Paige. Is she okay?" His breath was coming in gasps now. The two broken ribs screamed with each inhale.

"She appears to be with him voluntarily. I don't see a gun. He's not holding onto her arm."

"Where are they?"

"Headed the same direction you are, toward the lot where you parked. Maybe seventy-five, eighty yards ahead of you. I'll send help for you, too."

Now all he had to do was close most of a football field without running out of gas or spooking them.

CHAPTER TWENTY-NINE

"A LDO, SLOW DOWN. You're walking too fast for me. I've been on my feet for hours." Not to mention a busy day before and more sex last night than in the last year. Make that two years. And with a guy who disappeared when she needed him the most.

"We need to get out of sight. I don't know what that ruckus was back there, but if it was gangs, we're not safe here."

Paige plopped down on the grass. Gangs weren't the problem. "I've got a rock in my boot and I'm not going another step until I get it out, plus I ought to call my...driver...and let him know where I am." Leaving without telling Noah where she went was plain wrong. No matter how aggravated she got at the man, he was doing his best and she had no right to worry him just because she was pissed.

She toed off one boot and shook it until a piece of gravel fell out, then massaged her foot where it had been rubbing. She needed to call Noah before any more time passed, but she dreaded it. She'd seen him irritated, but never angry. Odds were, that was about to change.

The boot slid back on, but instead of getting up, she reached for her phone.

"What are you doing? We need to keep moving. You can make your phone call once we're in the car." Aldo was beginning to look a little irritated himself.

"I'm not taking another step until I talk to my driver. If he says to keep going, I will. Otherwise, I'm heading right back."

Aldo tugged on her arm. She tugged back. She didn't like this new Aldo. She stood and brushed grass off her rear. "This has been a mistake. Thanks you for your concern and offering to help me, but I think I should have stayed where I was."

As soon as she twisted toward the park, she glimpsed Noah jogging up the hill. She strained to see in the fading light. Was that a gun in his hand?

Noah sent up a silent *Thank you* for Conner's assistance. He couldn't afford to wander aimlessly looking for Paige and her abductor. He could always depend on Conner to have his back. That's what partners were for, but Conner did it better than most.

The guy in the plaid shirt must be somebody Paige knew. They could worry about who later. For now, she was safe as long as she went along with him willingly. As soon as she resisted, he was likely to show his true colors.

He'd been thrilled when Paige sat to shake out her boot. He was able to close the gap by a several yards. But then Paige seemed to notice him and plaid shirt became more agitated.

Was the guy upset because Paige was slowing him down or because he spotted Noah following them?

Even if he did see me, does he realize I'm a cop or just think I'm a band member?

Plaid shirt must have been tailing Paige this whole time, spying on her, but he'd never noticed the guy and he'd been looking.

He needed Paige to stay calm a little while longer. Not set off any alarm bells until he got a lot closer.

But then, Paige had never been one to do what he wanted her to, even when she knew what it was.

That fucking cop. He didn't know when to quit. Any hope of doing this the easy way just disappeared.

Aldo grabbed Paige's arm. "We need to head this way." He tugged her along beside him as he raced for the worker's parking lot and his car. They hadn't taken ten steps when he saw a uniformed officer coming their way.

He veered to the left, but Paige picked that moment to resist.

"Let go of my arm. I'm going to wait here for my driver."

Her driver? That cop? He wasn't her driver. He was a paid pig. Only doing what he was told. He didn't care about Paige.

"We'll talk about that later. For now, you're coming with me." He reached into his pocket and pulled out the gun he'd taken from the old fool. Paige's eyes went wide. He'd never seen anything that blue in his life.

"Think about this, Aldo. You can't get away. There're police all over this area."

"Then I don't have anything to lose, do I?" He pointed the gun in her general direction and tugged on her arm. This time she followed him without protest.

If he made a big circle past the Fallen Police Officers Memorial, he could come back to his car from the opposite direction.

Noah had slowed to a brisk walk when he saw plaid shirt grab Paige's arm. Things ahead were escalating and he was still too far back.

The radio he'd clipped to his belt squawked and his normally cool and collected partner's voice came through with an edge of tension. "Did you see that?"

"She's starting to resist."

"More than that. I think he might have a gun."

Had the guy taken Earl's weapon? He hadn't asked or checked. He was too involved in this case and it was causing him to make bonehead errors. That's what happened when you let the victim into your own world. He'd allowed his feeling for Paige to cloud his mind. As a result, he'd not only made tactical mistakes, he'd endangered those around him.

He wouldn't make that mistake again. As soon as this case was wrapped up and Paige was back in Nashville, Sweet Pea, Rachelle, and his nieces would be the only females in his life.

Conner was back to his business-like self. "I've made an Officer Needs Assistance call for you, but the closest help is coming under the freeway from the service parking lot. I think your guy saw him because he appears to have swung slightly left, up the hill."

He lived in Houston fucking Texas. The flattest city in the country. How could everything be up hill? There had to be a corresponding downhill somewhere.

Noah slipped his Smith and Wesson under the back of his shirt—too many people about to run around waving a gun—and picked up his speed.

The city had invested millions in landscaping over the last year. Street lights covered all the jogging/biking paths. Portable spotlights illuminated the concert area. Hiking trails leading to and from the bayou were well lit. The food trucks had their own generators. But once you stepped past the periphery of the lights, you were in deep shadow.

And that's where Paige's abductor was heading.

Conner held the binoculars so tight he was likely to have bruised raccoon eyes. He'd assigned the plainclothes officers to the wrong places. He should have ordered more protection around Paige herself instead of throughout the crowd.

It didn't help that the decision was made well above his pay grade. He'd agreed to it.

Earl was a dependable cop, but one person couldn't have eyes in every direction. So this cluster fuck was his responsibility.

Now Paige and the perp were disappearing over the hill and into the dark where he couldn't help Noah.

And he was left on lookout with nothing to look *at*.

He knew Noah well enough to figure out he'd take off after any reasonable suspect, but without guidance, he'd be chasing shadows.

He needed to find a new vantage point, but by the time he got anywhere, they'd be long gone.

His partner depended him and he was impotent. Not a feeling he was comfortable with.

There was one call he could make. One place he could count on for help.

Aldo kept one hand around Paige's arm and the other held the pistol he'd taken from the gray haired cop. Paige tried to slow him down, but he maintained a steady pressure.

The darkness hid them from anyone trying to follow, but made his footing unsure. The farther he got from the concert venue the quieter the night became. Cars zipping past, crickets chirping, frogs croaking in the bayou, and his own heavy breathing were the only things he heard.

Between practically pulling Paige up the hill, and carrying a hunk of metal heavy as a bowling ball, he was wearing out. Even if he got her to the cabin, she wouldn't go in quietly.

His whole plan was falling apart. He'd be lucky to get out of this alive.

He couldn't think that way. He'd always given up. Too shy, too timid to pursue his dreams. He'd believed his father's mantra. *You're a loser, a freak. Even your own family can't understand you. You'll never amount to anything. We'd be better off if I'd let your mother abort you like she wanted to.*

It wasn't until after the old man died that he'd discovered the truth. His father had been trapped into a marriage he didn't want. Maybe that's why the guy decided to fuck up Aldo's life every way he could. And his mother let him do it.

The man had a job. Not a great one, but it was steady. And he had insurance. Sure, the speech therapy Aldo needed would have cost money, but they could have managed. The old man's argument that he didn't trust doctors only held water until he required prostate surgery for himself. Then he trusted doctors just fine.

Paige was the only one who'd ever been nice to him. She'd smiled at him in school instead of laughing. She'd talked to him at his job at the ball park. She'd shown him what he was good at. Where his passions lay.

Then as abruptly as she'd stepped into his life, she stepped out again, leaving him more lost than ever.

He wasn't going to let her go a second time.

CHAPTER
THIRTY

A SOFT BLUE GLOW beckoned and Noah headed that direction. No way of knowing if that's where he'd find Paige and plaid shirt, but that's the course they'd been taking last time he saw them.

To the right, a wrought iron fence rimmed the park, separating visitors from Allen Parkway's constant traffic. To the left, a steep-sided ditch, ten feet deep and twice as wide, filled with briars, brambles, and bulrush fronted a chain link fence. Even pointing a gun, it would be hard to get her across either of those. He took a chance and continued forward.

Static buzzed through his radio and he turned off the useless instrument before it warned plaid shirt he was coming. He was on his own. No one knew his current location. No one would be coming to help.

The run across the park had him panting, and his busted ribs let him know they didn't like it. He'd ignored them last night with Paige. He could ignore them now.

The evening was mild, but muggy. Sweat dripped down his back. Paige had rolled the sleeves of his shirt to a knife-edged crease just under his elbows. What he'd give to rip those sleeves off now.

As he topped the hill, he realized where he was. Four towering light poles formed a massive square and cast a soft blue light on the Houston Police Officers Memorial. After complaining that every step tonight had been uphill, he'd found his corresponding downhill, leading to the granite, multi-tiered monument.

Starting approximately four feet below ground, the marker rose in stair-steps which, from above, formed the shape of a Greek cross. At the top, water trickled down over the names of all officers who had given their life in the line of duty. In the past, he'd served his time standing guard here. Now, a mini-station was manned twenty-four hours a day.

A couple that might have been Paige and her captor walked down the hill, still in shadow. If he cut straight across, he could catch up with them.

If he was wrong, and that wasn't Paige, she might be lost forever.

They had almost made it. The white brick building with the police department seal appeared quiet. The lights were on, but Aldo couldn't see anyone inside. The area was peaceful, but families strolled the grounds. Couples climbed to the top of the monument. Children ran down the hill.

Even this late, they wouldn't stand out.

"We've only got a little farther to go. Don't make a sound

and I won't need to hurt you. I just want to find someplace we can talk. I have a lot to tell you. Then you can go home."

Paige nodded, but didn't say a word. Maybe she believed him.

Ten more minutes and he could relax.

Light spilled onto the ground as the door to the station opened. Shadows silhouetted a man's face, but Aldo instantly recognized his blue uniform. *Damn.* The officer hitched up his pants and surveyed the grounds before heading their direction.

Kiss his clean getaway goodbye.

He still had a chance, if Paige kept her mouth shut. He yanked her toward the monument and pretended to study the structure. Near the back, he ducked into the sunken portion, pulling her with him. If they kept the granite between them and the officer, they could work their way around to the front and make a break for it while the officer faced the other way.

He bent low, keeping his head below ground level and eased through the multiple turns. Behind him, Paige jerked her hand from his and stood. "Help. Over here," she screamed.

Within seconds, the officer was standing over them. "Is that you, Ms. Reimer?" He didn't wait for an answer, but pulled his weapon and pointed it down at them.

Because they were in a narrow channel, the officer didn't have much to aim at. Aldo didn't have the same problem.

He wasn't used to the gun, but he had already found the safety and switched it off. He aimed for center mass and pulled the trigger. The officer's eyes went wide with surprise. He gasped for breath and went down.

Paige's scream seemed as if it came from a different planet. Near but far away.

Was it really that easy to take a life? Did fulfilling his own dreams entitle him to end someone else's? Right or wrong, he couldn't turn back now.

Aldo climbed out and pointed the gun at Paige. "Come on. This is all your fault. Now get out of there. We have to hurry if you don't want anyone else to get shot."

Noah's heart lodged in his throat at the sound of the gunshot. He couldn't see what was going on, but screams echoed from near the monument. People ran in all directions.

If something had happened to Paige, he couldn't live with himself. Not again. Not when it was his fault, the result of his poor decisions.

He broke into a run but his legs protested. After trudging uphill for so long, heading down felt unnatural. He had to concentrate on how to place his feet.

A pair of heavy shoes, toes pointed to the sky, and the hem of dark trousers showed from around one corner of the memorial.

Noah slipped the S&W from his waistband and hooked his badge on his front pocket. No more hiding. He was a Houston police detective. On duty.

He hunched down to make himself a smaller target as he burst around the corner. An officer lay prone on the ground. A shiny new name plate read *Officer Oscar Nguyen*. Fuck it all. How many deaths could he carry on his shoulders?

Noah knelt to check for a pulse, touching skin that was cool and clammy. The man opened his eyes and blinked.

"What the hell? I think that asshole shot me. Am I

bleeding?" Officer Nguyen's voice came in gasps.

The beams illuminating the monument reflected off the white granite, offering only a soft glow. "Too dark for me to see. Where does it hurt?"

The blue cast gave the officer's face a sickly pallor. He struggled to sit and yelped in pain. "Everywhere."

"You wearing your vest?"

"Always."

"Don't move." Noah reached for his radio when Lefty Bob windmilled down the hill to his side.

"Is he hit?"

"Probably broke some ribs." No point telling the guy every breath would ache for the next two weeks. "I think he's okay, but you never know. Better call an ambulance."

"I'll take care of that. You go after the son-of-a-bitch who did this. He went that way." Lefty Bob pointed toward Glenwood Cemetery.

Wonderful. The dickwad could get lost in its vast acreage. In the dark, winding, tree-covered paths, where hundreds of antique markers, statues, and obelisks offered places to hide in ambush. If the gates weren't locked, concert goers may have parked there. Plaid shirt could carjack some unsuspecting soul and slip away into the night.

Not on his watch. He'd made enough blunders already. This adventure ended now.

He raced back up the hill, his own broken ribs forgotten.

They had made it out of the light and into the shadows of the tree line without getting shot. Highly unlikely anyone could see them now as the night grew deeper, darker. Clouds covered the quarter moon.

It had been necessary to give Paige a solid punch to the jaw to ensure her cooperation. The pain in his right hand surprised him. He'd spent years sitting behind a computer or tinkering with equipment. Even his "part time" job relieving over-privileged hotel patrons of their extra cash had been mostly sleight-of-hand. His father's snide comments were correct. He was soft, a weakling. That ended today.

Aldo regretted hurting Paige, but as his father always said about his mother: *Sometimes you have to get their attention before they understand you're serious.*

Ahead, a white formation showed in the distance. He'd use that as a marker, then work his way down the other side, near where they started. With the entire police force heading for the monument, maybe he could disappear into the park.

Paige acted as an anchor. A dead weight he had to tug behind him. Her hiccupping sobs grated on his nerves just when he needed to concentrate the most. Exactly like his mother.

For the first time, he understood his father's need to silence her with a slap.

As he topped the hill, the structure came into focus. A bridge. A way out. Behind the bridge, an opening in the chain link fence. A gate into a place they could hide for days.

They made it to the edge of the bridge when Paige dug her feet in and refused to budge. She removed the hand she'd used to cradle her jaw, wrapped both arms around the railing and hung on. He tugged on her waist, but he couldn't dislodge her.

"Stop it, Aldo. You know this won't work. I'm not going

any farther. You can escape faster without me, anyway."

The sobbing had stopped. Her entire demeanor had changed. Her jaw was swollen but ridged. Determination flared in her eyes.

She was slim, but after running more than a football field, up and down hills, dragging an unwilling companion behind him, he didn't have enough gas to carry her the rest of the way.

His father's voice echoed in his head. *Loser. Worthless. Quitter.*

Not this time.

Okay, Plan A and Plan B had fallen through. If he could get her to the cabin, he'd come up with Plan C.

He pointed the gun in her face. "Finding your body would slow them down even more. Now shut the fuck up, bitch, and get your ass in gear."

The fire in her eyes cooled, if it didn't die completely, and she allowed him to grab her arm.

Listening to his father through paper-thin walls finally paid off. That's who he should have emulated all these years. Not his weak-willed, pathetic mother. Always on her knees, praying for an angel to swoop down and save her.

Paige was his angel. And he'd make his own salvation

CHAPTER THIRTY-ONE

BULLFROGS AND CRICKETS were busy with their courting rituals on what at any other time would have been a fine spring evening when their songs ended abruptly. A man's voice floated across the still air. Close enough to recognize the angry tone, too far to make out the exact words.

Noah paused to catch his breath and check his bearings. *Where are you, you worthless piece of shit? Say something else so I can find you.*

A cloud drifted past, uncovering a fragment of the moon and lengthening the shadows. The silver necklace Paige had borrowed from Rachelle reflected the light and flashed like a beacon.

Paige and plaid shirt were on the edge of the bridge. If they made it across, he'd never find them.

He dug his toes into the spongy grass and sprinted up the hill, praying his football knee wouldn't pick this time to give out.

Three more strides. Two. One. "Halt. Police." His voice wasn't as forceful as he intended, but he wasn't wheezing.

Paige swung toward the sound, but plaid shirt wrapped his arm around her waist and held her in front of him. He squinted into the dark and pointed the gun Noah's general direction. "Is that you Daugherty or Daniels or whatever name you're using these days?" The words were slurred. Could the guy be drunk?

That would make him even more unpredictable.

"Noah Daugherty, HPD homicide."

"Homicide? At least you're working in your own field now."

Not drunk, but something was wrong. An accent? Conner hadn't checked for any foreign nationals. If that was the lisp Earl mentioned, he'd never heard one like it.

"You haven't killed anybody yet. Let's keep it that way."

"You're a little behind the times, cop. I count two down tonight. Not the way I planned it, but I can't turn myself in now."

"You're wrong. Earl, the guy by the bandstand? He may be old and slipping, but he's got the hardest head I've come across in all my years on the force. When I left him, he was sitting up cussing to make a sailor blush." *Keep him talking, it's the only hope.*

"What about the cop? I know I hit him. I saw him go down."

"The young guy? He was wearing protection. You knocked the breath out of him. Maybe cracked a couple of ribs. I won't lie to you. You're in trouble. But turn yourself in now and it won't amount to much."

Paige twisted her head toward the man. "You should listen to him. Stop this before things go bad for you." She faced Noah again. "We were just looking for someplace quiet to talk about old times when the officer startled us. Aldo didn't mean to pull the trigger. It was an accident. He'd never hurt me or anyone else." Her voice was calm as a sea breeze after the rain had passed. No one would have guessed she was being held at gunpoint after witnessing a violent altercation.

Maybe they had a chance to end this now. He didn't want to have to shoot the guy. "Is that your name, son, Aldo?"

Plaid shirt didn't answer, so Paige spoke up. "This is my friend Aldo Rodgers. We knew each other in high school and he worked with me when I sang the National Anthem at ball games."

"Worked with you? You bitch! I got you that job. I sent the video to YouTube. I made you famous. And how did you repay me? By dropping me like a steaming dog turd."

There went any chance of ending this easily. Aldo tried to drag her back a step but Paige didn't cooperate. They were too far away for Noah to grab him and with Paige in front, he couldn't get a clean shot.

Movement at the edge of the ditch caught Noah's eye then disappeared as clouds covered the last corner of the moon. Weeds swaying in the wind? An animal? His imagination? As long as Paige and Aldo stayed on the cement bridge, they were visible, even in the pale light.

"That's not true, Aldo. Remember, I saw you at the ball park and waved to you. When you came over, I asked what you were doing and you told me about your job. That's when I said I'd always dreamed of singing the National Anthem and asked how I could get that gig."

"Exactly. Without my help, you'd still be flipping burgers."

Keep him talking, sweetheart. I need to be a little closer.

"You gave me the name of the person in charge of entertainment. I sent him a letter with a demo."

Noah risked moving a step nearer.

Aldo never took his eyes off Paige. "What about the video? I made that for you."

"I borrowed the equipment and set it up. All you had to do was push a button when I started singing. I *do* appreciate everything you helped me with. I would have given you tickets to any concert. I'm sorry if you feel I abandoned you. I had a free ride to Nashville and a place to stay for a few nights, but I had to leave right away."

"You twist everything. Like I wasn't even there."

The edge of the bridge where Aldo and Paige stood was still too far away. Noah tried another step, but it was one too many.

"Stay where you are. I'll shoot her if you come any closer." Aldo shoved his weapon into Paige's back. It made a solid *thunk* even Noah could hear.

A splash sounded to the left and Aldo froze until a frog croaked in the distance.

He switched his hand from around Paige's waist to the front of her dress. "What the fuck is this? Are you wearing a bulletproof vest? Well, it won't do you any good." He shifted the barrel of the gun to the side of her head.

From where he stood, Noah couldn't see if the safety was on or off, but the guy had already shot once so he had to assume it was off. As long as the fool held the gun in that position, he'd only graze Paige's head. Not kill her. Still, it wouldn't do her any good. He had to distract him. "It was my idea. I insisted she wear it on stage."

Yellow flowers on the tip of the bulrush swayed, catching the dim light. Something dark scurried up the far side of the ditch.

Paige struggled to get away, but Aldo pulled her closer and pressed the gun against her temple. Noah's breath caught. He had to make a move.

"Take me instead of her."

"Why would I do that?"

"I give you my word I won't fight you and I know this area. I can lead you out of here. The cops will be twice as careful if I'm out there."

Aldo paused, as if considering. "Are you wearing a vest?"

"No. I gave mine to her."

White teeth showed a misshapen smile as Aldo grinned his direction. Darkness had hidden the guy's face, but could he have some type of deformity? Was that why he was so hard to understand?

"Drop your gun and kick it away."

Noah laid his weapon on the ground and gave it a gentle nudge at an angle, forward and two feet to one side. The black matte finish blended into the dirt and grass.

"Now, take one step forward so I can see you better and lift your shirt. I need to make sure you're not hiding anything from me."

Noah took a half step closer. He held up his shirttail and preformed a slow pirouette. When he faced Aldo again, he lifted first one leg of his jeans, then the other.

"Is that a holster?" Aldo loosened his grip on Paige as he leaned forward to get a better look.

"It is and as you can see, it's empty. There's no way I can hurt you."

"I don't know, man. You seem pretty dangerous. If I didn't know better, that shiner would make me think you'd been in a fight. Looks like ramming into a cement barricade didn't slow you down any."

No question now. This was the asshat that murdered Lola.

A breeze kissed Noah's cheek and the moonlight grew brighter.

Noah stared into Paige's eyes and pointed his hand at Aldo. "What do you expect me to do, ask you to play dead? Make a gun out of my finger and say *Bang*?"

Paige's legs went limp and she fell to the ground, breaking Aldo's grip around her waist. Noah threw himself to the side. His hand swept the grass until it touched his S&W.

Before he could close his fist around the cold metal, a shot rang out. The back of Aldo's head exploded. Bits of blood and bone and brain matter showered down. He swayed to one side and went down in a heap, his arm draped around Paige.

Noah grabbed his weapon and sprang onto the bridge. He vaulted over Paige and kicked the gun from Aldo's lifeless hand.

"Get him off me. Get him off me." Paige's voice held an edge of panic.

He pulled her to a sitting position and tried to brush bits of matter from her hair. "I've got you, honey. He's not touching you. Ever again."

Tears pooled in her eyes, but she blinked them away. "There better be a treat waiting for me. And I mean one made with tequila, not liver."

CHAPTER
THIRTY-TWO

Noah switched on his radio. "Officer needs assistance at the bridge leading to Gatewood Cemetery. Suspect down. Send for a bus and the ME."

"Did I get him?" Conner stumbled onto the far side of the bridge. His shoes were more mud than leather. His pants, once starched khakis, looked like he'd slept in them for a week or more. Angry red scratches stood out despite a layer of filth. Dirt caked under his fingernails.

Noah almost didn't recognize him. And wished he hadn't.

Killing someone, even someone who deserved it, ate a hole in your soul. He knew it all too well. And he'd have given his own to spare Conner the pain.

Another fuck up to carry on his shoulders. If he'd been faster, he'd have taken out the prick himself. Better all the way around. His soul was already Swiss cheese. The only thing he could do now was to help Conner. Reassure him he'd done the right thing.

"He's gone. Good shooting. You saved my life for sure, and probably Paige's. Two seconds more and I was toast. And if he'd missed, no telling where that bullet would have gone. He could have hit an innocent bystander."

Conner would receive plenty of pats on the back and *Atta boys* from fellow officers. The department would put him on desk duty for a while and insist he talk to someone about his feelings.

The shooting was clean, and while Internal Affairs would investigate, nothing would come of it. In fact, Conner was likely to receive some type of commendation. All this would help, as would the passage of time.

But somewhere deep inside, Conner would be forever changed. And Noah couldn't do a thing about it.

The circus had arrived. Lights were set up, yellow tape strung. Paramedics, investigators, Internal Affairs, Crime Scene, Homicide, plain clothes, uniforms, nosey neighbors, and Lieutenant Jansen all hung around and watched the ME work. Everyone crowded under the big top except the clown.

Scratch that. The Chief of Ds made a brief appearance. Long enough to mutter to Noah in passing, "I though your instructions were to keep this quiet."

No, my instructions were to keep Paige safe.

And he'd have to work with the asshole until something changed.

The detectives hadn't interviewed Noah yet. He paced while he waited. The only thing that hurt more than the back of his legs was his ribs. That dive for his gun hadn't done them any favor.

Ambulances had taken Earl Sparks, and the young officer, Nguyen, to the hospital. A star-struck, baby-faced paramedic suggested Paige join them for a complete checkup, but she refused to leave.

An investigator Noah had met but never worked with had Conner off to the side, demonstrating every move he made. Conner should know better. The shooting might be righteous, but he was a fool to talk to anyone without his representative present.

Noah tried to cross the bridge, but Crime Scene techies wouldn't let him pass. He growled at them and used his *I'm-a-police-officer-get-out-of-my-way face*. They brushed him off. They dealt with police officers every day and weren't impressed. Twerpy little nerds.

He telephoned Conner, but his partner didn't answer. He texted with the same result. Damn it. He'd have to call Jeannie.

She answered on the first ring. "Noah, is Conner okay? He said he wasn't hurt, but you know he wouldn't tell me."

"He's fine. Scratched from climbing through the weeds, that's all. I hate to bother you with this, but I think he needs a lawyer. He's talking a blue streak and I can't get him to shut up. I don't think anyone's trying to hang him out to dry, but everything he says is taken down and could come back to haunt him someday."

"I suggested it when he called me. He said he hadn't done anything wrong. That answering questions now would get this over with faster."

"The idiot."

"Don't worry. I ignored him. Tom Meyers should be there

any minute."

Tom Meyers? Fuck. Where did they get the money for him? "Give him my number. I'll make sure he gets through."

"I already did. Call me as soon as you know anything."

Damn, that woman was something else. No wonder she and Betsy were best friends. Conner might be a pain in the ass, but he was one lucky man.

He'd barely returned the phone to his pocket when he felt a tap on his shoulder.

"Detective Daugherty? I'm Tom Meyers. I'm looking for my client, Conner Crawford."

Who wore a two thousand dollar suit, wingtips, and a silk tie at ten o'clock at night for an outdoor interview? The guy better be worth every penny.

"Conner's on the other side of the ditch, running his mouth off to Internal Affairs." He nodded toward the crowd working on the scene. "These jerks wouldn't let me cross."

"That won't be a problem." Meyers ran a hand through a full head of snow white hair and straightened his jacket. The man was several inches shorter than Noah, yet approached the bridge with the attitude of a giant. "I'm Mr. Crawford's attorney. I wish to pass."

The young turd who ignored Noah didn't glance up from his work. "Sorry, sir. This is a crime scene."

"Are you seriously trying to prevent me from seeing my client? That's a criminal offense." Myers had a steely glare Noah could only hope to imitate after years of practice.

Blood drained from the techie's face. He moved to one side and pointed to the far edge of the structure "Step here and here. Nowhere else."

Meyers didn't acknowledge the techie with a word or glance. He strode across the grass and onto the bridge. Noah followed close on his heels until Meyers twisted and held up his hand. "I can take it from here. Thank you for your help."

Noah slunk back where he had been for the last hour and resumed pacing.

Lieutenant Jansen spent half an hour questioning Noah before telling him to go home and get some rest. The lieu's attitude wasn't as hostile as the Chief of Ds, but wasn't exactly warm, either.

Noah glanced around the area. Most of the onlookers had gone home, leaving only official personnel at the scene. "Where's Paige?" She'd been there a minute ago.

"I assigned an officer to drive her back to the station for a formal statement."

She didn't have any business giving a statement after all she'd been through today. Or was it tomorrow by now?

"Not tonight. She hasn't had anything to eat for hours and then just a yogurt. I'm taking her back to her hotel. I'll bring her by in the morning at ten."

Jansen cocked his head and studied Noah from under bushy eyebrows. "Watch it, Daugherty. Don't cross the line with her."

"That's not it, sir. I've worked with her all week. She trusts me. And she needs that right now." He didn't wait for Jansen to answer. Taking a deep breath, he spun on one heel and raced down the hill after a pink dress disappearing in the distance.

As he got closer, he called out, "Paige." Even in the dark, he could see the relief on her face.

The officer offered only a feeble protest when Noah commandeered his charge. He handed Noah the vest and blue jean jacket he'd been carrying.

Paige flinched when Noah took her arm. How could he have not noticed a bruise that size? What else had he missed? Was she injured? "Are you sure you don't want go to the hospital and let them check you over?"

"No. I need food and a chance to wash up. Then to sleep till noon and pretend this day never happened."

The beautiful pink dress Paige had spent so long picking out was now drenched with blood and brain matter. A glop of something Noah didn't want to think about hung in her disheveled hair.

She definitely couldn't go into a restaurant looking the way she did, if one was even open this late. "I'll take you back to your room and order something to eat while you jump into the shower."

As far as he knew, she hadn't cried yet. Now her eyes filled with tears. "Thank you," was all she managed.

Neither spoke until they reached the hotel. The same receptionist shot him the same glare she gave last time he dragged in looking like a refugee from Abu Ghraib prison. Only this time, Paige looked worse than he did.

Paige toed off her boots and headed for the shower when Noah flipped open the room service menu.

"What do you want?"

Exhaustion swept over her. Her mind refused to cooperate.

"Surprise me." The look of indecision in his eyes made her stop. "I'm too tired for anything heavy, too hungry for anything light, and it's too late for anything spicy. Does that help?"

"I've got just the thing."

She dragged across thick carpet like trudging through knee-deep water. The solid thud of the bedroom door slamming behind her lifted ten pounds from her shoulders. How long had it been since she'd been alone, had one minute to herself?

Her fingers fumbled at the neckline of her dress. If she had to stay in those disgusting clothes one second longer she'd lose what little control she had over her emotions. She gripped the soft fabric and yanked.

Pearl sized buttons showered everywhere, *pinging* as they bounced against the dresser. She shimmied out of the dress and dropped it into the trash can. She couldn't bear to see it again. The new underwear followed.

Buttons crunched underfoot as she trudged into the bathroom and switched on the light. A scream caught in her throat at the sight in front of her.

No, it couldn't be.

Her mother's face stared back from the mirror.

The same cold, dead eyes. The same dark circles. The same lifeless skin. The only difference was the color of the hair, and that was wild and matted.

Was it possible to wash away memories? She cranked the faucet as hot as she could tolerate and let the water beat down on her. Which was dirtier, her body or her hair? She washed and rinsed her hair, scrubbed her body from head to toe, then washed her hair again before applying conditioner. She still didn't feel clean, but hunger pains kept her from repeating the process.

The mirror had completely fogged over when she stepped out of the shower. Thank goodness she didn't have to see those sorrowful eyes again.

She shrugged into a hotel terrycloth robe and wrapped a towel around her wet hair. Noah would just have to take her the way she was. The door to the suite clicked shut as she dragged into the living area.

Noah rolled the room service cart to the formal table, now set with placemats, napkins, water glasses, and utensils. He grinned as she slipped into her chair.

"Voila." He lifted the silver dome covering the food. "Grilled cheese sandwiches and tomato soup."

An almost-smile reached her lips. The first in over four hours. "That's the most delicious looking meal I've seen in my entire life."

Noah sopped up the last remnants of soup with a crust of bread. He watched Paige as she used a napkin to blot her lips. She looked better. Not her old self, but a dramatic improvement from the woman he almost carried back to the hotel.

"I know you're tired. You've had a hard day. A hard week." He took her hand. *A hard life.* "No one can hurt you now. You're perfectly safe here. Why don't I go home and let you get a good night's rest? I'll pick you up in the morning and drive you to the station to make your formal statement."

Her eyes sprang open. Sheer terror flashed across her face. That had been a mistake. He'd made so many he'd lost count. "Or I could stay here with you if you'd rather."

She glanced around the suite as if seeing it for the first time. "I don't want to be here at all. Can we go to your house?"

The case was closed. Why the hell not?

He'd helped women pack before—for a planned trip, weighing the pros and cons of every item, and in a rush to get out before an abusive boyfriend returned—but he'd never seen anyone move like Paige.

In ten minutes she'd dressed in jeans and a T-shirt, scooped her toiletries off the counter into a bag, and wadded, shoved, and crammed things into a suitcase.

She couldn't be ready, could she? "Have you got everything?"

"If I don't, they can mail it. Or keep it. I don't care. I don't want it. I don't even want these things." She dropped the handle of her rolling bag and lurched toward the door.

"We can decide that later." Noah took the suitcase and held the door for her.

In the lobby, the same receptionist eyed them suspiciously. Paige slapped the plastic key card on the counter. "Checking out of the penthouse." She waltzed through the revolving door, her head high.

He'd driven five miles before he dared broach the subject weighing on his mind. "I've got something I need to talk to you about."

Her head snapped around, eyes narrowed to pinpricks.

"You know the guy I ran after at the concert?"

"Aldo?" Venom dripped from her voice at his name.

"No. The other one. The one I thought you meant. He had on a reddish shirt."

"That's where you went? I couldn't figure out what happened to you."

"I had seen him around your first hotel and he seemed overly interested in you. That's why I was suspicious of him."

Her breath came in short gasps. "So do I have to worry about him, too?"

Crap. He couldn't do anything right. "No. No. This will make you happy." *At least I hope it does. If not, I'm batting zero for a thousand.*

"His name is Evan." What the hell? He didn't know the guy's last name. Lefty Bob would have it. "He's the man who adopted your daughter."

Her face lit up the inside of the car. "Are you sure? I don't want to get too excited and learn there was a mistake. How did he find me, anyway? Those things are supposed to be secret."

"That's the problem he wanted to talk to you about. The little girl, they call her Josie, wants to meet her mother and there were some...irregularities...with the adoption. His partner worked at the hospital and knew you weren't going to keep the baby." *Shit.* He'd done it again. There had to be a way to say this without causing her any more pain.

"When you signed the papers giving her.... Signed the legal forms, he, the partner, slipped in an extra sheet stating you wanted Evan to have the child. They still had to pass inspection by the state before the adoption was approved. I've never seen the partner and only met Evan briefly a couple of times, but he appears to be a stable, dependable guy. They both have steady jobs and worry about Josie's welfare. But, if you want, you have an opening to…. You could…. Because they didn't follow procedure, this is your chance to make some changes, if that's what you want."

CHAPTER
THIRTY-THREE

S WEET PEA BARKED excitedly, her tail wagging so fast it blurred. The Yorkie ignored Noah and ran to Paige, begging to be picked up. Now what? She'd never owned a pet in her life. Never been around them.

She stooped over and held out one finger. Would the dog bite her? Those teeth were tiny but sharp. Sweet Pea danced in a circle, rubbing against Paige's outstretched finger. The fur was smooth, silky. She scratched behind one floppy ear and the dog almost grinned.

Paige scooped up the ball of fluff and cradled her in front of her face. The dog lunged forward and Paige jerked back. Instead of a nip to the nose, Sweet Pea licked her with a warm, wet tongue.

Kind of yucky, but kind of pleasant. It might be nice to have a pet. To have a live body happy to see you come home. Something to talk to even if it didn't answer back.

Not now, but someday. She couldn't even keep a plant alive

now. She'd been known to kill a hundred-year-old *bonsai* tree. Plastic plants wilted and turned brown with one glance from her.

And she was seriously considering taking a child into her home? A child who would resent her for tearing her away from the only family she'd ever known. Loved.

She'd have to give up traveling. Stay home and do what, flip burgers? She couldn't feed them both that way. But that was the only thing she knew how to do. And what would happen to her mother?

She was in the exact same position she'd been in ten years ago. At the time, she was sure she'd made the right decision.

How she had ached to hold that sweet little thing, but Josie wasn't little now, was she? The picture in her mind was still the same minuscule pink face wrapped in a blanket covered with ducks and bunnies. Josie was a young girl with her own wants and likes. Did she eat her vegetables? Had she lost any teeth? Did the tooth fairy come and leave a dollar?

Her decision had never been based on what she wanted. It had always been about what was best for the baby. Had anything changed?

This was too much to think about. Not after all that had happened today. If she could just sleep, her head would be clearer.

Noah let Sweet Pea out for a final run, turned off the lights and locked the door. He took her hand and led her to his bedroom. She stripped off her clothes and slipped between sheets that held his scent.

The bed dipped as he slid in beside her. He stroked her back gently and showered whisper-soft kisses on her bruised arm. She snuggled against him and felt safe. Warm. Clean.

She drifted off, dreaming of ducks and bunnies playing on a field of pink flannel.

Paige wandered into the kitchen about half an hour after Noah got up. She had a severe case of bed head and no makeup, but could still out shine any other woman he'd ever met.

She must have decided she wanted the items in her suitcase after all. She wore heels, skinny jeans, and a frilly blouse. Casual yet elegant.

A look he could never manage to pull off unassisted.

"I've got coffee in the pot and tea on the counter by the microwave. Actual food is slim pickings around here, but I can manage toast and raspberry jelly."

She stumbled to the counter without a word, filled a mug with water, dunked in a tea bag, set the microwave for ninety seconds, and folded into the nearest chair.

"I've been thinking about Josie." A dreamy expression passed over her face, "I just love saying her name—and I think I've reached a decision."

"Are you sure? You don't have to rush this." Forget Evan and his partner. Let them live with the results of their actions. They didn't follow the rules in the first place. If Paige made a mistake this time, she and Josie were the ones who'd suffer.

"I must have been chewing on the problem all night. I woke up knowing what to do…sort of. First, I need to meet Evan and his partner. Get to know them. See how they live, what their home is like, how they treat Josie, how she reacts to them. See if I feel love there."

"Lefty Bob has their contact information. I'll get it for you."

"Thanks. They may have passed the state's inspection, but now they need to pass mine. I was raised in a house without love. I'll know immediately if it's not there. And it won't have anything to do with money or good jobs. If Josie truly loves her parents, and they love her, then taking her away from them could cause her immeasurable harm."

The bell *dinged* and Paige got up to fix her tea. Noah set out the toaster and dropped in two slices of bread. "It sounds like you've come up with a good plan. What happens after you meet them?"

"If they fail, I'm bringing Josie home with me. Nothing in the world can stop me. I'll scrub floors if I have to."

Noah refilled his mug and set the toast on the table. "What if they pass your test? Can you live with that?"

"I won't take her away from them or cause any trouble, but I have conditions. I want to be part of her life. I'll have to go slow, give her time to get used to me. I'll move Mom back to Dallas. When I visit her, I can see Josie. Take her to lunch or to the movies. In time, maybe she can visit me in Nashville for a weekend or over summer holidays."

Wow. She had given it a lot of thought. He'd never have worked out a plan that logical and fair. If she moved her mother to Dallas, seeing her on a regular basis would be more difficult but that was him being selfish. "I'm proud of you, honey. As soon as this other mess is settled, I'll drive you to Dallas myself and wait while you talk to them. Meanwhile, Conner will check into their background. If either one of them has ever had a parking ticket, he'll find it."

Noah glanced at the clock over the oven. Where had the

time gone? "We're due at the station by ten o'clock, if you're up to this. If not, I'll call and postpone."

"I'm ready. I want this over and done with so I can have my life back. Just give me fifteen minutes to finish dressing."

Noah poured another coffee and flipped on the TV while Paige darted into the bedroom. His least favorite sexy anchor was babbling on and he reached for the remote to change the channel when he saw twin photos of himself and Conner displayed behind her.

"—questions about the shooting and the way this entire incident was handled."

And now it begins.

An image of Houston's most prominent cop-basher appeared. "Putting aside the fact that the entire Houston Police Department couldn't protect an important visitor to our city, we must be concerned about the cowardly behavior of these two officers in particular."

What the fuck?

The screen switched to a dark, grainy video. Reflected moonlight made Paige and Aldo visible as they stood on the white concrete bridge. A figure, appearing only as a deeper gray area, stepped out of the shadows.

Wonderful. Someone had used their phone to make a video instead of calling for help.

Paige's body hid the gun Aldo held. She seemed to be standing in front of him of her own free will. Without warning, she sank to the ground. Anyone watching would have thought she fainted.

The shadowy figure threw itself to the side, out of view.

The station froze the video with Aldo standing alone. No

weapon was visible in the pale light.

How long before someone showed the rest of the footage? The part where Aldo's head exploded.

The camera switched back to the anchor, an expression of sorrow painted on her perfectly made-up face. "One officer ran from a confrontation and the other shot a man in the back, without any warning. Is this what we expect from those we depend on to protect and serve?"

A crash sounded behind him. Noah swung around. Paige's tea cup lay shattered on the floor. Her hand covered her mouth. The color drained from her face like pulling the plug on a sink full of water.

He fumbled for the remote, but not before the anchor got in one last dig.

"Both officers are under investigation and the victim's mother has indicated she plans to file suit."

Noah stared at the now blank TV screen. "You can't be seen with me."

"What?" Her voice trembled.

"If we show up together, anything you say will be suspect. I'll drive you to that diner where we stopped for coffee. Lefty Bob will meet you there and take you in to make your statement."

Blinding sunshine halted Paige as she left the florescent lights of the hallway and she put a hand up to shade her eyes. Lefty Bob took her arm and led her to the edge of the steps. He'd been unendingly patient, guiding her from one office to another, fetching her water, keeping her calm, but he wasn't

Noah. Where was Noah when she needed him so much?

A cacophony of voices reached her.

"Miss Reimer, Miss Reimer. Can you tell us what happened in the park last night?"

Reporters with microphones and cameras crowded in front of police headquarters. Why couldn't they have been at her concert instead?

"Will you make a statement for us?"

She took a deep breath. Stale air and exhaust fumes from downtown traffic filled her nose. "I've just spent four hours making a statement to police. I'm sure they can tell you anything you want to know."

'What do you think of the actions of the police last night?"

"I couldn't be prouder or more grateful. If it wasn't for them, you'd be covering a very different story today."

"Did you see the video?"

"I refused to watch it. That man held a gun to my head." She pointed to her temple. "He threatened to kill me. I had just seen him shoot a police officer, so I didn't have any doubt he meant business. When I foolishly refused to cancel the concert, Detective Daugherty insisted I wear his bulletproof vest, yet he set his gun down and offered himself in trade for me. Leaving him without any protection. That's what I call heroic. I owe my life to detectives Crawford and Daugherty. Without their quick thinking, I'd be dead, or worse."

She held onto Lefty Bob's arm and hurried down the steps to a waiting car, driven by an out-of-uniform Tracy Barrows, who whisked her to the airport for her flight home.

She shouldn't run. It wasn't fair to Noah or Conner. But she couldn't face the reporters, the questions, the lingering fear. Too much had come down on her already. She needed her own apartment. To be surrounded by her own things. Most of all, she needed time to think.

Sitting alone, cocooned in a metal tube, hurling through the air, was surreal after everything she'd faced in the last twenty-four hours.

The band beat her home by twenty-four hours, and when Kevin met her in Nashville, she collapsed into his arms, sobbing.

CHAPTER THIRTY-FOUR

NOAH BRISTLED AT instructions to take the next three days off—the orders came from his Lieu, but he suspected they originated higher up—so he filled his days by spending time with his nieces. He picked them up after school and took them to the park, the library, and the bouncy house place. One evening they went for Mexican food and the other for fried chicken, saving James Coney Island hot dogs for the last night. He got them home, dirty and tired, ready for a bath and bed.

His sister didn't approve, but let it go. He needed to be with them as much as she enjoyed some space of her own.

On Wednesday, he got Lola back from the body shop. Good as new, he was promised. Driving her was both right and wrong. She felt good, comfortable, but the sense of pride he'd always felt for her was gone.

He and Paige texted several times during the day and talked each evening. Somehow, it wasn't the same. The night he told her that her father was still alive but would spend the rest of his life in a Florida jail, was the hardest. It would have gone easier if he could have done it face-to-face as he wanted.

He'd never been so ready to get back to work in his life.

Paige's impromptu press conference had solved his problems and most of Conner's. Tom Meyers would take care of the rest.

The first thing he saw when he booted up his computer was an email from Lefty Bob containing an attachment with an inventory of the contents of the cabin Aldo Rogers had prepared for Paige.

Each item on the list made the noose around his chest to tighten until he had to force his lungs to work. If he'd been five minutes later....

No point thinking about that. It would drive him crazy.

A hand on his shoulder caused him to swirl his chair around. "Conner, I thought you had the week off."

"I do. They wanted me to come in today and, *talk to someone*." He made quotation marks with his fingers.

"Good. Good. How did that go?" If he'd *talked to someone,* all those years ago, would he be a different person today?

"Okay. Awkward at first, but better after we got into it. Seeing Lefty Bob's list of chains and padlocks did as much for me as the department shrink. The handwritten contract he had waiting for her signature explained a lot. He was to be her manager and agent for only a measly twenty-five percent. That's not all. I just got a fax from Tennessee. Guess whose mom moved to Knoxville two years ago and just happens to drive a 1998 Ford Taurus, spray painted navy blue? They haven't found a plane ticket for Aldo yet, but I'm betting they will. I did the right thing. I'll learn to live with it."

Yes, but it wasn't fair. He shouldn't have to. Best to change the subject. "How's Jeannie?"

"She's sticking so close to me I jumped at the chance to come in today. Which brings me to the reason I stopped by to see you. I think they call it *nesting*, but Jeannie's cleaning and cooking and arranging from one end of the house to the other. She's planning to cook beef bourguignon tomorrow night and she wants you to come over for supper."

"I'd love to partner, but I have plans."

Conner raised his eyebrows.

"Paige's guitar player is still on the mend and I'm driving to New Orleans immediately after work to sit in with the band. They've got a weekend gig at one of the bigger clubs and need my help."

The only thing left to do was stop on the way out of town for a bag of jelly beans.

The round, industrial-style clock over the Leiu's door moved like an icicle in the first spring thaw. Tick, tick, tick instead of drip, drip, drip. It must need a new battery. Noah checked the time against his cell. No. Still fifteen more minutes.

Due to overtime, he was off at noon. Lola was loaded, gassed up, and ready to go. If nothing held him back, he'd be in New Orleans by five o'clock.

He gritted his teeth when the phone rang. No, not now. Not after nothing all day.

"Detective Daugherty? This is Naomi Reasnor Henderson, Paige's friend."

"Yes, Naomi. How are you?"

"Upset. The more I learn about that awful shootout, the worse I feel. I knew Paige had Finlay Brown wrapped around her little finger, but I forgot about Aldo Rogers. He was somebody you'd walk past and forget you saw him, but I guess he and Paige were friends. At least she smiled and spoke to him. That was more than most people, including me."

"I can't imagine that would have made any difference." Really? Aldo wasn't in hiding. He had a job and an address. They'd definitely have questioned him. That might have been enough to stop him. At the very least, he'd have recognized the guy at the park and stayed with Paige instead of running after Evan.

Paige had told him about singing the National Anthem several times. If she'd mentioned her friend Aldo, who helped her get the gig, just once in all the times he'd asked, none of this would have happened. Conner wouldn't have to live with the results and he wouldn't have to carry fifty pounds of extra guilt.

"Thanks, Detective. That makes me feel better. I guess he had kind of a thing for Paige. I think he helped her with her math homework sometimes. Well, actually, I believe he did it for her. I suppose that doesn't matter now." Her laugh was self-conscious. "It's not like that's going on her permanent record at this point."

"No, we all did things in high school we'd just as soon forget. I'll tell Paige you called. She's thinking of moving her mother back to the Dallas area so it's possible you'll run into each other."

He promised her again that nothing was her fault, then

he hung up. It was time to go. He grabbed a Diet Coke and a bag of chips from the vending machine, hopped into Lola and pointed her east.

Two hours later he crossed the state line and three hours after that pulled into New Orleans, The Big Easy.

But nothing was easy about it. He'd spent the whole drive thinking, pondering, worrying, wondering. Going over every minute, every detail, every conversation. What had he asked? What had she answered? What had she omitted? Did he fail to do his job because he'd been blinded the same way Finlay Brown and Aldo Rodgers were?

By the time he reached the hotel, his head felt like it was ready to explode.

Noah didn't have time to talk to Paige before the gig. He greeted the guys and helped set up. Without having to stay on the alert for stalkers or pretend to be someone he wasn't, he enjoyed the hell out of performing.

Later, they all went out to eat and he downed the best po'boy in recent memory. On the way out, he bought a carton of pralines for Mrs. Powell.

It was after one o'clock before he and Paige were alone for the first time.

"Ready to go up to the room?" she asked.

He glanced around the pocket-sized courtyard. Moonlight had turned the flagstones silver. Wrought iron benches waited under fragrant magnolias. "Let's sit out here for a minute. Enjoy the night air."

"What's the matter? Something's been on your mind all

night."

"You knew Aldo Rodgers."

"I told you I did. He went to my high school."

"It was more than that. You were friends. He helped you with your homework in school and with your career later."

"What's your point, Noah? I knew him as a quiet, timid, shy person. I never would in a million years expect him to pull a fire alarm or break into my hotel room and leave a dead rose. You saw the chains and padlock. You know what he had in store for me. Don't you think I would have told you if I did?"

"True, but you suspected him of slipping that first letter under your door. You called the concert promoter, the mayor, and the chief of police with every intention of reaping the benefits of any publicity."

She sighed and pulled back her shoulders. "I got a letter from him just before I left for Houston. He congratulated me on how well I was doing and said I needed one more big push to make it into the big time. He claimed he had some ideas, but he never said what. I didn't encourage him. Hell, I didn't even know how to contact him."

"And you didn't think to give us his name when the shit hit the fan?" She certainly hadn't forgotten Aldo existed if she'd had a letter from him.

"You're right. I did suspect him after the first note. But I didn't KNOW. The deed was already done, so I decided to enjoy whatever publicity came my way. Later, when you told me what type of person you were looking for, I thought that couldn't be him. It had to be just what you suspected, a stalker. By then, it was too late to give you Aldo's name."

No, that would have been the exact right time to mention

him.

"I didn't do anything illegal. I didn't ask him to do anything, or give him permission to do anything for me or know for sure he had."

"What about Finlay?"

She actually had the nerve to look surprised. "Finlay? What about him? He didn't have anything to do with this."

"You begged him for months to take you to Nashville. You knew he was broke. How did you expect him to pay for the gas when you stopped in Plano?"

"I don't know. I didn't ask."

He'd held out hope she might deny some of it, all of it. A strange calmness settled over him. He wasn't angry, just sad that life had worked out this way. "You never do. You just bat your eyelashes and wait for others to do your dirty work for you. Were you using me the same way?"

He picked up his guitar and stood.

"What are you going to do?" Her voice had the slightest tremble. Real or fake?

"Not a thing. As you said, you did nothing illegal." True, nothing she did was illegal. He wasn't even sure it was immoral. He was just sure Betsy wouldn't have done it.

He preferred hunting for murderers. At least he wasn't disappointed when they lied to him.

The fact that he was being overly critical probably showed he wasn't ready for this. He reached into his pocket and pulled out the bag of jellybeans. "Here, you take these." He kissed the top of her head and turned away before he changed his mind.

His footsteps echoed on the flagstones as he strode toward Lola. He didn't have the slightest temptation to look back.

Paige wasn't a bad person, just not the right person for him. Maybe that person was out there somewhere, or maybe he'd already had his turn.

Trying to figure that out was like guessing the next lightning strike during a summer storm.

For now, Sweet Pea was waiting at home and he owed Rachelle a night of babysitting.

ACKNOWLEDGEMENTS

Contrary to popular opinion, writing is not a solitary occupation. Many individuals were involved in making this book a reality:

My son, Ron Muller, who drove me to Eleanor Tinsley Park, Glenwood Cemetery, and The Houston Police Officers Memorial so that I could get out, walk around, and absorb the atmosphere.

J.E. Handcock who chauffeured me through downtown Houston while I made notes about what was where, how far apart locations were, how much traffic passed at night, and if areas were dark or well lit.

Members of the Houston Police Media Department who graciously answered questions from an inquiring writer.

Shawnna and Jan and the ladies in Critique Corner who read my work and offered suggestions and encouragement.

Christie whose gentle prodding kept me on tract.

My daughter Angela and son-in-law Jason, my daughter-in-law Karen, and my wonderful grandchildren, Andrew, Sam, Caroline, and Bode.

Kimberly who helped me get organized.

My friends who stuck by me when I was too busy writing to pay attention.

To all these people and more, I send my love and a heartfelt *Thank You.*

Did you enjoy Spring Shadow?
Try these other books in the Seasons Pass series. Follow Noah
and Conner as they solve other cases throughout the year.

WINTER SONG

Homicide detective Noah Daugherty is on a mission: solve cases, lock up murderous scum, and get on with what's left of his life. He's on the clock, and his time is steadily ticking away. His path leads him to an icy Houston street, where a car has careened out-of-control and crashed, its driver, a beautiful young socialite, is dead. All the clues lead straight to her husband, but Noah's intuition screams the case is more than meets the eye.

Not willing to give up until he solves this cold-blooded murder, he finds the unthinkable . . . a hitman no one saw coming, with a chilling personal agenda that now targets Noah.

Can he solve the case and save himself before winter is finished singing her song?

SUMMER STORM

It's a scorching Houston summer, and homicide detective Noah Daugherty's only consolation is his life's work: solving crimes to atone for the sins of his past.

When the high-powered CEO of Beneficial Products, a company dedicated to the production of healthy foods, is discovered drowned in her hot tub, what appears to be either an accident or suicide, quickly escalates into something much more sinister. As the body count rises, the link between victims becomes all too clear.

Can Noah find a killer bent on vigilante justice before the storms of summer strike?

AUTUMN SECRETS

The harvest moon has arrived and homicide detective Noah Daugherty is drawn into one final, harrowing case when the search for clues leads him to the middle of a killing field. Desperate, he enlists the help of a woman from his past. Together they discover a serial killer, hell bent on reaping his own depraved version of social sanitation.

As Noah continues his urgent search for justice, the demented madman seems to stay one step ahead, taunting him and threatening everyone he holds dear.

Can Noah put a stop to the killing, or will he be buried along with autumn's secrets?

Join me on Facebook: Susan C Muller, author
Checkout my website: www.SusanCMuller.com
Sign up for my newsletter and be the first to learn about new releases: http://eepurl.com/cibhMn
Can't wait? Join my Review Group:
https://goo.gl/forms/1o9gJcQbDedZJXW62

* 9 7 8 0 9 9 6 0 7 9 7 5 4 *